THE TRACKER

Thomas McDonald

To order additional copies of this book, contact:
Bookwhip
1-855-339-3589
https://www.bookwhip.com

Prologue

Kristine sat on her bed crying. How could she have been such a fool? James Lopez had been good looking and the perfect gentleman when she met him in Dallas. He had wined and dined her sweeping her off her feet. James was rich and had the best of everything. Kristine thought he lived in Dallas. He had a large estate on the west side of Dallas. The house had twenty rooms and a garage filled with ten expensive cars. Kristine couldn't believe he wanted her. He could have had his pick of any woman he wanted, but he picked her. They had made love many times in the huge bed in the master bedroom. James was a great lover.

James wanted Kristine to take a trip with him on business. He told her it would only be for a week. They took a flight from Dallas to Cartagena Columbia. The city was called the city of romance. Kristine loved the city, but the next day they left by car into the outback. After several hours of driving they came to a large valley. The house looked like something a King would live in. There were many buildings and barns around the back of the house.

Kristine expected to be taken to the big house, but the car pulled around back to a small cottage. She soon found out she would live in the cottage. James lived in the big house with his wife and several children. She would be his mistress.

It was dark and Kristine sat on the bed crying when a man dressed in black busted in her locked door. It scared her. A large wolf stood in the doorway as lookout. "I'm here to take you home."

Chapter One

Gary finished packing his things and carried them out to his new Ford Mustang. He was going to Houston for his first job since High School. He had his real estate license and was ready to set the world on fire. Mrs. Mitchell came to the door. "Gary come in and eat, breakfast before you head out for Houston."

"I'll be right in."

His Mother fixed a full breakfast consisting of eggs, bacon, grits and toast. Gary was enjoying his last home cooked meal for a long time.

"Mom, tell Dad so long for me. I don't know when I'll be home again."

Gary hugged his Mother and headed out to his car. He got in the car, waved to his Mother and turned the nose of the car toward Houston. He drove upon the square and took a last look around. He had a lot of good memories from High School. He wandered how his friends, Punky, Leroy, Rex and Mike were making it. Punky was in the Navy, Leroy was in Dallas in the Police Force and Rex was in Dallas working for Texas instruments. Mike still lived out in the country from Boonville on his own piece of land. He was married to Linda Love. The Carson's moved to Texas from Oklahoma and Mike got a job working for them. He was a poor country boy, but Linda fell in love with him. Mike trained horses for a movie company. Linda had finished college and had a good job. Gary realized he was just now starting out. He decided to go out and see Mike and Linda before he left for Houston.

Gary pulled across the cattle guard, Thunder and Lightning followed him back to the house. He liked the two horses. They were pure white. Gary stopped in front of the corral where Mike was working a black stallion.

"Hi Mike, how is the stallion coming along?"

"Not too good. He is a beautiful horse, but as dumb as a doorknob. What are you up to?"

"I'm on my way to Huston to my new job. I got my real estate license and I'm going to work for Houston Associates Realtors. They are a very big company and sell a lot of industrial property. They sell land to build on. I hope to make it big. I'm a late starter and have to catch up with you guys. Where is Linda?"

"Linda went to work early. I'm sorry you missed her. I'll tell her you came by. You want to stay for a beer?"

"No thank you, I had better get on the road. I saw it on the news it's raining between here and Houston. Come to see me when you can."

Gary headed his car toward the gate and waved on his way out. Thunder and Lightning ran along beside the car until he crossed the cattle guard. He was on his way to Houston. The weather was nice until he got past Huntsville and hit a rain storm. It was raining cats and dogs. He had to slow down to thirty miles an hour. Gary arrived in Houston at one o'clock. The real estate company he was going to work for had gave him keys to several apartments. He was going to pick one and start work in the morning. The third one he looked at suited him. It was a two story, living room, kitchen, den and a full bathroom downstairs. Two bedrooms and a full bathroom were upstairs. He liked the layout of the apartment. He unloaded his car and parked in the rear in a carport. He unpacked his clothes putting them in the closet and dresser. Gary stored his rifle in the closet and his 45 automatic in the dresser. He liked guns and shot them when he had time. He was a sharpshooter with both guns. After making his bed he decided to find a place to eat.

The next morning came too soon. Gary liked to sleep late because he wasn't a morning person. He had bought a supply of food that night and had a good breakfast, toast and coffee. He picked his briefcase off the table and headed out the door to his car. He lived on Pasadena and Houston. Association of Realtors was located on loop 610 and Pasadena. Gary was close to his work and didn't have to fight a lot of traffic, only taking him five minutes to get to work. He pulled into a large parking lot and found a space with his name already on it. He was thirty minutes early for work. He didn't have to be there until eight, but he wanted to be early on his first day.

Gary went through a large double door into the lobby. The receptionist sat at her desk, Rebecca Currie on her name plate. She looked up from her typewriter as Gary approached. She smiled as she looked him over like a prize bull. He was six feet tall, light brown hair, broad shoulders, brown eyes and a trim waist. She liked what she saw.

"How may I help you? Do you have an appointment?"

"I'm Gary Mitchell and I start work for the company today."

Rebecca looked at her appointment book and found Gary's name. "Mrs. Chadwick is expecting you. Go down the right hall and her office is the third door on your left."

Gary knocked on her door and opened it. Mrs. Chadwick was on the telephone and motioned for him to take a seat in front of her desk. She finished her call and hung up. "Good morning Mr. Mitchell and how was your trip to Houston?"

"I ran into a rain storm and it took a lot longer to get here, but I made it and I'm ready to work. Thank you for hiring me. I'll do the best I can."

"I'm sure you will fit right in. All your sales will be on commission, but if your sales are outstanding you will get a large bonus. We divide up the clients among the sales people to give everyone a fair chance. I'll want to introduce you to each sales person as they come to work. Some of our people only work part time. Your office is on the right next door to mine. Your client's folders are on your desk. There are cling on signs on your desk for your car. Do you have any questions?"

"Not at this time, but I'm sure I will have in the future. Thank you for giving me a chance at the job."

Gary went next door to his own office. The client folders were on his desk with the stick on signs. Everything was so organized at his new job. Even his parking space was marked before he arrived. He opened his briefcase and put away his things. It was time to go to work and earn a pay check. He picked up the top folder and read it through. Each folder was about the same. It gave the location, a description of the property, price wanted, lowest price the owner would take, lowest down payment and when the new owner could move in. The standard price for selling the property was six percent. Gary would get three percent for selling the property and the company got the other three percent. A list of interested clients was with each folder. He picked the most expensive piece of property and called the first name on the list. The third name on the list seemed the most likely to buy so Gary made an appointment to show the property the next day at eleven o'clock. He used the same song and dance with all the clients, until he had appointments for all the properties. The next few days he would be busy.

Tommy Greg and Philip Knox came into Gary's office. "Welcome aboard," Tommy said. "We came in to get to know you. Where do you hail from?"

"I'm from a little town called Booneville in east Texas. I lived there all my life. Where are you from?"

"We are both from Houston," replied Philip. We're going to a singles bar tonight after work and thought you might like to come with us. It's a bar that a lot of good looking women hang out at and they are easy to pick up. Some like sex the first pickup and some you have to go with a few times, but sooner or later you get them in bed. The chase is well worth it in the end. How about it, do you want to go?"

"I'm tired from my trip, but I would like a good Coors lite. Yes I think I'll tag along with you. It might be fun. I'll follow you to the bar when we get off work. I might get lost in the big city."

Tommy and Philip went back to their offices. Tommy made an appointment to show a house on the south side of Houston and Philip was working his clients to get a showing from one of them. He wasn't having any luck. Sometime you had good luck and some time you couldn't get a showing if your life depended on it. Philip hadn't had a sale in two weeks and needed a sale real bad. He was running low on money and had bills coming due.

After work Gary followed Philip to the singles bar. It was a large bar with a dance floor, tables around the dance floor and a D.J. playing music. They got a table close to the dance floor and ordered a round of drinks. Tommy said, "The first round is on me."

The dance floor was full, the couples dancing to a fast two step. Country music was the kind of music Gary liked. He liked to slow dance and some fast dances. He watched as the couples passed their table. Philip was right. There were a lot of fine looking girls there tonight. He might even try to pick one up. She could give him a massage for his sore body.

Tommy and Philip both kept asking girls to dance trying to make out. Gary sat and watched them trying to pick up a girl. Maybe the girls weren't horny tonight. They came back to the table looking like they had lost their best friend.

"You not having much luck picking up a girl are you? Maybe you should change your bait. Try a new pick up line."

Philip said, "What would a small town boy know about picking up girls? Do you have single bars in your town? I bet you have never picked up a girl in a bar, have you?"

"No I haven't, but picking up a girl should be the same every-where. Booneville is a dry town and you have to go out of county to get booze. When you want to pick up women you watch their body language to see if she wants you to pick her up. Then you make your move."

"I think it's a lot of bull shit if you ask me," said Tommy. "Come on Phillip, it's time to get a woman for tonight."

After Tommy and Philip left Gary looked around the bar. He was pissed off the way they tried to put him down. Maybe he would hook up with a woman tonight. It was still an hour before closing time. He scanned the dance floor and the long bar. A flaming redhead was watching him. She smiled at him and that was all he needed. Gary smiled back at her and she put her hand on the barstool next to her. He picked up his Coors lite and walked toward the bar. "Is this stool taken?" Gary asked.

"It is now, sit down and take a load off. Did you have a bad day?"

"I had a long day. I drove to Houston from Booneville and started a new job with Houston Association of Realtors. I hope to make some money working there."

"You should do well there. They are a very big company. I have some friends that work there and they make a big paycheck. Your beer is almost empty. Do you want a refill?"

"I'm ready," smiling at her, it had a double meaning. She smiled back as she picked up on his meaning. She looked him up and down and noticed his fly to his pants was bulging. She knew he had a big hard on.

Sandy became aroused looking at his fly. She looked into his eyes and saw a man that wanted her. They stared at each other as they finished their drinks. They both got up at the same time and headed toward the front door. Tommy and Philip were on their way back to their table when Phillip saw Gary leaving.

"Would you look at that? Gary is leaving with the redhead that I have been trying to make out with for months. How did he do it?"

"I don't know, but he is doing something better than us. That is one hot chick he just walked out the door with," said Tommy.

"By the way my name is Sandy Foster. What's your name?"

"Gary Mitchell is my name, at your service. You want to go to my place or yours? I'm not sure how to get to my place without getting lost at night."

"I live a few blocks from the bar. Follow me in your car, ok."

They both got in their cars and Sandy led the way while Gary followed her tail lights. She pulled her car in a parking space in front of her apartment and cut the engine. Gary pulled in beside her and killed his engine. He locked up and followed her into her apartment. Her apartment was made the same as his. The bedrooms were upstairs. Gary was ready to go upstairs and make love, but he let her set the pace. Sandy was ready for some hot sex, but she didn't want to look too easy. "Would you like a beer?"

"Yes thank you." Gary starred at Sandy and she stared back while they drank their beers. He knew she was hot and ready. If Gary read her body language wrong he was about to make a fool of himself. "We have had enough foreplay, are you ready to make love?"

It took Sandy by surprise, but she took Gary's hand and led him up the stairs to the master bedroom. The room was large having a king size bed, dresser, makeup table and nightstand. Gary reached for the buttons on her blouse and she reached for the buttons on his shirt. He pealed her blouse off, unsnapped her bra letting them fall to the floor. He touched her nipples with his hands and got a moan out of her. Gary lowered his head and took a nipple in his mouth and began to suck on it. That got another loud moan from Sandy. While sucking on her nipple he unsnapped her skirt and let it fall to the floor. Gary slid his hand in her panties and lowered them to the floor. Sandy stepped out of them and stood naked before him. He touched her heat with his finger and knew she was ready.

"Gary you have on too many clothes. It's my turn to undress you." Sandy pulled off his shirt, unbuckled his belt pulling down his zipper and reached inside to feel his shaft. It was big and hard. She tugged at his pants until he stepped out of them. Pulling off his briefs let his large shaft stand at attention. Sandy stared at the size and wandered if she could take all of it. "Gary I don't know if I can take that into my body. It's so big it will probably tear me up."

"We'll take it slow and you will love the feel of it when you have it all inside you. I'll turn on my back and let you on top. You will have control to how much you want at a time."

Gary lay on his back with his hard on standing straight up toward the ceiling. Sandy licked her lips and starred at it. It was time to get the show on the road. Her body was burning up with desire. She straddled his hips and positioned her body over his large erection. She slowly lowered herself until it penetrated her lips and eased down a little bit at a time. She finally had every inch of his shaft inside her. Sandy smiled down at Gary, "I took it all and it feels wonderful."

Sandy sat still and let her body adjust to his size. She moved around in a circle as she moved up and down slowly increasing her speed. "Oh yes, oh yes, it feels so good," Sandy moaned.

It was time for Gary to join in the action. He slammed up each time to meet her on her way down. Sandy cried out loud as she started to have a climax. Her climax went on and on. She shuddered and tightened her muscles on his shaft. Gary went wild slamming into her hot passion until he came. Sandy went limp and fell on his chest. They lay there exhausted, but still locked together. Sandy reached back and pulled the sheet over them. They drifted off to sleep still locked together in a dream world.

Sandy sat up in bed, what had she done? There was a man in bed with her. Then it all came back to her. She was sore in her private place, but she remembered what happened last night and smiled. She had a wild night like nothing she had ever experienced before. They had made love three times and each time it got better, each climax lasting longer. Sandy watched as Gary slept enjoying looking at him. He was on his back with a big hard on and he was smiling. She wandered if he was dreaming about her. He didn't talk in his sleep.

Finally Gary opened one eye and caught Sandy watching him. "Why are you watching me? Tell me you aren't sorry about last night. I did come on a little strong."

"Last night was fantastic. I have never been so thoroughly loved in my life. I loved every minute of our making love. By the way the flag pole is standing straight up," laughed Sandy.

Gary reached for Sandy and pulled her into his arms while sliding his hand between her legs. She was wet and ready and she grabbed the flag pole and pulled it between her legs. They made love very slow before they got out of bed. Sandy made breakfast while Gary took a shower. She would shower after they ate. It was Saturday and they were both off work. They could relax and enjoy the day. "What would you like to do today?" asked Sandy.

"I would like you to give me a tour of Houston. I have never been here before and I get lost easy. Show me all the clubs, good eating places, a park where you can run and how to find my way around without getting lost."

"Ok, it sounds good to me. We can make a day of it. I'll drive and you watch where we are going since I know the city by heart."

It was a little cool in the morning so Sandy pulled a light jacket out of her closet. She locked up as they left the apartment fishing in her purse for her keys. Sandy started the car as Gary settled in the shotgun seat. She backed out into the street and headed south. "We'll start with the Space Center first. Have you seen it?"

"No I haven't, but I hear it is a must see attraction."

Sandy parked in the parking lot and they took a tour of the space center. Next she showed him the movie theatres and good places to eat. She showed him how to follow the back streets to avoid the traffic rush in the morning and the evening. She pulled into a fish place for lunch.

After lunch they continued to explore Houston. She showed him where the ball park for baseball was played. They found all the night clubs and bars.

Late that evening they went to a steak house for supper. Gary ordered a rib eye steak, bake potato, and a salad. Sandy had a large chicken salad. They had tea to drink.

It was dark by the time they finished their meal. Gary paid their check and they went back to the parking lot. He opened the driver door for Sandy and went around the front of the car to get in the passenger seat.

"Are you ready to go dancing?" asked Sandy.

"It sounds good to me. Where are we going?"

"I thought we would go to Mickey Gilley's, if it's alright with you."

"Fine with me, let's do it."

Sandy pulled out into traffic and headed toward Mickey Gilley's. The traffic was heavy, but Sandy knew Houston like the back of her hand and was a good driver. She pulled into the parking lot and parked. It was crowded and they had to park a long ways from the front door.

They were lucky and got a table close to the dance floor. Gary ordered beer and Sandy had a fancy mixed drink. When they brought their drinks Sandy's drink was large and looked to pretty to drink.

Sandy laughed, "It is more fruit and juice than liquor."

They watched the couples dance as they sipped their drinks. Sandy stared at Gary and wished he would ask her to dance. She was hot and ready to tear up the dance floor. She wanted to feel Gary's body close to her. She wanted to rub her breasts against him and see the effect on his face. She wanted to see if she could get a rise out of him. She glanced at his fly and it was flat. Well it wouldn't be after she got him on the dance floor. She stared at him, but he was still watching the couples on the dance floor. The band changed songs.

Gary stood up and reached for her hand, "Would you like to dance?"

"I thought you would never ask," replied Sandy.

It was a fast two-step and they circled the floor at a fast pace, dodging couples as they made their way around the dance floor. They were exhausted by the time the song ended, but a slow belt buckle shining song started and they stayed on the dance floor. As they danced Sandy could feel Gary getting a hard on and she giggled. "Did I do that? Better not walk off the dance floor that way or you will embarrass yourself."

When the song ended Gary walked close behind Sandy and she giggled all the way back to their table. Gary ordered more drinks.

"Sandy I don't know anything about you, not your last name, where you work and I would like to know."

"My last name is Carson and I work for an investment advisory service, so we have something in common our working with real estate. We look for good real estate for customers to invest in. We also look for good stocks and bonds or anything a customer can invest in and make a good profit. We keep a close eye on the investments and if we see them going bad we advise the customer to sell to get out from under."

"Do you want to dance some more? I'm ready to leave if you are." Sandy reached under the table touching his fly.

"If you put it that way, yes I'm definitely ready to go."

They finished the rest of their drinks and left the club. When they were on the road, Gary slid his hand between Sandy's thighs and touched her hot spot. She moaned, but kept her eyes on the road because she didn't want a ticket or have a wreck. Gary stroked the fire until she thought she couldn't stand it any longer. Sandy parked in her parking space and killed the engine. She got out of the car and her knees were so weak she couldn't walk without Gary helping her.

When the door was locked, they made their way up the stairs to the master bedroom without turning on the lights. They were frantic to get in bed and make love, so they undressed themselves and jumped in bed. Gary turned on his back with his shaft straight up toward the ceiling. That was Sandy's clue that she was in charge of the love making. She didn't hesitate, straddling his legs, positioning her body over his shaft as she twisted her body while lowering her body until she had sheathed his shaft. She sat still while her body adjusted to accommodate his large shaft. She had learned how to keep from hurting when they made love.

Sandy leaned over and kissed Gary while ramming her tongue deep into his mouth to stroke his tongue. She sucked hard on his tongue as her body jerked from side to side. "Are you ready for some fast loving? I'm so hot I may catch fire if you don't put it out."

Sandy started at a slow pace, but picked up speed fast, up and down on his shaft. Gary heaved up to meet each thrust. She moaned and twisted her head from side to side. It didn't take long for her to have a wonderful climax. "I'm coming I'm coming, give to me harder."

Gary slammed into her, felt her muscles tightened around his shaft and he couldn't hold out any longer. He shot his load deep into her body. "Oh baby that felt so good."

Sandy fell forward on Gary's chest kissing him and rolled off him shifting her back up close. He pulled her closer spoon fashion and they went to sleep.

Gary raised his head remembering the love making last night. He smiled and reached over to wake Sandy. She turned over and smiled at him. They were both still naked. He reached and softly touched her bare breast. "Do we have time to make love," asked Gary.

"We'll take time, but I need to go to the office. I got some work to do before my first client comes in tomorrow." They did a quickie. After breakfast, Gary went to his apartment while Sandy went to her office. She would have liked to spend another day with Gary, but a girl has to eat and pay her bills.

Gary studied his client's accounts. His bank account was getting low and he needed a big sale. Monday he made his first big sale and the rest of the week was fair. He worked hard to make sales and by the end of the week he was top salesman for the week. Tommy and Phil were both mad at him for beating them in sales and dating the redhead. Gary didn't care what they thought. He was there to make money and make out with the girls. All's fair in love and war.

Sandy and Gary dated every week they could get together. He wandered if he was falling in love or was it just good sex. Sandy had never mentioned love or commitment, so he didn't say anything about loving her. They continued to date and make love. Gary told her he was looking for some property that would be a good investment to be used for industrial.

Two weeks later Sandy called Gary and told him she thought she had just what he was looking for. He went and looked at the property and it was exactly what he had in mind. An old couple was moving out of Houston and wanted to sell it cheap. They would take five hundred an acre if he paid cash. He went to the bank to empty out his checking account leaving only one hundred dollars in the bank.

Gary went to Sandy's office where the couple was waiting. They signed the papers and he was the new owner. All he had to do was keep the property until the right moment and he would make a killing on the property. He thanked Sandy for helping him.

Sandy grinned, "I'll collect this week end. I want some good loving."

"You got it," replied Gary. He went to work since he had to show a house to a young couple. He made the sale and it put him over the top at the moment to be top salesman for the week.

He wanted top salesman for the month because it paid a big bonus. He called Sandy at her office and gave her the good news of his sale. "What do you want to do this week end?"

Sandy thought for a few seconds, "Would you like to go to Galveston? We could get a hotel on the beach."

"Sounds like a plan to me, could be a lot of fun." What Gary was thinking was making love to Sandy. He could see them in a big king size bed and all night to make love. He remembered what she had said about wanting some good loving and he could handle that. He had a hard on thinking about it.

"I'll call and make reservations for a hotel and maybe we can get a room at the Flagship Hotel overlooking the water. That would be romantic, don't you think?"

"It sounds good to me. I'll pick you up at eight Saturday morning. I don't get off until late Friday because I have a late showing. We only have one night, but I'll make sure you get enough loving."

"I hope so because I have been hot and I need you to cool me down. I got a phone call, talk to you later."

Gary was looking forward to the week end and some good loving. He could almost feel her hot muscles closing on his penis causing him to have a big hard on. Making love with Sandy was fantastic. It was time to call it quits for the day.

Tommy walked in his office as he was on his way out. "Hi, I'm meeting Philip at the singles bar. Do you want to join us?"

"I don't think so, it's been a long day and I am dog tired. I'm on my way home, eat a bite, watch a little television and go on to bed. Thanks for inviting me, but I'll take a rain check." He really didn't want to go with Tommy, for some reason he didn't like him or trust him.

"Ok, talk to you later," replied Tommy.

Gary went home, stopping at a fast food place for a hamburger, fries and a drink. When he entered his apartment, his answering machine was blinking. He put his food on the kitchen table and sat down to eat. He was hungry as a bear, the phone could wait.

His first call was from Sandy letting him know she had got reservations for Saturday night at the Flagship Hotel. Maybe they could get in a little fishing Saturday afternoon since it had been a long time since he had put a hook in the water. He didn't know if Sandy liked to fish, usually most girls hated to go fishing. They hated to bait a hook. Well, there were other things to do, shopping, eating out in a good restaurant, sightseeing and they could just stay in their room making mad passionate love until they were too tired to do anything but sleep. He went to sleep dreaming about Sandy and making love. He slept all night and woke up to his alarm. He jumped out of bed ready to face another day. He worked long hours the rest of the week, but it was worth it.

He had made a good pay check and now had money for the coming week end. He went to bars, eating places and clubs that industrial people hung out at after work. He was looking for a buyer for the land he purchased and sooner or later he knew he would find a buyer. He worked late on Friday. He hadn't talked to or seen Sandy to confirm for Saturday. She answered on the third ring and sounded out of breath. "I just walked in the door. I have been working late trying to get caught up, but it is a losing battle. We are going to Galveston come hell or high water. I've been looking forward to our trip all week."

"Me to, I'll pick you up at eight in the morning."

"I'll see you in the morning. Good night and sweet dreams," giggled Sandy.

Gary ate supper, packed his bags and went to bed. He wanted to be rested for the next day. He had gassed up his car on the way home so everything was a go for tomorrow. His alarm went off at six. He was out of bed, showered and dressed in record time. He cooked eggs, bacon, grits and toast for breakfast. He had two cups of coffee and was ready to hit the road.

He arrived fifteen to eight. Sandy came charging out the door, loaded her bags in the car, went back and to lock her door and was in the car ready to go. She smiled at Gary and he leaned over and kissed her good morning. He pulled out into the morning traffic which was bad even on a Saturday. Thirty minutes, they were out of Houston and making good time. Sandy sat close to him, running her finger tips up his leg until she touched his bulge in his pants causing a fast response to her touch. She laughed because he had a hard on. She liked to tease him every chance she got.

"You had better behave yourself or we may have to stop and get a hotel."

"Then we wouldn't make it to Galveston on time." teased Sandy. "I guess I had better behave myself for now, but wait until we get to the Flagship and then it's fun time. We may just stay in our room and make mad passionate love."

They stopped to get a bite to eat. They discussed what would be the first thing they were going to do. Gary suggested going fishing, but she vetoed that one. He figured she would since most girls didn't like fishing. They decided to go swimming if it wasn't too cold. Good luck on that one.

Gary pulled into the parking lot at the Flagship Hotel and killed the engine. The weather was beautiful, waves crashing upon the shore, seagulls were making a lot of noise, some people were swimming and everything looked great. Gary grabbed their bags and followed Sandy in the front door to the reservation desk. The clerk gave her a key and she headed toward the elevator.

"We are on the second floor facing the water. I didn't want to look at the parking lot. We can look out and watch the people swimming." She opened the door to their room and walked in the room as Gary followed close behind. The room had two double beds. "Sorry they didn't have any king size beds, but we each have a bed," she giggled.

It didn't phrase Gary. "We can make love in one bed and change beds making love again. That way we can mess up both beds."

"Let's go for a walk along the beach since the weather is so nice out and we can find a place to eat. There are some good restaurants along the boardwalk, prices are reasonable and the food is delicious. I have been to Galveston several times and know which restaurants are good versus the ones that are bad."

"Ok Sandy, you make the call. I haven't been to Galveston."

They changed clothes, Sandy put on red short-shorts, a white shirt tied under her breasts, exposing a lot of skin. She put her hair in a ponytail. Gary put on short pants and a t-shirt. He stared at Sandy's breast, wanting to take her in his arms and kiss her until she wanted to stay in the room and make love, but he decided they could make love all night. They decided not to eat anything at the Flagship. It had good food, but the prices were extremely high.

They left the hotel hand in hand and strolled along the beach. The crowd had picked up and there were a lot of people swimming. Gary enjoyed the scenery since there were a lot of girls in skimpy swim suits showing a lot of skin.

"See something you like?" asked Sandy.

Gary had been caught red handed and blushed like a school girl. "Well you caught me. I always liked to watch girls. My buddies in High School and I always checked out all the girls on the first day of school. We were looking for a girlfriend for the school year."

"Did it work, did you find one?"

"Sometimes we had one picked out we wanted, but we didn't always get her. Usually it was a girl that went out for cheerleader and the football guys claim them. They hog all the best looking girls, so we took seconds."

They walked further down the beach until they were getting tired. They sat down on the beach and watched the swimmers. A couple came out of the water and walked over where were sitting. They stopped to talk.

"Are you guys down for the week-in?" Sandy asked.

"Yes we are. We go to college at Sam Houston in Huntsville. My name is Shirley Alley and my friend's name is Charles Overton. We wanted to relax after a week of tests. We are staying at the Flagship Hotel. Where are you staying?"

"We are staying at the same place and we are on the second floor room 206," replied Sandy.

"We are on the first floor in room 101. Would you like to hang out together?" asked Shirley.

Sandy looked at Gary and he shook his head yes. "Sounds like it would be fun. We are on our way to get something to eat. We can eat at a great fish restaurant on the boardwalk. Do you want to come with us?"

"Sounds good, let us slip our clothes on." They were almost dried off, so they put their clothes on over their bathing suits.

They walked up to the boardwalk and crossed the street to a fish restaurant. Gary asked the waitress for a table for four. She showed them to a table overlooking the water. It was a beautiful view. They ordered beer around and studied the menu while the waitress brought their drinks. When she returned they were ready to order. Charles and Shirley ordered fish and chips. Sandy ordered lobster and Gary had fantail shrimp. They had a great salad bar, a large pan filled with col slaw, beets, pickles, tomatoes, peas, pickled tomatoes, corn, peaches and much more. They made a trip to the salad bar and filled their plates. They finished their salad bar plate just as their main dish was served.

"Would you like to go dancing?" Sandy asked. "There is a good club a couple of blocks back toward the hotel. After we leave the club you can come to our room and we can finish off the night."

Charles and Shirley answered. "Yes in unison."

"Then what are we waiting for, let's go dancing," replied Gary.

They walked the two blocks and found the club. The sign read "Fifties Night." They looked at each other and entered the club. With a live band they paid to get in. They found a table close to the dance floor. The music was loud, but good. They ordered a round of beer and hit the dance floor.

"They seem like a nice couple," remarked Gary.

"Yes they do. Do you like fifties music?"

"Some, but I like country western better. That's what I grew up on."

When they got back to the table, Gary asked Shirley to dance a fast jitterbug with him. He liked to fast dance. He tossed her all over the place, on his left hip, on his right hip, over his back, up in the air over his head, down between his legs, pulled her back up and swung her around several times. They were burning up the dance floor. Sandy and Charles cheered them on. They swapped partners several times during the night.

When Shirley danced a slow number with Gary she could feel his manhood pressing against her belly and it made her nervous and hot. She wandered how big his shaft was and what It would feel like slamming into her folds. He wasn't her date, but she couldn't help wandering. A girl could dream, couldn't she? After all, Shirley and Charles were just friends, but they did sleep together when they got horny. She wandered about their relationship. Were they going steady or were they just friends?

Gary and Sandy danced the last dance together which was a slow dance. Gary held her close and promised her a good time when they got back to the hotel. She would hold him to that.

They left the club and walked the short distance to the hotel. Gary and Sandy went up to their room and made ready for their company. Sandy put dip and chips on a small table while Gary put four beers on the table with napkins. Charles and Shirley changed clothes and hung their bathing suits in the bathroom. She put on short-shorts, combed her hair and put on makeup while He put on short pants and a shirt. They went to the second floor and knocked on their new friend's door. Gary opened the door and invited them in.

"Come right in." Gary escorted them to the chairs around the small table. "We have chips with dip and beer. If you want something else we can call room service."

"I think this should do just fine," replied Charles.

Sandy entered from the bathroom, "Hi everyone, make yourself at home. What would you like to do?"

"We like to play cards of any kind," replied Shirley. She would like to play strip poker, but thought she should feel the other couple out first. They played strip poker all the time back at the college. She was good at cards and usually won.

Sandy surprised everyone, "Why don't we play strip poker. I haven't played since I finished college. We played all the time in college. It was fun to watch the guys. They were shyer than the girls. We had fun teasing them. Oh, cut for deal."

Shirley had an ace and won the deal. "Ok, five card draw is the game and losers take a swig of beer and take off one piece of clothing. Only clothing, shoes and socks are used." Shirley won the first hand and everyone took off a piece of clothing. She was good and won three hands before Sandy won the deal. Gary and Charles had lost their shoes and socks already, now the clothes would fall off. Sandy won the next two hands until Charles won the deal. Gary was the big loser so far. He was down to his pants and briefs.

Sandy and Shirley teased Gary and he blushed red. This wasn't happening since he was usually good at cards. He wandered if the girls were cheating, but if they were he hadn't caught them in the act. Charles dealt the next hand and won. Gary took off his pants. If he lost the next hand he was in big trouble. The girls couldn't keep from laughing at him. Shirley was becoming hot watching Gary undress. She licked her lips and hoped he would lose again. She wanted to see how big his shaft was and if she thought she could take all of it. Gary finally won a hand, but lost the next hand. It was show and tell time. Shirley held her breath as Gary pulled off his briefs.

"What do we do now?" asked Gary.

"If you lose again, you have to do what the winner wants you to do."

It was Shirley's deal. Everyone was getting a little drunk from drinking after each hand. Shirley slowly dealt the next hand and won with three aces. "I get to ask Gary to do my bidding." He was naked and standing proud.

"I want Gary to go to bed with me and screw my brains out."

Everyone looked at Shirley. "Do you care if I make it with Gary?" she asked Sandy. "You and Charles can watch and the two of you can make out if you want to."

Sandy replied, "Sure go for it. It might be fun watching you try to take all of his, large shaft. I call it the flag pole."

Charles and Sandy watched from their seats at the table as Gary jumped in bed and turned over on his back. "Are you ready for this?"

Shirley stared at Gary's large shaft while she took off the rest of her clothes. She had a beautiful figure with curves in all the right places and breasts that pointed straight out. Her nipples were hard and she could feel her juices flowing down below. She crawled up on the bed and took his shaft in her hand and started to slowly stroke it. She lowered her head and circled the head with her tongue. It surprised Gary and he about came off the bed, his penis throbbing as he ran his fingers through her hair, pulling her head down on him. He couldn't believe what a deep throat she had. Shirley stroked the bottom of his erection while she sucked on the rest of it. It was so good.

Shirley stopped before he came. She straddled him and guided his erection to the tips of her hot spot. She eased the head into her folds and twisted her body as she slowly lowered herself until she had almost all his length. Gary arched up and she sheaved all of his erection. She sat still while her body adjusted to his size. It felt wonderful as she started to bounce up and down on his big shaft. She twisted, turned and thrashed her head from side to side. She had never taken anything that big before. She increased her speed and knew she was about to have a climax.

"Gary, drive it in me hard, I'm coming I'm coming."

"Hang on just a little longer and I'll come with you."

Gary slammed into her a few more times. He felt her muscles throbbing around his shaft and punched her hard one more time before his shaft jerked as he shot his load into her hot body. Shirley collapsed on Gary's chest, her hard nipples digging into his chest.

Shirley was trying to get her breathing back to normal. That had been some ride. She enjoyed every minute of it. They were still connected, but Gary had gone limp. She didn't want to get off of him and he didn't push her off. Shirley glanced over at Sandy, "Now it's your turn. Charles will give you a good ride."

Sandy removed the rest of her clothes and crawled into the other bed. She turned over on her back and spread her legs in invitation. She smiled at Charles, "What are you waiting for."

"I'll be right there." He ripped the rest of his clothes off and jumped in bed. Charles positioned himself between her legs and kissed her, running his tongue deep down her throat. He ran a hand down to touch her moist folds while the other hand pinched a nipple. He lowered his head and took a nipple in his mouth causing Sandy to arc her back inviting him to take her. She whispered, "I want you inside me now. I am burning up."

Charles positioned himself between her thighs with a hand on either side of her head. Sandy grabbed his erection to guide him home. She sheathed all of him and started to move. She was hot and ready for a good ride. He slammed into her hot body while she met each thrust. She could feel her muscles tighten around his erection and knew she was having a climax. "Give me all you got. I'm coming, I'm coming and it feels so good." It went on and on and she didn't want it to end, but all good things come to an end. Charles thrust into her one more time and arched his back as he had a climax. Sandy could feel his come go deep into her body. He rolled off her and lay beside her totally spent.

"That was quite a show," giggled Shirley.

"Charles was good," replied Sandy.

Shirley could feel Gary's shaft starting to throb inside her body and she wiggled on it bringing it to a full hard on. "It's my turn to pleasure you. Assume a position on your hands and knees so you can be my mare."

Shirley rolled off Gary and positioned herself for his assault. He positioned himself behind her and touched her hot folds with his erection. She moaned as he grabbed her hips and slammed his shaft deep into her body. "Give it to me fast and furious. Oh yes, oh yes ---!"

It didn't take long until they both went over the edge at the same time. Gary glanced over at Charles and Sandy. They were both asleep. "Well I guess you sleep with me tonight." Shirley curled up on her side and Gary slid in behind her spoon fashion. They were asleep in record time.

They all slept late Sunday morning. Charles was the first to wake up. He took a shower before he made noise to wake the rest of them. Everyone finally had their shower and was dressed. It had been a fun time, but it was time to leave and go back to the everyday grind. They loaded their cars. After talking a few minutes they went their separate ways.

"That sure was a fun time, don't you agree?"

"Yes it was," replied Gary.

They didn't discuss the partner swap. They arrived back in Houston that afternoon. Gary dropped Sandy off at her apartment and went straight home. He had phone messages on his phone.

The ones related to work could wait until the next day when he returned to work. The last call was from his Mother wanting to know when he would be home to visit. He called home and talked to his Mother. He told her everything he had done in the past weeks except his sex life. He promised he would be home the next week-in.

Gary put in long hours so he could go home on Friday evening. He sold several houses and made a good paycheck to build up his checking account. He called Sandy and told her he would be out of pocket for the week-in.

Gary made it home Friday night by nine. His Mother had fried chicken, mash potatoes, green beans, corn-on-the-cob, biscuits and cherry pie for desert, waiting on the table for him. It was the first home cooked meal he had eaten since he left home. Mrs. Mitchell told him Leroy was home from Dallas visiting his parents. He called Leroy and asked him to meet him at their old hang out, the Dairy Queen.

"Hi Gary, what's up?" Leroy greeted him as he came in the door.

"Not much, just work."

"That doesn't sound like the person I know. Now tell me about all the girls you have gone out with and if you have made out with any of them. You can't fool an old buddy."

"I don't kiss and tell, but you won't know any of them anyway." He gave Leroy a run down on his sex life and swapping girls in Galveston.

"You have been busy since you went to Houston, but are you serious about any of the girls? Do I hear wedding bells?"

"No, I'm working and enjoying sex with the girls. I plan on hitting it big before I even think about getting serious and getting married. Are you serious about a girl?"

"As a matter of fact I am. I'm going out with a Newspaper reporter in Dallas and it is serious. I think I have found the one I want to spend the rest of my life with."

"Well good luck if you are sure about her."

After a long visit they parted and went home. It was good to see Leroy again. Gary wasn't sure he could ever do the job Leroy had picked for his life's work. Being a Policeman in Dallas was dangerous work. He knew that wasn't his cup of tea. It had been a good visit, but it was time to go back to Houston.

Mrs. Chadwick called Gary into her office Monday morning. "Gary, there are some gentlemen asking about industrial property that we don't have a listing on. Do you know anything about the property?" She showed him the address.

"Yes, I know about the property, I own the property. I used all my savings to buy the property hoping some company would come along and want it. Do they want to buy it?"

"Yes, Exon wants the property for an office and warehouses. That is choice property and it will bring a lot of money. What do you plan to do about it?"

"If it is ok with you, I'll sell it through the company. The company will get half of the selling fee and I will get the rest. That way the company gets the listing and makes money. I'll make the sale for the company and get credit for a big sale."

"I see you got it all figured out. Good thinking on your part. This will make you rich, but I guess you already knew that. Here is the number to Exon. Mr. Goodnight is the contact for your sale."

Gary was shaking all over with excitement as he called Mr. Goodnight and set up an appointment to look at the property. Ten days later, Exon owned the property and Gary had a huge bank account. He was a rich man. He vowed to never be poor again. He had made it to the top. It had one drawback. Women would want to marry him for his money. He would have to be very careful who he went out with from now on. He read in the newspaper about a ranch near Sugarland for sale. It had fifteen hundred acres, house, barn and livestock. It didn't give a price. He decided to take the afternoon off and go see the property. He decided he wanted a home and maybe a family if the right woman came alone.

Gary saw the sign before he got to Sugarland, L.J. Ranch. It was just outside the city limits, but still close to town. He slowed down and turned right, crossing a cattle guard and drove up to the house. It was a two story wood home with a large porch on the front of the house. Trees and grass were well kept. There was a large coral beside the barn. Gary gazed across the fields and saw livestock grazing. He fell in love with the ranch.

Mr. Leroy Jones met him as he walked up the porch steps. "How may I help you?"

"My name is Gary Mitchell and I'm here about your ranch. I would like to see it and probably buy it if it is still for sale."

"Yes, I have to sell my ranch or lose it to the bank. I have a big loan on the ranch. Come on and I'll give you a tour of the ranch."

The house was huge with five bedrooms, three full bathrooms, living room, dining room, kitchen, tact room, washroom, office and a three car garage on the side. It had a cottage for the foreman and a small bunkhouse for the hands. The barn was large enough for livestock, feed, hay and equipment. It was a working ranch. The land had a creek running through it and a small lake for water. It had some trees and good grass for the livestock. Gary had seen enough, he wanted the ranch.

They talked price until they came up with a selling price. Mr. Jones paid off his loan and had a good nest egg to live on. He was getting too old to worry about keeping the ranch afloat. Gary gave him plenty of time to move out. He kept Joe, the old foreman and the one young hand Sam. They knew the running of the ranch and would be a plus to the sale.

"Joe I won't be here only on week-ends. You will be in charge of the ranch when I'm gone. I'll set up a line of credit at all the places we buy supplies. Do you know what is needed to keep the ranch going?"

"Yes sir, I buy all the supplies for Mr. Jones."

Gary gave Joe his phone number at work and at his apartment. "Call me day or night if you have a problem and I'll try to take care of it. I don't have any ranching experience, so I'll depend on your advice a lot. I'm going now and I'll see you next week-end." He didn't tell anyone he had a ranch.

Sandy called Gary just as he stepped in his apartment. She had good news for herself and wandered if Gary would be mad or happy for her. "I got a job in Dallas making twice what I make here."

"I'm proud for you. We were going together for fun and sex. I hope you do fine in Dallas. The name of the game is to make money and get ahead. I sold that piece of property you let me know about. I got a good price for the land." He didn't tell her how much.

"Come to see me if you make it to Dallas. I got to go and finish packing. I'm leaving in an hour for Dallas. It was fun while it lasted."

"Yes it was," replied Gary. "I wish you all the luck."

Gary had mixed feelings about Sandy. He knew he wasn't in love with her, but he enjoyed their time together. He was going to miss her.

The next week was hectic to say the least. He didn't make a sale until the middle of the week. Finally, he made a good sale, but he had to work hard to make the sale. He couldn't wait until Friday. He wanted to return to his ranch and was looking forward to the week-end.

As Gary walked by Rebecca on his way to his office, she called to him. She had several messages for him. As he reached for them, she bent forward showing a nice set of breasts. She was wearing an uplift bra and her breast looked good enough to eat. He took the messages from her hand and took an extra amount of time as he stared down her front. She smiled and took her time straighten back up. She had heard through the grapevine that Sandy was gone and it was open season on Gary. She wanted to be his new girlfriend.

Rebecca wanted him to ask her out Friday night, but he turned to go back to his office. She decided to be bold. "There's a country western band at Mickey Gilley tonight that is out of sight. Would you like to take a lady out?"

"Yes I would like to take you out, but I already have plans for the whole week-end. I'm going out of town. I'll take a rain check. Maybe we can go out one night next week."

"I'll hold you to that."

Gary arrived at the ranch at seven Friday night. He brought food and a sleeping bag.

The house had water, lights, electric stove and a refrigerator, but he would have to buy some furniture. Early Saturday morning he went to Sugarland to buy furniture for the house. After buying out the furniture store, he went and stocked up on food. He went back to the ranch to wait on his furniture delivery. They showed up a couple hours later. After they unloaded and set up each room, the house was fully furnished.

Joe and Sam knocked on the back door and wanted to know if he needed any help. He didn't need them, but he asked them in for a cup of coffee from his new coffee pot. They talked ranch business for over an hour while drinking up the pot of coffee. Gary wanted to look over the cows and horses that evening. "Joe, I'm a little embarrassed because I have never been on a horse."

"Don't worry, there are several tame horses for you to ride and I will teach you how to ride. Come down to the barn when you are ready."

Gary arrived at the barn. Joe had two horses saddled and ready to go. After a short ride, Gary was riding like he had always been on a horse. Joe showed him the things to check on, down fence, water, cattle or horses in trouble and plenty of grass or hay for the animals.

He needed to keep up with everything that went on at the ranch. Joe showed him a cow that had delivered a calf that morning. He explained that they cut and bailed their own hay. They had the equipment in the barn for that task. Gary wanted to purchase more cattle and horses. He wanted the ranch to make a profit. It would take time and money.

Gary gave Joe a check and told him to buy some more good livestock. They spent the rest of the day riding fence. Gary was so sore he could hardly get off his horse. They gave the horses a rubdown. He wished he had a good looking woman to rub him down.

That night Gary went to Sugarland to check out the eating places and nightlife. He found a fish place and had catfish, hush puppies, cold slaw, pickled tomatoes and tea. He was as full as a tick. It was time to check out the nightlife.

He found a country western club and paid the door charge. He found a table in the corner where he could watch everything and have his back to the wall. You never knew when a fight would break out and he didn't want to be involved in it.

Gary didn't ask anyone to dance. He enjoyed watching couples as they twisted around the dance floor. He was tired and sore from riding a horse all day. He wasn't sure he could get up out of his chair. He watched awhile longer and called it a night. He went home and took a cold shower, had a cold beer and went to bed. The new bed felt wonderful and it didn't take long before he was fast asleep. He was so tired he didn't even have a dream.

He woke up late. He fixed bacon, eggs, toast and coffee for breakfast. He stayed around for a couple of hours before heading back to Houston. He arrived back at his apartment at one in the afternoon. He answered his phone messages until the last one. He stared at the number. It was from Rebecca telling him how much she missed going out with him. She was giving him the come on. Gary didn't know if he wanted to go out with Rebecca or not. He decided to take it slow and see what happens.

He had a dream about a girl out of the country in big trouble. She had a great body with curves in the right places. It was so real, like out of the body experience. He had a hard on watching his dream. It was like watching a movie and he was the main player. Gary knew he was there to save her. He grabbed her hand and started for the door. A huge wolf was standing in the doorway. He woke up from the dream. He sat up in bed and starred around the room totally confused. What had just happen? He had dreams, but nothing like this one.

Rebecca smiled at Gary as he walked by her desk on the way to his office. "Good morning Gary, did you have a nice week-end?" She wanted to know where he went, but he didn't tell her.

"Yes, I had a productive week-end. I got things done I needed to do." He walked on to his office. He knew she was curious about where and what he did, but he didn't want to tell her. He enjoyed going to the ranch and working. It was his way to relieve the week's stress.

Every chance Rebecca got, she came into his office. She was always dressed fit to kill. He decided to give it a couple more days and he would ask her for a date. He had to get his mind back on his sales and make a paycheck. He always managed to make at least one good sale every week.

Friday, Gary made a date with Rebecca for Saturday night. He took off early Friday and went to his ranch. He went to Sugarland to start a bank account. He transferred a bundle of money from his

Houston bank. That would be his operating money until the ranch turned a profit. He wanted to use only the bank in Sugarland for the ranch.

Gary drove across the cattle guard and looked up at the name. He wanted a new name, but he didn't know what he wanted to call the ranch. He decided to wait until he could come up with a new name. He gave Joe some checks to use if he needed something where they didn't have an account. "Joe I want you to make out the payroll and keep a log."

He gave Joe a log book labeled expenses and payroll. Joe would take care of things until he finally moved out to the ranch to stay. He hoped to do that one day. He wanted to find his true love and get married.

He wanted to raise a family. He didn't want to get married right now, but it was in the plan. Finding the right woman would take some time. He thought about his date tonight and got a hard on. He hit the road back to Houston. His date wasn't until seven, so he had plenty of time to shower, shave, and put on clean clothes. He put on jeans, white shirt and cowboy boots. He didn't like to dress formal. He didn't care what his date wore. If she didn't like his dress they could call the date off or stay home.

Chapter Two

Gary picked up his date at seven. "Where would you like to go tonight?"

"I'll leave it up to you," purred Rebecca. She didn't care where they went as long as she was with Gary. He didn't know it, but she planned to seduce him tonight, if she could make it happen.

"Then I'll take you out to eat while we decide what we want to do tonight." She looked good enough to eat. Gary wandered if she was a tease or was she ready for some good loving. He took her to a bar and grill that wasn't formal.

"This looks like a nice place and even has a small dance floor. Would you like to dance after we eat?" She wanted to rub her body on him while they danced. She wanted some good loving tonight and she didn't care what she had to do to get it.

They both ordered steak, a bake potato and a salad. Gary had a beer and Rebecca ordered a cocktail. They stared at each other while they consumed their food. After their meal they ordered another round of drinks.

"Would you like to dance?" Gary asked.

"I would love to dance."

Gary stood and took her hand. He led her out onto the dance floor, took her in his arms and slowly moved around the dance floor. It was a very slow dance and Rebecca rubbed her body against him. She felt a hard object against her belly and knew Gary had a big hard on. By the time the dance was over he was ready to scream because he couldn't control his erection. He walked behind her back to their table and sat down. They finished off their drinks.

"What would you like to do now?" asked Gary.

She surprised him. "I want to go home and get screwed all night."

"I like a girl who knows what she wants, let's get out of here."

They drove back to Rebecca's place in record time. She unlocked the door and they hurried inside. Gary pulled her into his arms and kissed her hard, running his tongue deep into her mouth. Her tongue met his and they twisted together.

She had her arms around his neck and pressed her body against his chest flatten her breasts, digging her nipples into his body. She was on fire. He reached around her and slid her zipper down, pushed the thin straps off her shoulders letting her dress fall to the floor. She wasn't wearing a bra. He reached down and slid her black lace panties off her hips and let them fall to the floor. She stepped back so he could see all her body.

"Gary, you have too many clothes on. Let me help you undress." She unbuttoned his shirt and pushed it off his shoulders letting it drop to the floor.

Next, she reached for his belt, unbuckled it, pulling down the zipper she reached inside his pants and grabbed his shaft. He stepped out of his boots. She pulled his pants down along with his briefs. "Gary, let's go to the bedroom." She starred at his large shaft and licked her lips. She grabbed his arm and led him to her bedroom.

This was going to be a great night. Gary sat on the bed while Rebecca pulled off his socks. He lay on his back with his shaft standing straight up toward the ceiling. It was hard as a rock and ready for action. She slipped off her shoes and moved up between Gary's thighs. She took his shaft and stroked it as she slipped it into her mouth. She circled it with her tongue and sucked on it. He put his hands on her head and helped her move her head up and down.

"Rebecca I can't take much more or I'll come in your mouth." He reached for her shoulders to pull her up. She slid his shaft out of her mouth. "Then do it," she said as she took it back in her mouth. Gary shuddered as he came in her mouth.

"You taste a little salty."

"Now it's my turn to pleasure you." He pulled her over on her back and started to move on her body. He slid between her legs and kissed her hard. He nibbled on her ear, shoulders, down to her nipples which he sucked the right one until it was hard and gave the other one the same treatment. He licked his way down to her fuzzy patch. He spread her lips and stuck his tongue deep into her folds. She arched her back to get all of his tongue. It didn't take long for her to have a climax. "I'm coming, oh I'm coming." She shuddered and went limp. She felt like a contented cat. He lay beside her while they rested. They turned over and faced each other as he pulled her into his arms.

"Oh Gary, that was so great."

After they rested for a few minutes, Rebecca felt his penis poking her in her belly. She knew he was ready to make love again. She turned over on her back and spread her legs in invitation. He poised above her and lowered himself down as she grabbed his erection and guided it into her folds. She arched her back and sheaved his large shaft. It felt so good she wanted to scream. Gary slammed into her harder each time he thrust into her hot body. She was bucking like a horse and tossing her head from side to side. She cried out each time he hit bottom. She wanted it to last all night, but she could feel her muscle's tightening around his erection and her juices flowing.

She couldn't wait any longer. Her body shuddered as she had a climax. "I'm coming, I'm coming, sock it to me hard." Gary came right behind her and she squeezed every drop out of his shaft. "Oh Gary, it was so good. I would like to do it all night."

"Turn over with your back to me. Yes like that, now stick your butt up." He slid up behind her spoon fashion. He slid his shaft inside an inch into her folds. It was still limp, but in time it would turn hard again. "When my shaft turns hard and even if I'm asleep push back and take it all."

"Hey, I like the way you think."

They dozed off to sleep still connected. Now that was a way to sleep. Rebecca had never done sex that way before and liked it. She woke up first and felt Gary's hard erection an inch inside her folds. She pushed back against him until she sheathed his shaft. She rocked back and forth until Gary moved against her. "Oh Gary, it feels so good, do it faster." It didn't take long before they both came.

They showered together and got dressed. After a big breakfast of eggs, bacon, grits, toast and coffee, Gary left for his apartment. He had a lot of work to catch upon. He took a nap that afternoon. Too much sex had exhausted him. He dreamed about Rebecca and how good she made love.

Monday started off fast with clients looking for homes, but a large number were just looking which killed a lot of time. Maybe one of them would come back. The rest of the week was slow and Gary was glad, when Friday quitting time rolled around. Rebecca wanted to spend the week end with him. He informed her he had business out of town. She was not a happy camper.

Gary picked up some clothes at his apartment on his way out of town. He wanted to spend time at the ranch working. He wanted to go into town and get to know the locals. He wanted to relax and enjoy the week-end. When he arrived at the ranch Joe was feeding some new mothers and their young offspring some feed. Sam was busy repairing a fence.

Joe explained that they had more livestock. He had gone to the sale and bought some horses and cattle. He explained they would have a calf crop to sell off in a few months. That would put the ranch in the black. Gary couldn't wait for that to happen. He told Joe to hire someone to train horses. He wanted to start selling trained horses. Joe was all for it. If he was lucky enough to find a good horse trainer, he would board other horses for training. He wanted to cover all bases to make a profit.

That night Gary slept like a log. It was so nice on the ranch. He would quit his other job as soon as the ranch was up and running. It would have to turn a good profit. He hoped to marry and bring a wife with him. He didn't know if Rebecca would be the one. He had strong feelings for her, but was it love? He didn't know how you felt when you were in love.

Gary was up early Saturday morning. He drove into town to eat. He wanted to get to know the locals. The restaurant he picked was owned and operated by a local man. It served good food and the service was good. The customers were friendly and he had a second cup of coffee.

He shopped around town, even if he didn't need anything and met a lot of the local merchants. When he was tired of shopping, he headed back to the ranch. He spent the rest of the day riding fence and checking on livestock. He loved the ranch because it was his, lock, stock and barrel. He had paid cash for it. He was tired that night and got a good night's sleep. He got up late and after breakfast he headed back to Houston.

When he walked through the door, his phone was ringing off the hook. He picked it up and Rebecca was on the line. She wanted him to come over for supper. He told her he would be over shortly. He knew what she wanted. She wanted to make love. He had never gone with a girl that wanted sex all the time. He was exhausted each time he went with Rebecca.

That night after supper, they made love over and over until they finally went to sleep. The next morning, Gary ask, if Rebecca would like to move in with him. They would be out only money for one apartment. She said she would in two months when her lease was up.

Two months later Rebecca moved in with Gary. He wouldn't let her pay any of the bills and she loved that. She could build up her bank account. It worked out perfect except Gary was pussy whipped all the time. Rebecca never got enough sex. After a couple of weeks they slowed down some.

Gary still went out of town some weekends to his ranch. He never told her where he was going and she didn't like that one little bit. "I love you," she purred as he was leaving.

"I love you to. I'll be back Sunday by noon."

Gary went to his ranch Friday evening and by noon Saturday he was caught up on everything. He sat at the kitchen table thinking about Rebecca. He decided he would pick up an engagement ring on his way home and surprise her. He would tell her about the ranch and his plans. He would ask her to marry him if she wanted to. He stopped at a jewelry store on his way home and got a beautiful ring. He couldn't wait to see the look on her face when he pulled out the box.

After Gary unlocked the door, he eased inside wanting to surprise her. Rebecca wasn't downstairs and he eased up the steps. At the top of the stairs he heard grunts and groans coming from the bedroom. It blew his mind when he entered the bedroom. Rebecca was between Tommy's thighs with a mouth full of his erection, while Philip banged her from behind. They didn't see Gary come in the bedroom.

"What the hell is going on?"

"Just having a little fun," replied Rebecca. "You were gone and a girl has needs."

"Get out of my house now, all of you." Gary reached in his dresser and pulled out his gun. He pointed the gun at them. "Get out of here before I do something terrible." They stared at Gary. He fired the gun exploding the ball on the left side of the headboard, then took out the ball on the right side.

Tommy, Philip, and Rebecca made a dash for the door picking up their clothes on the way. A couple of minutes later he heard the front door slam. Somebody called the Police that shots were fired. Five minutes later the cops were knocking on his door. Gary didn't try to lie out of anything. He showed them the bedroom and told them what happen. "I'm surprised no one was killed," replied the Cop. It was hard to keep from laughing while he wrote up the report.

He finished the report and handed Gary the report to sign. He read the report and was surprised. It read, gun went off by accident and no one was hurt. Gary looked at the Cop and he grinned. He signed the report and the cops went on their way. Gary was devastated. He pulled the ring box out of his pocket and hurled it across the room. He slammed his fist into the wall and put a hole in the wall. How could she do that to him? He thought she loved him. He finally took a shower and went to bed. Gary didn't get much sleep and got up tired. He knew what he was going to do.

Rebecca saw Gary coming and ran to the bathroom to hide. He went straight to Mrs. Chadwick's office and knocked before he opened the door. Tommy was in her office and he beat feet. Mrs. Chadwick stared after Tommy wandering what was happening. Gary came right to the point.

"Mrs. Chadwick I'm quitting as of right now."

"May I ask why? I thought you liked it here."

"I did, but I can't work here now."

"You can ask your employees. I'm leaving town and would like my pay now if I can get it. I won't be back."

"Gary, I'm sorry to see you go. You can pick up your pay before you leave." She called payroll and ask for a final check for Gary to be delivered to her office. A short time later she handed him his check. He left the building never to return.

After Gary was in his car, he drove to the bank and transferred all his money to his bank in Sugarland. He went back to his apartment and packed. He paid all his outstanding bills and gave the landlord his key. He headed home to his ranch.

When he pulled in front of the house, he saw Joe and a new man at the corral working a new quarter horse. At least things were going good at the ranch. He killed his engine and walked over to the corral.

"Hi Joe, how's it coming?"

"Good as to be expected training a new horse. Gary this is Ben Hodges our new horse trainer."

"Good to have you on board. I want to be able to give our customers anything they want in the way of a horse. If we don't have what they want, we can buy it and train it."

"Sounds good to me," replied Ben.

They talked business for some time before Gary retired to his house. When he was inside he thought he would relax, but he was still wired. Nothing could seem to relax him. He got a beer out of the refrigerator and went to his office. He went over the bills and sales of the calf crop.

Joe had sold the first calf crop. Joe was right about the sale. It put the ranch in the black. From now on he planned to keep it that way. With the ranch in the black he should be on cloud nine, but he felt like a black cloud was hanging over him. He had a hard time getting over Rebecca even after what she did. He finally realized why she did what she did. It was simple she was a woman who had to have continuous sex. There was name for it, but he couldn't remember what it was. At least now he knew why she did it. He would try to move on with his life and time put it behind him.

Gary worked and slept. He tried to move on, but it was hard. He went to town a few times and went to the local bars. He had a few beers and danced with some of the women, but he couldn't make himself get interested in a certain woman. Maybe in time he could date again. He hung around the ranch for a couple of more weeks, but he was restless.

Hunting season was coming up and he decided to take a trip deep into wild country out in west Texas. He got his 45 automatic and his 30 cal. Carbine. He packed plenty of shells for the trip. He used a large backpack to fill with food and other things needed for the trip. He filled a suitcase with clothes. Last he packed his sleeping bag and tent.

Gary found Joe in the barn and explained where he was going. "Look for me when you see me coming. I don't know when I'll be home. Take care of the ranch while I'm gone. I got a lot on my mind and need to get away for some time alone."

The next morning the weather had turned cold, but that would make the deer move around. Cold weather was good for deer hunting. Gary had bought an old Ford truck for the trip. It wouldn't win any beauty prize, but it ran good. It would get him there and back.

Gary headed west not knowing where he was going, but he knew he would know when he got there. He stopped and ate lunch along the way. He drove several more hours before he found himself in land without fences, houses or people. He turned off the road and drove deep into the wilds. He drove until he found a small creek with running water.

After looking around, he drove back up the hill and parked under the only tree for miles. He set up his tent, laid out a sleeping bag, backpack and supplies. He had a small gas stove to cook on. He looked around for some firewood to build a fire in case it got real cold.

Gary found some branches that had fallen off the tree and some dry leaves to start the fire. He gathered some rocks to circle the fire. After fixing the fire, he broke out his stove to fix supper. He warmed some beans and sat down to eat. As it turned dark he watched the stars come out. There were hundreds of them, pretty and bright. He finally started to relax and blank his mind. It was hard, but he wanted to forget what had happened. Wild animals started to make noise as dark came. Wolves started to howl at the moon. Gary crawled into his sleeping bag and got his first good night's sleep in a long time.

Early the next morning Gary was up and at them. He made breakfast of eggs, bacon, bread and milk to drink. After he was full he strapped on his backpack, strapped on his 45 automatic and picked up his carbine. He had some bottle water to take with him. He wanted to explore the area and see what game was out there to hunt.

Gary started off south from his camp. He walked along at a distance from the creek as he followed it south. He saw a deer in the distance, but it was too far for a shot. He saw some wild hogs on the other side of the creek. He saw quail and dove flying overhead. This was a hunter's dream. After he had walked about a mile, he turned and headed back to camp. Gary wanted to live off the land as much as possible.

On the way back to camp a rabbit jumped and ran in front of him. He brought the rabbit down with a head shot from his carbine. He picked up the rabbit and headed back to camp. Gary had his supper. All he had to do was skin, gut the rabbit and cook him. He thought he could taste the rabbit already.

After Gary had the rabbit on a rod over the fire, he made coffee. The rabbit smelled good as it cooked. He sat and licked his lips as he watched the rabbit turn brown. When the rabbit was done he ate his fill and packed the rest away for a meal tomorrow.

As it got dark, the wolves started to howl again. Gary was getting used to the sound. The only difference was they were a lot closer than last night. He went to his tent and crawled into his sleeping bag. He laid his carbine beside him just in case. Better to be safe than sorry. He got another good night's sleep.

The next morning after breakfast, Gary packed up and headed north to explore. As before, he saw plenty of game to hunt. He saw another deer, but he was too far away to get a shot. The carbine was only accurate at two hundred yards. After about a mile, he turned around and headed back to camp. He seen several rabbits, but he still had part of a rabbit left from last night.

Gary angled down close to the stream and discovered cat tracks. That put him on alert. He wasn't sure what kind of cat tracks he was looking at. They were large whatever they belonged to. He angled back up to higher ground so he could see further ahead and behind him. Closer to camp, he ran across the cat's trail again. It was headed in the direction of the camp. Picking up speed, Gary saw the black cat going through his supplies. Most of it was packed in metal boxes to keep animals out.

Chapter Three

Gary fired his carbine in the air to chase off the cat. It looked like a panther, a big one. He went through his supplies and the only thing missing was the rest of the rabbit. He should have shot one on the way back to camp. He put his supplies back in place and wandered what he would have for supper. Looks like it would be beans again with some beef jerky. He made coffee on his stove and sat down to eat. He was more relaxed than he had been in a long time. He didn't have to make decisions except where or what he wanted to do with his time. Tomorrow he would explore a different direction. He liked to explore places he had never been.

Each day it was starting to get colder, but Gary didn't mind. He was up early and finished breakfast in record time. He put on his gear and headed back toward the way he came in. He wanted to make sure he was the only one in the area. He made a sweep back and forth as he got further from camp. He ate lunch of beef jerky and water. He planned to kill something on the way back to camp for supper. Half way back he killed a large rabbit. That would last him a couple of meals unless he had another visit by the cat.

The rabbit tasted like a steak. He dreamed he was in a steak house in Houston. He cooked a large potato to go with the rabbit. After a couple cups of coffee he was full and ready for bed. After dark the wolves started their usual noise, but Gary had got used to it and went to bed. He got another good night's sleep. The next morning he slept late. It was cloudy and the wind was picking up. There was a storm on the way. It was getting colder as the day wore on.

Gary hadn't shaved since he left the ranch and had a dark beard. It would help keep him warm. He fixed him a good breakfast of bacon and eggs with coffee to drink. He heard a wolf howling real close. It sounded like it was coming from the creek.

After he cleaned up breakfast, he strapped on his 45 automatic and backpack. He filled a canteen with water and picked up his carbine. Gary walked down to the edge of the cliff and scanned the area. He didn't see any wolves.

Suddenly he heard a rattling noise behind him. He turned slowly to face a rattlesnake ready to strike. He eased back slowly and lost his footing. He fell off the cliff and landed hard on the ground below.

His leg hurt like hell as did the rest of his body. His leg was turned at a crazy angle. He knew it was broken. Gary moved his other leg and knew it was broken or a bad sprain. The wind was picking up and the storm was getting closer by the minute. He looked around for some shelter. There was a cave right behind him. It was starting to rain. He had to move fast, but that was impossible. He grabbed his carbine and dragged himself into the cave. It was larger than it looked. It had a small entrance, but it got larger the further you went into the cave.

Gary leaned against the wall and tried to keep from passing out. He had some pain tablets in his backpack. He found them and took a couple with the water from his canteen. He leaned back against the wall and wandered what he should do next. He knew he had to do something for his broken leg. He found some masking tape in his pack. What could he use for a splint? The only thing he had was his rifle. He didn't like using it, but that was all he had. He still had his 45 automatic for protection.

Sliding the rifle along his leg, he pulled on the leg until it looked right. Gary wrapped the masking tape around the leg and the rifle. He wasn't a Doctor, so he wasn't sure he did it right, but it would have to do. He took his flashlight and shined it into the back of the cave. There were bones all over the floor and he knew he wasn't alone. He knew he would have company soon. He pulled out his automatic and waited. He didn't have long to wait.

A large wolf stood in front of him. They stared at one another. Since the wolf didn't look like he was going to attack, Gary put his weapon down beside him. He held out the back of his hand for the wolf to sniff it. The wolf walked right up to Gary and sniffed his hand. He pulled out a piece of beef jerky and held it out to the wolf. The wolf took it from his hand.

Gary relaxed and held out his hand. The wolf let him touch him and then pet him. Gary petted him some more. He had found a friend, a wolf, but a friend.

It was dark when the rest of the pack came home. Gary put his hand on his automatic ready to defend himself. He knew he didn't stand a chance with a broken leg and so many of them. Suddenly the wolf in front of him stood up between him and the other wolves. He stood his ground until the wolves went into the cave. He curled up in front of Gary and went to sleep. He couldn't believe his protector was a wolf. Would he continue to look after him?

After a good night's sleep, Gary woke up and his protector was still there. He fed his new friend and petted him. The wolf stood up and walked around in the front of the cave, but he kept an eye on Gary.

The wolf pack left the den to hunt, but his protector remained with him. There was something very strange about their friendship. Gary tried to move around, but it was too soon. The wolf continued to roam around, but stayed within sight. Gary closed his eyes, but something was wrong.

Gary could see things in front of his vision. He blinked his eyes and closed them. He opened his eyes and looked where the wolf was looking. He realized he was looking at the same thing the wolf was looking at. He opened and closed his eyes several times with the same results.

It was a crazy feeling. How could it be happening? Gary closed his eyes and spoke to the wolf. The wolf looked as confused as he was. He realized the wolf could understand him. He didn't speak to the wolf out loud. There was a large limb close to the wolf. Gary stared at the limb and whispered for the wolf to bring it to him. The wolf walked over and picked it up. He looked confused, but brought it back to Gary. Maybe things wouldn't be so bad while He waited for his leg and body to heal.

After resting awhile, Gary decided to experiment more with the wolf. He whispered to the wolf to go to his camp. The wolf looked at him and trotted off in the direction of the camp. Gary closed his eyes and he could see through the wolf's eyes. The wolf waited for his next command. Gary told him to go in the tent, pick up a bag filled with supplies and return to the cave. The wolf returned with the bag and dropped it at Gary's feet. He patted the wolf on the head.

"Good wolf. Now you go fetch the rest of my gear."

The wolf made several trips until Gary had all his equipment and supplies. He pulled out beef jerky and fed the wolf. The hard part had been bringing the stove, but the wolf finally got enough in his mouth and made it back to the cave. Gary rolled over onto his sleeping bag. He closed his eyes and went to sleep. The wolf curled up beside him and went to sleep.

Each day Gary woke up, his leg didn't hurt as much. He thought it would take six weeks to heal. He didn't have enough food and water to last that long and he knew he couldn't make it to the camp for his truck. Wolf would have to take care of him. The next day Gary ran out of water. He took the cap off his canteen and attached a strap to it. He held it up.

"Wolf I need some water. You can fetch it from the creek."

He handed the canteen to wolf and pointed to the creek. Wolf waded into the water and let the canteen fill with water. He returned to the cave with the canteen. Gary took the full canteen and took a drink. The water didn't taste bad coming out of the creek.

Gary dug in his sack and came up with a can of spam. He gave wolf half and he ate the other half. His supplies would last longer if he rationed them each day. What he needed was a deer to get a good supply of meat, but that wouldn't happen anytime soon. Gary checked his leg for infection, but it was healing just fine. It would just take time.

The next day wolf went hunting and came back with a rabbit. That would last a couple days if they didn't make a pig of themselves. Wolf brought limbs from the camp and Gary made a fire to cook their rabbit. He gave the scraps to the other wolves and kept the choice parts for wolf and himself. He was amazed at what wolf could do. It was like they were as one. He couldn't explain any of it, but he didn't care. He realized he wanted wolf to go with him when he was well enough to go home. He was like a brother to him. Gary started sleeping beside him and couldn't image going home without him.

The next morning Gary opened his eyes and saw a small deer drinking from the creek. He eased his automatic up and aimed at the deer. He fired two rapid shots and dropped the deer. Wolf jumped to his feet and stared at the downed deer. The other wolves came running out of the cave into the open. They didn't go far, before they realized there was meat on the table.

Wolf dragged the deer over to Gary. He took out his knife and started to skin the deer. Wolf and the other wolves watched as he cut up the deer. He kept the best pieces for wolf and himself. He threw pieces to the other wolves which they ate. He couldn't believe his luck.

Gary prepared chunks of meat to cook over the fire while wolf gathered wood for the fire. He put the rest of the deer away for future meals. They would have plenty to eat for the next few days and save the can goods for hard times. The weather was cold enough to keep the meat from spoiling.

Four weeks later Gary and wolf had everything down to a science. When they ran low on meat, wolf would bring something back to the cave. He filled the canteen over and over. Gary was moving around some and his sprained leg was well. His body was also. It wouldn't be long before he could make it up to his camp and leave. He was holding off so he wouldn't break the leg again trying to get to the camp.

It was over six weeks since Gary fell. All the supplies were gone. It was time to leave. He loaded wolf with most of his gear and left what they couldn't carry. Gary and wolf worked their way around the cliff to a place he thought they could climb out. It was slow, but they finally made it to his camp. He broke down the tent and loaded his equipment in the back of the truck. It was time to go.

Gary opened the passenger door and starred at wolf. "Do you want to come with me?" Wolf stared at Gary, then back toward the cave and his pack. They had followed them to the camp. "I'll understand if you want to stay with your pack, but I think we are a team and should be together."

Wolf looked at the wolves, back to the open door and back to the pack. Suddenly he made up his mind and jumped in the door on the passenger side. Gary smiled as he got under the steering wheel and started the truck. He was going home to the ranch. He wandered what had gone on while he was gone. He was filthy and had over six week's growth of beard. He didn't want to stop on the way home, but he would need gas.

Gary stopped at a service station, filled up with gas and got some junk food. The clerk looked him over, but didn't comment. They stopped at a roadside park one more time before they reached the ranch. He looked at the ranch and the sign over the cattle guard.

"Now I know what to name the ranch. I will name it G&W Ranch, Gary and Wolf Ranch. How does that sound to you?" Wolf barked his pleasure. Gary laughed at him.

Joe saw them coming and came out to meet them. He saw the huge wolf beside Gary on the passenger seat. He didn't know what was going on. Gary got out and Wolf stood beside him.

Joe took a step backwards. "What is going on?" asked Joe.

"Joe, I would like you to meet my new partner. This is Wolf. He saved my ass and came home with me. I want the sign changed out front. I know what I want now." He told Joe what he wanted. He would tell Joe and the rest of the hands his story later on.

"Come on Wolf, let's get cleaned up and get something to eat." Wolf followed Gary into the house. He looked around, it sure beat the cave. Gary shaved, took a shower and put on clean clothes. Wolf was waiting on him in the kitchen. "I see you found the food." The kitchen had an indoor grill just for steaks. Gary got two big steaks out and put them on the grill. He fixed a salad and two baked potatoes. He didn't know what Wolf would eat besides meat.

When the steaks were done, Gary served them. He had a beer to drink and Wolf had a bowl of milk. Wolf ate a little salad and some of his potato. After supper Gary went to his office to catch up on his mail and be sure Joe paid all the outstanding bills.

Wolf roamed the big house and checked it out. He didn't understand why Gary had such a big cave for only one person. When he went to bed, Wolf parked himself in front of the door. Gary smiled, once a protector, always a protector. He got another good night's sleep. He knew nobody or anything would get past Wolf.

The next morning Gary was up and feeling great. "How about you and I take a trip to town? I want people to see you and get to know you since you will always be with me and have my back." They took the truck to fill it with gas. He finished and paid for his gas. Wolf was standing beside Gary.

Suddenly from across the street, a man with a gun came running out of the grocery store and headed for a parked car. Gary whispered to Wolf. "Take him down, but don't hurt him."

Wolf hit the man in the back and sent him sprawling on the payment. He dropped his gun and a bag of money. He turned over as Wolf planted his paws on his chest. Wolf stared down at the man.

"I wouldn't move if I were you," advised Gary. He heard a cop car coming. It stopped just short of the scene. The cop got out and slowly walked over. "You don't have to worry, the robber isn't going anywhere until you want him," said Gary.

The cop starred at Wolf. "That's a wolf," he stuttered. He didn't believe what he was seeing.

"Yes, that is Wolf and my partner. When you are ready to take the robber I'll have Wolf get off him."

The cop pulled out his handcuffs and Wolf stepped back. "Where did you get the wolf? He is so big. I have seen a lot of wolves, but never one his size."

"I didn't find Wolf. He found me and saved my life." Gary told the story to several people gathered around them. Wolf didn't know what all the fuss was about.

A newspaper reporter approached them and took pictures of Wolf and Gary. Gary stared at the reporter. She was about five foot five inches, long blond hair, blue eyes and curves in all the right places. She smiled at Gary and wanted him for an interview. Wolf stood beside Gary like a dog would do.

"My name is Judy Adams and I am a reporter for the local newspaper. Where did you get the wolf and how did you train him? He acts like a trained police dog."

"My name is Gary Mitchell and this is Wolf. The wolf found me when I fell off a cliff and nursed me back to health. I didn't have to train him. He knows what I want and does it without questioning my command." He didn't tell her how everything was. She wouldn't believe him anyway. She took down the details about the robbery. "Thank you for your story. It will sell a lot of newspapers."

Judy walked back to her car. She would like to have more contact with Gary. He made her feel warm all over. It had been a long time since a man had any effect on her that way. She turned and Gary was still standing there staring at her. She blushed red. What was wrong with her? She was acting like a schoolgirl on her first date. Judy willed him to follow her.

When she reached her car, a hand reached around her and opened her car door. Judy turned around to face Gary. "Thank you."

"It was my pleasure. I'm new around here and wandered if you might show or tell me about the area. I have a ranch just outside the city limits."

Judy couldn't believe what he was suggesting. She would turn him down. "I would love to." Had she just said that? Her body was warm again.

"Fine, would you like to come out to the ranch? If you ride, we could cover the ranch on horseback. It would be fun."

"Yes I ride. When would you like me to come out?"

"Would tomorrow be too soon, how about nine tomorrow morning?"

"Sounds like a plan. I'll be there." She started her engine and drove off. She smiled and couldn't believe she had a date for tomorrow with a handsome man.

Gary had a hard on thinking about Judy. She was a fine looking woman. "Well I guess I'm over Rebecca and what she did to me. It's time to move on with my life." He would start over tomorrow.

The newspaper was plastered with the story about the robbery. It gave step by step account of the robbery. Gary and Wolf's picture was on the front page. The local radio station had picked up on the story and ran with it. Gary and Wolf ate breakfast while they waited for Judy to arrive.

Wolf went out on the front porch to watch for Judy. When she drove up in front and parked, Wolf howled. Gary came out to meet her as she walked up to him.

"I have never been announced like that before."

Wolf came over to be petted. Judy hesitated only a second before she put her arms around his neck. She couldn't believe she was hugging a huge wolf. "Don't I get a hug?" asked Gary. Judy walked over and gave him a hug. The sparks flew when they touched. She stepped back and caught her breath. Judy's heart skipped a beat and her nipples became hard. It was only a hug and her body went crazy. She stared at Gary and wandered what it would be like if he kissed her. Judy glanced at his zipper and saw a big bulge. She wasn't the only one affected.

"Come on in the house and have some coffee before we go riding." Judy and Wolf followed Gary into the kitchen where he had two cups on the table. Judy sat down while Gary poured the coffee and put sweet rolls on the table. They drank coffee, ate sweet rolls and stared at each other.

They couldn't think of what to talk about. Both of them were shook up. They finished their coffee and rolls. Gary broke the silence, "Are you ready to go riding? Joe saddled two horses for us to ride."

Judy nodded as she still was having trouble talking. What was wrong with her? They walked out of the house and headed for the barn. "You have a beautiful ranch," Judy said. They finally started to talk about the ranch.

They mounted their horses and Gary led the way. He showed her the land and all the livestock. Judy was impressed by what she saw. "This is a working ranch. We raise cattle and horses. I have a trainer which trains all the horses we sell. It takes a lot of work, but we manage to keep the ranch in the black. If we keep growing, in a few years it will be a fine ranch. Judy watched Gary and knew he loved the ranch.

"Is there a Mrs. Mitchell?" Now why had she asked that? "I shouldn't have got that personal. I'm sorry I asked."

"It's ok there isn't a wife or girlfriend." Now why did he say that? Gary wanted her to know he was open for dating. He could see her breasts straining at her blouse trying to get free. He couldn't keep from staring and hoping a button would pop off. He scolded himself for being a dirty old man.

"Would you like to race back to the barn?"

"You're on." She kicked her horse in the flanks and got a large jump on Gary's horse. She beat him back to the barn by a couple horse's length.

"You cheated," Gary said as he stopped beside her.

"All's far in love and war," laughed Judy.

Wolf had followed them the whole time. He was tired and went upon the porch and lay down. These people were crazy. They ran all over the country for what? He realized he didn't understand people. He knew Gary liked Judy, so why didn't he just take her, that's how he did it when he wanted a female wolf.

People were funny and wasted too much time trying to get what they wanted. He would have to train Gary how to get a woman.

Gary and Judy went to the kitchen for something to drink. He had a beer and she had a diet coke. She told him about the locals, good food places, entertainment and where to find girls.

"I don't need to know the last one. I hope I've found a girl." He stared at Judy and hoped he hadn't stuck his foot in his mouth. Judy stared back and blushed.

"Maybe you have." She couldn't believe she said that. It had been a long time since she dated. The Newspaper took up too much of her time. Maybe it was time to have a little fun in life. All work and no play, makes for a dull person.

"I got to get back to town. I had a wonderful time. I got a human interest story to write." She didn't tell Gary it was about him. She gave him her home phone number and told him to call.

Gary walked Judy to her car and opened the driver door for her. She turned to say she would see him later. He was standing real close, "I'm going to kiss you." He pulled her into his arms, before she had time to resist. She looked up as his mouth covered hers. They fit perfect together. Her nipples became hard as she put her arms around Gary's neck. Finally, Judy got into her car.

Judy looked up at Gary, "You sure know how to get a girl's attention." She waved as she drove off. She smiled and touched her lips. Her lips were tingling. Gary was a good kisser.

Gary watched Judy drive off and missed her company already. She was fun to be with. He hoped it didn't turn out like his last love affair. He was still having trouble trusting women. He had been playing with an idea about Wolf and himself. He wandered how good Wolf was at tracking. It didn't take long to find out.

Joe came in the house very excited. "Boss we have a cow missing." He had saddled two horses for them to ride. They rode out to where the cow was located. Wolf went ahead of them. They found the cow and she was having a fit. She had some scratch marks on her flank. Gary closed his eyes and looked through Wolf's eyes. Wolf knew what Gary wanted him to do.

Wolf sniffed the ground and took off at a run. Gary walked his horse. "Shouldn't we try to keep up with Wolf?" asked Joe.

"No, we don't have to hurry. I know where Wolf is at all times. We'll go to him when he catches up with the cat." Gary picked up the pace just a little. Joe stared at Gary and wandered how he knew where Wolf was. He closed his eyes for a second. "Ok, let's roll. Wolf has the cat up a tree and it is a large bobcat." Gary let his horse have his head and they were at the tree in a few minutes. The bobcat looked down at them. "Joe, you bring him down." Joe took his rifle and dropped the cat with the first shot.

Wolf stood and looked at the cat. He didn't want to eat the bobcat since he was still full from breakfast. Joe put the bobcat in a bag to carry him home. He wanted to have him stuffed.

Gary looked at Wolf, "Good job Wolf."

Wolf trotted ahead of them with his head and tail in the air. He liked to be praised. Joe smiled at Gary, "Would you look at that."

Thanksgiving was the following week and Gary went home to visit his parents. Leroy and Rex were also home visiting. They got together at Mike's ranch. Leroy was still a cop going with a reporter for the Dallas paper. Rex didn't have a girlfriend at present. Mike was still training horses for the movie company. Gary had brought wolf with him. His friends couldn't believe he was running with a wolf. He told his story of survival. They bought the story until he told them he could see through Wolf's eyes and talk to him far away from him.

"Bull shit," said Leroy. Rex agreed with Leroy, but Mike didn't. He could talk to horses, so why couldn't Gary talk to Wolf.

"Ok nonbelievers, I'll take a test. Put a blindfold on me and we'll play what Wolf is doing." Mike put a blindfold on Gary. "Leroy, take Wolf with you in your car. Take a little trip and I'll tell the guys where you are and what you are doing." Everybody looked at Gary like he was crazy.

"Leroy, go to your car, Wolf will follow." When Leroy was in his car with the passenger door open, Gary looked at Wolf. Wolf got in the car. Leroy went down the road toward town. Leroy stopped at a service station. Wolf scratched on the door and Leroy let him out. He walked over to a coke machine and put his paw on the coke button. Leroy got out and put money in the coke machine. Wolf pushed the coke button. Leroy handed him the coke. Wolf got back in the car. Gary was telling everything that was happening.

When they returned, Wolf walked over to Gary and dropped the coke in his hand. Gary removed the blindfold. "Thanks Wolf, I wanted a coke." Everyone stared at Wolf and Gary. They couldn't believe their eyes.

"How do you do it?" asked Leroy.

"I don't have a clue. I just know we connect as one. I see what he sees and I can command him with just a whisper. Wolf reads my mind and knows what I want done. I know it sounds crazy, but we are connected as one."

"Would you help me if I ever get in bind?" asked Leroy. "I get some pretty tough cases sometimes."

"You know I will, just give me a call and I'll come running. Don't tell anyone about Wolf and myself. The nuts would hound us to death for tests and everything."

"You got it," they answered.

They broke up and went their separate ways. They hoped to get together again soon. Gary's parents didn't know what to think about Wolf. He was like a good trained dog. Gary didn't tell them about their strange powers. He just told them he was his pet. Gary and Wolf went back to the ranch the next day. It was good to be home.

Joe had put up the new sign over the cattle guard. Gary saw it as he approached the ranch. "Well Wolf, how do you like our new sign G&W Ranch? The W is for you." Wolf howled his approval.

Gary pulled up to the coral where Ben was working a quarter horse. "How's it going?" Gary asked. "Great, we have three new horses in training. Business is really picking up. All three are already sold as soon as I complete the training." If things kept going good, Gary would have to hire some more men.

That evening, Gary put an ad in the newspaper. You lose them and we find them, Gary and Wolf. He got a surprise the next day when a rancher close by called. His prize Herford bull was missing and wanted Gary to find him.

"Come on Wolf, we got our first job." Gary hooked up the horse trailer to his truck and saddled a horse. It was time to rock and roll. About twenty minutes later they pulled into the Hard Luck Ranch.

The owner met them out front. He was worried about his prize bull. He had been missing for two days. The bull always came to the barn each day for his feed.

Gary unloaded his horse. Wolf and Gary started their search. The ranch had some rough terrain and took time to search it. One section was trees and underbrush. After an hour, Gary stopped his horse under a large oak tree and rested. He closed his eyes and could see where Wolf was searching at all times. He saw the bull in a bog. Wolf did most of the searching while Gary closed his eyes and watched. Gary rode the short distance to the bog.

"Good job Wolf, now we all have to do is get the bull out of the bog."

Wolf circled the bog as Gary took his lariat off the saddle horn and lassoed the bull. He tied the lasso around the saddle horn and backed his horse up until it was tight. Gary got behind the bull and twisted his tail. The bull bellowed as the horse slowly backed up. Finally the bull managed to get on solid ground.

Gary left the rope around the bull's neck and started back to the ranch with Wolf on his heels to keep him moving. The owner came out to meet them. The bull and Gary were muddy.

"Where did you find the bull?"

"We found him in a bog. It took some hard pushing and pulling, but we finally got him out of the bog. He needs a hose down and so do I."

They went over by the barn and used a water hose to wash the bull. Gary washed up the best he could. The owner paid Gary and thanked him for his services. Gary loaded his horse and they headed for home. "Well Wolf, we completed our first job. If we are lucky there will be many more to come."

In the next couple of months they were busy finding cattle and horses. Gary stared at his records and was amazed at the profit they made. How could people be so careless with their livestock? Most of the time a gate was left open or a fence was down.

Early the next morning, Gary was listening to the radio, when the announcer told about a little lost boy of six years old. It had rained that night and it looked bad for finding the boy alive. There was a ten thousand dollar reward to the person who brought the boy home. It was between Sugarland and Houston where the boy was lost.

"Wolf, it's time for another job, but this one is different. We will be searching for a little six year old boy. I hope the kid is still alive. Let's get our gear together and get on the road." Gary strapped on his 45 automatic in case of snakes. He didn't take the horse trailer. The woods were too dense for riding a horse. He pulled the truck out on the highway and put the medal to the floor. Every second counted for the little boy.

Gary pulled his truck off the road at the search area. There were people everywhere even a search and rescue team, but nobody had found the boy. The boy's home was a short distance up the road. Gary found the Father and talked to him for any information about the boy.

The Father stared at Wolf. "I read about you and that big wolf in the newspaper. Do you think you can find my son? It rained a gully washer, here last night."

"Sir, I don't want to promise you anything, but Wolf and I will do everything we can to find the boy. We'll be on our way now." Gary and Wolf headed out into the woods. The whole area was empty of people. They had searched the area and moved deeper into the woods.

Gary didn't think the boy had gone too far into the woods. They did a crisscross pattern trying not to miss anything. There was a swamp on the right side and dense woods on the other side. Gary took his machete with him to cut his way through the bush.

After two long hours, they stopped to rest. Gary was wet with sweat and scratches from the brush. They knew this was not going to be an easy job. "Well Wolf, we had better get back at it." The rain last night made it even harder. It was muddy in places and Wolf couldn't track the boy. He held his head up high in the air and tried to catch the boy's scent.

At lunch time, they stopped to eat a bite, beef jerky and water. They didn't bring a lot of food. They wanted to travel light. They ran across other searchers, but they weren't having any luck either. Gary was starting to worry that the boy wouldn't be found in time.

By four o'clock they were deep into the woods and still nothing. Other searchers were on their way back. Gary and Wolf stopped to rest and think. He thought about the swamp directly behind the house and decided to go back as close to the swamp as possible.

When they were close to the house, Wolf stopped and sniffed the air. He smelled human and it wasn't Gary. "What is it Wolf?"

Wolf let out a low howl. They heard the muffled sound of a child crying. "Find him Wolf." Wolf went as close to the swamp as possible with Gary following him. They saw a small island with a large log in the center. They also saw snakes everywhere. The rain the night before had made a small island.

With his machete in his hand, Gary, waded the water toward the small island. Wolf went ahead of him. When Gary reached the island he killed two snakes around the log. He looked inside the log and saw the boy. "Don't be afraid, we are here to get you out and take you home."

Gary finally got the boy out of the log. He was thirsty and hungry, but in fair condition. He had a coke and a candy bar with him which he survived on. His clothes were torn. He had bruises and scratches over his body, but he would be ok.

The boy stared at the big wolf, but he didn't cry. "What's your name little one?"

"Joey."

"Well Joey, how would you like a ride home?" Gary sat Joey on Wolf's back for the ride home. They slowly made their way out of the swamp. It was almost dark by the time they came out of the woods. There was a large crowd gathered waiting for them.

Joey slid off Wolf and ran to his Mother's open arms. "Mommy I rode Wolf home. It was fun."

Mr. Simmons handed Gary a check and thanked him for finding his son. Gary looked at the house they lived in and wandered where he got the money. Mr. Simmons, where did you get the money to pay?"

He hesitated a second before he answered. "I got a loan on the house."

Gary tore up the check and handed it back to him. "No charge for finding the boy." Mr. Simmons couldn't believe his ears. He thanked Gary again and if he could ever repay the favor he would do anything to help Gary. Joey came over, hugged Wolf and Gary. That was enough pay for the job.

Chapter Four

Joe, Sam, and Ben met them when they pulled up in front of the ranch house. They wanted to know if they found the little boy and everything about it. Gary told the story about them finding the little boy. "We heard it on the radio. The radio said you didn't take the money for finding the boy," said Joe.

"I couldn't take the money after I found out where he got it. He got a loan on his house to pay me. I don't need the money that bad. The ranch is in the black and we can pay all our bills and payroll."

Wolf and Gary went to the house to eat and get cleaned up. They were hungry after walking all day in the woods. Gary slapped two big steaks on the grill, two potatoes, made a salad and set the table. As soon as the steaks and potatoes were done, they started to pig out. Gary was so hungry he could eat a horse.

After supper Wolf took a shower first and Gary took his shower last. Wolf settled down in the office for a nap, while Gary checked for phone calls and mail. The last call was from Judy. She wanted to come out for a story. It had been a long time since he had seen Judy and he was looking forward to seeing her again. He remembered the hot kiss they shared when she was leaving the ranch. He got a hard on thinking about her. He called her to let her know she could come out tomorrow.

Gary was tired and went to bed early. Wolf curled up at the door as usual. He woke early after a good night's sleep. He fixed Wolf a steak. He cooked eggs, bacon, grits and toast for himself. Wolf had milk and Gary had coffee to drink. After washing dishes, Gary took a shower, shaved, put on jeans and a t-shirt. He was ready for Judy to arrive.

Judy arrived at eight and knocked on the door. Gary opened the door and wasn't sure how to greet her. Finally, he opened his arms and she walked into them. He hugged her and lightly kissed her.

Sparks flew as usual. She became heated and her nipples strained at her blouse wanting to be free. Gary had an instant erection. Judy looked down at his fly and blushed.

"We sure do have an effect on each other."

"Yes we do," stuttered Gary. He didn't release her right away, she felt good in his arms. Finally, He opened his arms and she stepped back. "I guess I better get on with the interview, the paper wanted the story from the horse's mouth," Judy laughed.

Judy got her interview, but didn't want to leave. "What have you been doing? I never received the phone call from you."

"I have been trying to get our new service off the ground. It has been fast and furious."

"I saw your add in the paper. That is a strange one. Has it got you any business?"

"Yes, lots of business and we could have brought home ten thousand dollars on the last job, but I couldn't take the man's money. He got it on a loan on his house. I don't need money that bad. If he was rich I would have taken the money. "

Judy liked this man, more and more as she got to know him. She wanted him to ask her out again. She finished her interview and went out to her car. Gary opened her car door and she turned to face him. "I'm going to kiss you." Gary opened his arms and she went into them. He covered her mouth with his and eased his tongue into her mouth. His tongue touched her tongue and her knees started to buckle. If Gary wasn't holding her so tight, she would have melted at his feet.

"Would you go out with me Saturday night?"

"Yes," Judy stuttered. She had lost her voice. She was blushing like a school girl on her first date. What was wrong with her? She had lost her cherry in High School, but she wished she had waited for her true love. It was too late to cry over spilled milk.

"I'll pick you up at seven and we can decide what we want to do." She gave him her address.

"I'll be ready," replied Judy. As she drove off, she smiled, she had a date for Saturday night and she was going all out to impress Gary.

Gary went to town and bought new duds for his date Saturday night. He went whole hog. He bought a western shirt, jeans, leather vest, leather coat, black western hat and boots. When he saw the bill, he about passed out. Was the date worth all that money to impress Judy? Yes it was if he made out. When he got back to the ranch, he put up his purchases and went to work. They had a strip of fence down and he wandered if rustlers had cut the fence.

Joe and Gary did a head count on the cattle and horses. There was twenty head of cattle missing. Did they go through the fence on their own or were they rustled. Gary called the Sheriff and reported the cattle missing. Gary and his crew saddled up and went looking for the cattle. Wolf lost the trail next to the highway. They found truck tracks where the cattle were loaded on a truck. Gary had insurance, but he wanted to catch the rustlers. The cattle were branded G&W. The rustlers would have to change the brand or sell them to a fly by night slaughter house. It didn't look good. The Sheriff told him there was a rash of cattle rustlers.

Gary wasn't giving up on finding his cattle. Wolf and Gary would do their own thing. They went to sales and checked for the cattle. They went to slaughter houses.

They checked out a slaughter house just outside the city limit. The owner was very nervous. Gary didn't know if it was Wolf or he had something to hide. Gary decided they would stake out the slaughter house and see what would happen. He divided the shifts with Sam, Joe, and Ben. They watched from a safe distance.

If the slaughter house was involved, it wouldn't take long to find out, with the amount of cattle missing. Gary asked the Sheriff to call him when some went missing. Two days later, Joe was on watch at midnight when a load of cattle rolled up to the slaughter house. It seemed odd to deliver that late. He called Gary and he called the Sheriff on his way there. There wasn't a report of cattle missing, but it wouldn't be until the next day and by then the cattle would be cut up into meat for sale.

Gary arrived before the Sheriff. Wolf walked ahead followed by Gary and Joe. They walked up beside the truck and could hear them killing the cattle with an ax. It was so much noise that they could walk right upon the thugs.

One thug turned and reached for a gun, bad mistake, Wolf broke his arm as he took him down. The other thug stared at Wolf. He dropped his gun and Gary picked it up off the ground. "Don't let that wolf get me."

"If you put your hands on top of your head and don't move, I'll keep him off of you." Two more men came out of the slaughter house, but they weren't armed.

"Put your hands on top of your head," ordered Gary. They did as they were ordered.

The Sheriff pulled up and got out of his car. "Gary what's going on?"

"I'll let you know as soon as I check the brand on the cattle." The Sheriff and Gary went to check the brand, while Joe and Wolf stood guard on the men. The Sheriff knew the brand on the cattle and wanted to see a bill of sale, which they didn't have. Another Sheriff's car pulled up and the Deputy helped handcuff the bad guys. They loaded the cattle rustlers into the two cars and headed for town. That was one meat packing plant that was out of business. They were making 100% profit, which was a lot of money. They would need it for a good lawyer.

Gary went home for a good night's sleep or what was left of it. He had a hot date tomorrow night and he didn't want to miss it.

While making breakfast, Gary called Judy and told her about last night. She wanted an interview to send to the paper. She was getting all the hot news lately. He gave her the details over the phone and she called it in. The Editor couldn't believe she had all the hot dope on the rustlers. He had a reporter at the Sheriff's office trying to get the scoop on the story. Judy dropped it in his lap on time to get on the front page.

"Are we still on for tonight?" asked Gary.

"You bet we are. I wouldn't miss it for the world. I bought a new dress to wear. Don't you back out on me or I'll sock you."

"I'm scared," laughed Gary, "See you tonight."

Joe, Sam and Gary checked all the cattle to make sure they had a brand. Some of them didn't have a brand. They rounded up the ones without a brand and spent the rest of the day branding cattle. Gary was filthy by the time they were finished.

Gary took a hot shower and put on his new duds. He looked in the mirror and decided he looked good. "Wolf, you stay home and guard the house, I got a hot date." Wolf thought it was about time Gary did something about his sex life.

When Gary left, Wolf curled up at the front door on guard duty. Lord help the person who broke into the house, Wolf would eat him alive.

Judy opened the door as Gary stepped up to the door. She had been watching for him. She was as nervous as a cat on a hot tin roof. Her heart was beating double time, her nipples were hard, pressing against the front of her dress and she was moist down below. That man sure had an effect on her.

Gary stepped inside and opened his arms. Judy stepped into

them and they shared a hot kiss. He smiled and stepped back a step to stare at her. "You sure clean up nice."

"Thank you, I think," Judy giggled like a school girl. "You don't look bad yourself."

Judy was wearing a clingy low cut black dress that showed off her curves. She wore black high heels to match her dress. Gary was in his new duds. He would like nothing better than to push the small straps off her shoulders and let the dress drop to the floor. He wandered what kind of panties she was wearing. He would bet they would be black with black lace. He had a hard on thinking about it. Judy looked down at his fly and blushed. "We better get going," she giggled.

After they were in the car, "Where do you want to go?"

"There is a small club on the west side of town and it serves a good steak. It also has a band and a dance floor. I would like you to take me dancing. I can't remember the last time I went dancing."

"I may step on your toes."

"I'll take the chance."

Gary drove while Judy gave directions. They pulled up in the parking lot thirty minutes later. He killed the engine and looked at the sign which read Local Bar and Grill.

"It's not fancy, but the food is good and the music is loud. I think you will like it. I used to come here when I was younger. I don't have time to come working at the paper. Tonight I want to eat, drink and be merry."

"I think we can manage to do all of that," laughed Gary. They went in and got a table close to the dance floor. Several people Judy knew stopped to talk. Several remembered Gary from the newspaper.

Pretty soon they had a large group around their table. They wanted to hear stories about Gary and the wolf. They were starting to call Gary "The Wolf Man" because he always ran with the wolf. After they had heard all the stories the people returned to their tables.

"You are a popular man around here. I bet you didn't even know it."

"No I didn't, but I'm glad they finally left us alone. I want to spend time with you." Gary flagged down a waiter and they ordered supper. They both had steak, baked potato, salad and wine to drink. The steaks came out thick and juicy with just the right amount of pink in the center. They found out they liked the same things. They liked the same type movies, books, riding horses, fishing and swimming. Gary wandered if they would make love the same way. Time would tell, he hoped.

Judy watched Gary and wandered what he was thinking. "I'll give you a penny for your thoughts." He came out of his trance and stared at her. "You wouldn't get much for your money," he teased. He wasn't about to tell her what he was thinking, not yet anyway, not until they had been together longer. She glanced down at his fly and she bet she knew what he was thinking. She giggled, she couldn't help it.

"What's so funny?" asked Gary.

"Nothing honey," she giggled.

"Do you want to dance?"

"I thought you would never ask. I would love to dance."

Gary stood up and pulled her chair out for her. He reached for her and pulled her out on the dance floor. They danced to a fast two-step. "You lied to me when you said you weren't a good dancer."

"Judy, anybody could dance with you as their partner. You float around the floor and make me look good." The song ended and a slow one started. Gary pulled Judy tight against him as they barely moved around the floor. She was having trouble breathing. Her nipples became hard, poking Gary in the chest and she could feel something hard poking her in the belly. She started to tremble. "Are you cold?"

"No, well maybe a little," she lied. They finished their dance and returned to their table. Gary ordered another round. He had a beer and she had a cocktail. Judy was week in the knees. She didn't want to dance anymore. She told Gary she was tired.

"We can leave when you want to go."

Gary finished his beer and stood. He helped her to her feet and they walked toward the door. He was ready to go himself. He wanted to spend some time alone with Judy. She was thinking the same thing. She knew what her body wanted to do, but she didn't know if she was ready.

They drove in silence back to her apartment, each one in their own little world. Gary wandered what would happen if he made a pass, was it too soon? He wanted to make love to Judy tonight. Judy was still fighting her body for control. Her body was hot for some good sex, but her brain said it was too soon. She didn't know what would happen. She could kiss Gary at the door and go inside. That's what she would do.

When they got to the door, "Would you like to come in?" Judy asked. Now why had she done that? Her body was against her.

When Judy closed the door, Gary opened his arms and she threw her arms around his neck. He tenderly kissed her, running his tongue into her sweet mouth. She tasted like wine. They kissed for a long time before he slipped her straps off her shoulders and let her dress drop to the floor. Gary kissed her neck and worked his way down to the top of her bra. The bra hooks were on the front which he took care of as the bra dropped to the floor. Judy couldn't believe she was standing in his arms with only her panties on and she was burning up with desire.

Judy decided it was time to take action. She reached for the buttons on Gary's shirt and had it off in a matter of seconds. She unhooked his belt and slid his zipper down on his fly. She slid his pants down, but realized he still had his boots on. He laughed, stepped back and took his boots off and his jeans. "Now we are even, almost, you `still have your shoes on." Judy kicked her shoes off. "Now we are even." She put her arms back around his neck and rubbed against him, her hard nipples digging into his chest.

Gary kissed her again, working his way down her slender body to her nipples where he took one in his mouth and sucked on it while using his fingers on the other one. Judy let out a low moan, she was on fire. He started to kiss his way down her body, stopping at the top of her black lacy panties. He stared at her panties. He was right in his dream about what she was wearing. He put a thumb under each side and lowered them until they fell to the floor. He stepped back and took his fill of her.

"You are beautiful and I want to make love to you."

Judy reached for his briefs and pulled them down. "You need to be rid of the briefs first." They stood for a few seconds staring at each other. "You are beautiful too," she giggled.

Gary pulled her to him, flesh against flesh until he lifted her up and she locked her legs around his waist. He lowered her until his erection entered her folds. She was tight and he took his time, slowly letting her take an inch at a time. He turned with his back to the wall to steady them and let her take all of his erection. Judy moaned and called Gary's name over and over as she twisted and turned on his shaft. He slammed up into her hard. She was having the time of her life and didn't want to stop, but she could feel a climax coming on.

"I'm coming, I'm coming, give it to me hard and fast," she moaned.

"You got it." Gary banged her as hard as he could until he felt her tighten around his erection.

Judy had a big climax with juices running out onto Gary's shaft. He slammed into her a couple more times before he came deep in her body. He held her until his erection went limp. He lowered her to the floor, but continued to hold her. They held each other until their breathing became normal.

"Oh Gary, that was fantastic. How soon before we can do it again?"

"Woman I need a little time to get my strength back. Do you have a bedroom?"

"Yes I do." He used the bathroom. Judy took his hand and led him up the stairs to her bedroom where they crawled in bed to rest. They were still naked. Judy was hot and ready to make love again. She stroked his shaft as it slowly came back to life. She turned over on her back and spread her legs wide while still stroking Gary's erection. "Stop that or you will make me come too soon." He slid between her legs while she guided him into her folds. He slammed home in one easy stroke and picked up a fast pace. It didn't take long until Judy had a climax and Gary was right behind her. He fell on her breasts and was struck by her hard nipples. He wiggled on them, it felt so good. He finally pulled out and lay beside her. They were both exhausted. Judy lay on her side and Gary slid up next to her spoon fashion. It didn't take long until they were both fast asleep.

At around seven in the morning, Judy woke up to something poking her in the back. She turned over and put her hand on a big erection. Gary was still sleeping and didn't know what he was doing. He must have been having a good dream because he had a big smile on his face. She hoped it was about her. It had been a fantastic night of love making. She was a little sore, but it had been worth it. It had been a long time since she had made love and she hadn't remembered how wonderful it could be. She stared at the man beside her and wandered if this was true love. It felt so right being with him. She knew some woman had hurt him badly in the past and he didn't trust women. She was going to change that.

Gary turned over on his back, but he was still asleep. Judy started to stroke his shaft until it was at a full erection. He finally woke up to the most wonderful feeling he could ever remember having. A beautiful face appeared above him. Judy lowered her body down to sheath all of his erection. She wiggled her rear end as she started to bounce up and down. She moaned his name and increased her speed until she knew she was close to a climax.

"Now, give me all you got. Yes, like that. Oh yes, it feels so good." Judy squeezed his shaft and shuddered as she had her climax which went on and on. She finally fell over beside Gary totally content. She was exhausted and wanted to go back to sleep.

"What's for breakfast?" asked Gary.

"Go back to sleep. I'm too tired to get up."

Gary got up and went into the bathroom to relieve himself. He took a shower and came back to get dressed. Judy was fast asleep. He smiled and finished dressing. He went downstairs to the kitchen and looked in the refrigerator for something to cook. The refrigerator was fully stocked. He pulled out eggs, bacon, butter and hash browns. He found a pan and started cooking. He made coffee and toast to finish off the breakfast. He found a tray and loaded it. He carried it to the bedroom and woke Judy up. Judy stared at the tray and couldn't believe she was being served breakfast in bed. "I have never had anyone serve me breakfast in bed." Her eyes misted over.

"Now you have, I'm going back to the kitchen and eat my breakfast." Gary walked to the door and smiled at her as he left. He didn't want to embarrass her. He was glad he made breakfast for her since it was special for her.

After Judy finished her breakfast, she showered and dressed. Picking up her tray, she went downstairs to the kitchen. Gary was just finishing the dishes and took her tray to finish. He would make some woman a good wife. She liked a man who knew his way around in the kitchen. He smiled at her and her body became warm. No man had ever had that effect on her before. She stared at Gary.

"Do you clean house and make beds?" Judy giggled.

"Not if I can get out of it, but I can do all of it I have to. Do you want to hire a housekeeper?"

"Maybe, the benefits will be good." Judy smiled and let him think on that. "Do you have to leave or can we spend the day together?" Gary thought on what he had to do at the ranch. It was Sunday and nothing would be going on at the ranch.

"I can stay until this evening. What would you like to do today?" He watched her and could see the wheels turning in her head. I would like something simple where we would be alone together. What could we do to make, it happen. I don't want to dress today unless we go to church."

"How would you like to come to the ranch? We can make a picnic basket and go riding. We can find a nice place on the ranch to eat and relax."

"Sounds like a plan to me, I love to ride. I have to put on my boots, make a picnic basket and I'll follow you." She was wearing jeans and a white shirt. Judy locked up and met Gary at their cars. "I'll follow you so you won't have to drive me back home."

Ben was working a horse when Gary pulled up next to the coral. "Ben, why are you working on Sunday?" He walked over to the gate.

"The new owners are coming for two cutting horses tomorrow and I wanted to be sure they are ready. Would you do a favor for me and ride the horses for me? You need to work a calf out of the herd. Let the horse do all the work." Gary took the horse and rode him around the lot using his knees to give the horse instructions what to do. The horse responded great.

"Ben, let Judy ride the other horse and we will see how well they are trained. She is a good horsewoman and can get the most out of the horse." Ben went to saddle the other horse. He came out of the barn leading the other horse. Judy took the rains and swung into the saddle. Gary opened the gate and caught the other horse. They rode off into the pasture looking for the herd. They found them down by the creek.

Gary pointed to a calf and let the horse have his head. The horse moved the calf out of the herd. After several more times, he was satisfied with the horse. "Ok Judy, now it's your turn."

Judy let the horse do all the work until Gary was satisfied with the horse. They rode back to where Ben was waiting on them. "How did the horses do?"

"They did great. You can take off. Judy and I are going riding and have a picnic." Gary got down and got the picnic basket Judy had prepared at home for them. They rode out again and Ben took the rest of the day off. They ended up on the far side of the ranch next to the creek. They got off their horses and dropped their reins on the ground. The horses stood there like they were tied. That was part of their training. Judy put a small blanket on the ground under an oak tree and laid out the food.

The lunch consisted of cold chicken, potato salad and beans. They were hungry and finished off the food in record time. Judy packed up what was left and set it beside the blanket. They were fat and lazy after all that food. Judy lay back on the blanket. She was ready for a nap. Gary lay down beside her and pulled her into his arms. They dozed off to sleep locked in each other's arms.

Two hours later, Judy woke up and sat up. It was getting late and she needed to go home. She punched Gary on the arm. "Get up sleepy head, time to go home."

Gary was sleeping sound and didn't want to get up, but he finally got to his feet. He pulled her to her feet. They loaded the leftovers on Judy's horse and headed back to the ranch. When they got to the ranch, they walked the horses into the barn, unsaddled them and gave them a rubdown. When they finished, Gary walked Judy to her car.

Judy walked into Gary's arms for a kiss. It was a long sweet kiss. She hated to go since they didn't get to see each other very often. She would miss making love with Gary, but they both had jobs to do. She drove away from the ranch and waved to him. He waved back at her.

Gary missed her already. They didn't spend much time together and he hated it. He could see it in Judy's eyes when she left how sad it made her to leave. He was lazy for the rest of the day and night. He fixed a small supper, ate and went to his office. He went over the books to make sure everything was in order. Gary and Joe were good with the books, making very few mistakes.

The next couple of days were work as usual. There was always something to do. The new owner had picked up his horses and Ben was training a new horse. Gary rode out to check livestock and fence.

Wednesday, Gary held a meeting with the crew. He had a new idea to discuss with them. He wanted their input since it would involve all of them. He had made donuts to go with the coffee. Ben, Joe, and Sam filled in and sat down at the kitchen table. Gary walked around the table and filled their cups with coffee. He then took the seat at the head of table. Everybody looked at Gary and waited to see what was up.

"Men, I have another idea how we can enlarge the ranch some

more and I want your input. I want to start raising our own horses instead of buying them. That way we get all the profit and cut out the middle man. We will build another barn and corral for that purpose only. We have to go shopping for mares and a stud. We will start with quarter horses and if we have good luck we can move on to other breeds. Joe and Ben, I want you to look for our new horses. I will have to hire a couple more men to add to our crew. Ben, find you an assistant to help train horses. Joe look for another man to help out as needed. That's all, now I'll take intake on the idea starting with Joe."

"Sounds like a good idea to me, but what if it doesn't go over in this area?"

"If it doesn't work, we will scrap it and try something else. Ben since you will be in charge of training, what do you think about the idea?"

"I can handle my end and hope we sell enough horses to make a profit. I don't think we will know if it will work until we give it a try. I'll start looking for a man to assist me."

"Sam, you have been quiet up to now, what's on your mind?"

"I was thinking if we keep adding men to the crew, you will need more quarters and a cook. I know that will add more expenses, but I don't see how we can get around it."

"Sam, I think you gave a good input and I think you are right on the money. If we are going to expand we should do it right. All hands in favor give me a show of hands." All hands were for the adventure. "All right, let's do it."

Friday, Joe and Ben went to the sale looking for horses, while Sam did the work around the ranch. They came back that evening with several new horses to start their adventure. Gary called a contractor to build a new barn and corral. They would start on the following Monday.

That night, Gary drew up plans for the barn and corral. He added the cost for the new adventure and found out it would cost a bundle to get started. He hoped he didn't jump in over his head. His bank account would take a big hit. What were the chances of failing? He didn't have any idea. He should have checked out the area before he jumped in over his head. Well nothing ventured, nothing gained. He was going for broke.

Gary called Judy to see what she was doing for the week-end. He was missing her very much. She answered on the second ring and was happy to hear from him.

Judy hated to give Gary bad news, but she had to go to Galveston for a news story and wouldn't be back until late Sunday night. She was packing for the trip. "I could give you a place to pick up a good looking girl," she teased.

"Thanks, but no thanks, I have a good looking girl and I'll wait for her. Maybe we can get together next week-end." He told her about his new adventure and hoped it wouldn't flop. Judy thought it was a good idea. She didn't want to go to Galveston, but it was her job to report news.

One of the mares Ben bought was with baby. Sunday, bright and early, ben was knocking on Gary's front door. They ran back to the barn just as the mother delivered her colt. She had an easy birth. They watched while the mother cleaned her colt. The colt finally stood up and stumbled around the stall.

"We got our first male colt," Ben said, "He looks healthy enough." Gary walked around the colt looking for flaws, but didn't find anything wrong with the colt. Ben cleaned up the afterbirth and put out fresh hay on the floor.

Wednesday, Gary got his first call from a rancher wanting information about his new program. He wanted the pick of the new colts, born. They reached an agreement and Gary couldn't believe his luck. He told the rancher about the new colt and the rancher was coming to look at him. If he liked the colt and bought him, Gary would keep him on the ranch and train him as he grew to a full size horse. Starting out young, the colt would be trained by the time he was old enough to ride. He wouldn't get as much for a colt, but he would get boarding and training fees.

Friday, the rancher showed up to look at the colt. He carefully looked the mother and colt over. He bought the colt. They would move the mother and colt into the new barn as soon as it was completed. It would take about three weeks to complete the barn and corral.

Gary was thinking about Judy all the time. They couldn't seem to get free at the same time. Gary and Wolf went looking for another lost bull. He couldn't pass up the job. He could use the money and he didn't want his reputation of turning down jobs. It took Wolf and Gary until Sunday before they found the bull on another ranch. The owner didn't know how he got on his land. He would check his fence for down fence.

Gary and wolf loaded the bull on his trailer and took him home. The owner was glad to have his bull back. He had repaired the fence where the bull had got out. He thanked Gary for his time and handed him a check for his time. Gary and Wolf made good money finding lost cattle.

"Well Wolf, another day, another dollar. We can go home and eat a big steak for supper, after we get some of the filth off our bodies."

Wolf stared at Gary. He didn't like to take a bath, but Gary wouldn't let him stay in the house unless he took one.

Wolf went in the shower with Gary and they finally got all the filth off their bodies. Gary dried off and then dried Wolf off. As he promised Wolf, he grilled two big steaks for supper. After supper Gary went to his office to catch up on his books while Wolf curled up at the door. He called Judy to check in with her. "When are we ever going to get together again?" asked Gary.

"I don't have a clue. You are working or I'm working. I miss you very much. Maybe next week-in we can try again." They talked about an hour before they called it a night. After Judy hung up, she sat and stared at the phone. Something had to give. She wanted more time with Gary. She dreamed of the last time they made love. Her nipples became hard, her body became hot and she could feel heat in her private part. Was it love or lust for Gary? She didn't know if she was falling in love with Gary, since she didn't know what love was really like. Whatever it was, she wanted Gary in her bed.

The next day, Gary woke to the phone ringing off the wall. Now who would be calling this early in the morning? He answered the phone and it was the Houston Police asking for his help. They had heard that Gary and Wolf could track anything. They had a danger-ous man that escaped his ride on the way to prison. He was in a large wooded area, was armed and dangerous. They were afraid they didn't have enough men to contain him and he would get away.

"Wolf and I are on our way, we'll be there as soon as possible." The police Chief said he would send a car to the city limits to escort them to the area.

Gary was driving his car and flashed his lights at the Police as he approached the city limits. The Police car pulled in front of him and led the way. They pulled up to a large wooded area on the west side of Houston. The Chief met Gary and Wolf to explain what was going on. "We need to catch this guy fast before he leaves the woods. We don't have enough men to cover the whole area. He is armed and dangerous. He doesn't have anything to lose. He was sent to prison for life."

"We are going in after him." Gary watched as Wolf crossed back and forth across the front of the woods. Suddenly he broke into a dead run into the woods. Gary leaned back against his car and closed his eyes.

"Aren't you going to follow him into the woods?" asked the chief.

"No, I couldn't keep up. I'll go to him when he catches the prisoner." Gary closed his eyes and watched where Wolf was headed. He had a compass in his hand and tracked Wolf as he changed directions. The Chief stared at Gary like he was crazy. If only he knew.

Fifteen minutes later, Gary saw Wolf approach the prisoner from behind and he whispered for him to take the man down. The prisoner never knew he was about to be hit. Wolf hit the man hard from behind knocking him face first on the ground. He dropped his gun on the way down. He turned over and Wolf put his paws on the man's chest. He was scared to death with Wolf's mouth open showing his teeth. He was afraid to move an inch. Wolf looked up and could see the highway and a store sign.

Gary could see the same thing Wolf was looking at. "Ok Chief, Wolf took him down, let's roll." He got in his car with several cop cars following behind. A few minutes later, Gary pulled off the highway and stopped. He jumped out of his car and ran into the woods followed by several Policemen. Wolf was still standing on the man's chest. The Chief picked up the prisoner's gun and stood staring at Wolf.

"Well I'll be dam, I wouldn't believe it if I hadn't seen it with my own eyes. How on earth did you do it.?"

"Trade secret, Wolf you can let the Police have the prisoner unless they want to give him to you for lunch. Wolf hasn't had his meat for today and he may be hungry." The Policemen laughed, but the prisoner didn't like the joke. "I'll get you for this," raved the prisoner. The Chief told Gary if he ever needed anything let him know. He thanked Gary for his help. Wolf stared at the Chief. And thank you to, Wolf for catching the bad guy. The look on Wolf's face, made the Chief believe he knew everything that was said.

"Come on Wolf, let's get some breakfast." They jumped in the car and took off. They didn't take time to eat before they left the ranch and Gary was starved. He pulled into a restaurant just inside the city limits on their way back to the ranch. "Wolf, stay in the car while I get some carryout." He let Wolf out to relieve himself and get back in the car.

A man came out of the restaurant and approached Gary. "Don't leave the wolf in the car, bring him in with you." Gary stared at the man. "Don't you know that you and the wolf are on the radio news? There's nothing too good for you and the wolf."

They followed the man into the restaurant where he seated them. "What can I get you?" Gary knew what he wanted. "I'll have a steak, two eggs over easy, hash browns, toast and coffee. Wolf will have two steaks rare and a bowl of milk. The owner gave the order to a waiter and told him to take care of the order. They were in a booth and Wolf was on a seat. Wolf looked at Gary, like I should be on the floor. Gary whispered, "Wolf, you will eat in style."

The food arrived at the table and Gary cut up Wolf's steaks to bite size pieces. Wolf looked at him like he was crazy, but he started to eat. Customers stared at Gary and Wolf. A family came by on their way out. "Mister may I pet the dog?" asked the small boy. Wolf stared at the boy, I'm a wolf.

"Sure you can, but he's not a dog, he's a wolf. The little boy petted Wolf and was thrilled to death. Wait until he told his friends, they wouldn't believe him. The father thanked Gary for his time and taking the bad guy off the streets.

When Gary went to pay, the owner wouldn't take any money. It was on the house. Gary and Wolf went to his car and headed for home.

"Well Wolf, at least we got a free meal for the job. Maybe this will bring more business that pays." Gary stepped on the gas, in a hurry to get home.

Ben was training a horse and had an assistant helping. Gary watched them working the horse before he went into the house. Gary's phone was ringing when he stepped in the front door. He picked up the phone and could guess who was calling.

"Well, you are making news again. It's all over the radio. Would you give me the scoop?" Judy was lucky to know Gary since he was always in the news. He gave her the full story. She hung up to get her scoop in the newspaper. She promised to call him back to talk about the week-end. So far, she would be off if nothing happened.

Judy called at eight to talk about the week-end. Gary didn't have anything going on. They decided to go to San Antonio for the weekend. Judy called and made reservations at a hotel on the River walk. They left as soon as she got off work on Friday. It was late when they arrived at their hotel, but they had reservations. Their room was on the second floor facing the River Walk. They unpacked and went downstairs onto the River Walk. They found a restaurant that served steaks. They were both steak eaters. They ordered steak, baked potato, salad and red wine to drink.

After they finished their meal, they walked up and down the River Walk. They held hands and the sparks started flying. They always had that effect on each other and couldn't wait to be in bed together. They stopped and watched a show put on at the end of the River Walk. After the show Judy was ready to go back to their room. She wanted to make love.

When the door closed on their room, clothes went flying everywhere. They were both naked at the same time. Judy got down on her back and spread her legs wide inviting Gary to take her. He crawled on top of her, putting his hands on either side of her head, while she guided his erection into her folds. He slammed all the way home as she put her legs around his body.

"Oh Gary, it's been so long since we made love. We have to find a way to be together more often." She arched her back to meet each thrust as he increased his speed. They made love until they were exhausted. They took a shower together and ordered room service.

When their food arrived, they took it out on the balcony. The River Walk was lit up and was beautiful at night. They ate and watched the people move around on the River Walk. They sat out there until they became sleepy.

The next day they went to Sea World and killed the day sightseeing. That evening they went shopping around town. They bought all kinds of junk they didn't need, but it was fun. When they got back to the hotel, they packed their stuff from shopping.

There was a Mexican Festival going on about a block from the hotel so they decided to attend. There was lots of music, food and drink. They ate hot dogs and drank beer until they were full. There was dancing everywhere. They tried to dance, but gave up on the Mexican dances. They both liked country western dances and they were in the wrong place for that.

They found some chairs, sat down and watched the people dancing while listening to the music. Eleven o'clock they returned to their hotel. They made love one time and went to sleep. It had been a fun trip. They slept late Sunday morning since they didn't have to be out of the hotel until noon. They packed their gear and headed home.

While they were in the edge of town, Gary asked, "Would you like to stop for a bite to eat?"

"Sounds good to me, then we should make it home without stopping for gas." Gary pulled off the road into a parking area and they went inside a fast food joint. They had hamburgers, fries and a coke then got back on the road.

They rode in silence for some time, Gary glanced over at Judy and she was smiling from ear to ear. He watched her until he had to know. "What are you smiling about? What's so funny?"

"I was thinking how you grunted and groaned when I made you climax." She continued to smile and finally laughed out loud.

"You made a lot of noise yourself when you climaxed. Tea kettle can't call pot black. We both make a lot of noise when we climaxed together. You did wear me out making love so long, but I loved every minute of it and if you don't stop talking about it, I'll pull off the road and do something about it." He made like he was going to pull off the road.

"Oh, no you don't, not out here in the middle of nowhere." Judy looked straight ahead at the road. Gary slipped a hand between her legs and stroked her thighs. She squirmed in her seat as heat built up down below.

Gary laughed and removed his hand from between her legs. She closed her eyes missing the heat from his hand. When he touched her, she went crazy with longing for him to make love to her, but this wasn't the time or place. They sat in silence most of the way home. Each one was off in a world of their own.

When they arrived at the ranch, Wolf was outside with Joe and came running to meet them. He followed them in the house to be with them. He liked Joe, but he liked Gary better. They were a team and worked great together.

Judy said she would stay and cook supper. Gary and Wolf was all for it any time food was involved. She pulled a cut up chicken out to fry and turned on the stove to heat up. She told them to get out of the kitchen while she cooked. Gary went to his office to check his phone messages and books. Wolf curled up in the doorway on guard duty.

Judy prepared potatoes to be cooked, fried the chicken and left the lid on the pan to keep the chicken warm. When the potatoes were done, she mashed them and made chicken gravy to go with the potatoes. She had cooked corn-on-the-cob for her second side.

Judy set the table and carried all the food to the table. She came to the office and looked inside. Wolf looked up at her. "Chow is on." Gary and Wolf were on their feet, they didn't have to be told a second time. Judy turned back toward the kitchen in a hurry to get out of their way or get run over. Food was delicious and Wolf finished off any leftovers.

"You're going to make some man a good wife," teased Gary. Maybe he shouldn't have said that, she might think he was hinting. Well to think about it, maybe he was. He had been thinking along those lines for some time. It would be nice to come home to a good meal and a nice warm body to curl up with in the cold of winter.

Judy stared at Gary, passed her hand in front of his eyes without any effect. He was lost in space or something like that. "Hello earth to mars, are you reading me?" Gary finally came out of his spell. He stared at Judy and realized he hadn't heard a word she had said.

"I'm sorry, what did you say?"

"Nothing honey," giggled Judy. "You were off in space. Thank you for the complement on my cooking. I love to cook, but I don't have time, working all the long hours I do." She got up and started to clear the table. Gary rose from the table and helped her. Wolf went into the living room and curled up by the front door.

They did the dishes together like an old married couple. Judy was thinking she could get used to being a wife. She liked the part of sleeping together at night and the mad love making they did. She always slept like a log the rest of the night. The next day she was sore, Gary being so large, but she wouldn't have it any other way. She got hot just thinking about them making love. She glanced over at him and wondered if he ever had the same thoughts. She hoped he thought the same way she did. She hoped he loved her. She realized she was already head over heels in love with Gary and the big wolf.

It was getting late, she had to go home and get ready for work on Monday. Gary walked her to her car and kissed her for a long kiss goodnight. She hated to leave and He hated to see her go. She started her engine and looked back at Gary. He stuck his head in the window and kissed her one more time. "I needed one more kiss for the road." She waved as she drove toward the highway.

All the way home Judy dreamed about what it would be like to be Gary's wife. She touched her lips and could still feel the touch of his lips. She relived every moment they had spent together over the week-end. It had been wonderful.

Judy opened her front door, went to the bedroom and took a cold shower. Wasn't that what men did when they were heated up and didn't make out? She put on a nightshirt and went to check on phone messages which were loaded, but nothing she couldn't put off until tomorrow. She went to the kitchen and made her a sandwich to eat. She filled a glass with milk. After she finished her food she went to bed.

Gary went in the house and took a cold shower. If he had Judy for a wife he wouldn't have to do that anymore. She was always hot and wanted to make love. He wandered what she would say if he asked her to marry him. She had her career and seemed to enjoy her work. Maybe they could work it out somehow. He laid awake a long time staring at the ceiling before he finally went to sleep and dreamed about making love to Judy.

The next day was work as usual. They had fence to fix, feed to put out, training a new quarter horse, help a cow give birth and a hundred other odd jobs. The ranch was getting large and required more attention all the time, but Gary loved it. It sure beat working in an office and selling real estate.

Wolf and Gary had two jobs all week looking for lost cattle. So far they had found everything they had been asked to find and it paid well. That night, Gary checked the books and was pleased that the ranch was in the black, plus plenty to fall back on in hard times. He decided to give the hands a small pay raise next payday.

Gary had been playing with the idea of having a big party and inviting all his neighbors to get to know one another. He talked it over with the hands and they were all for it. He sent Joe to town to get lumber for tables and benches. It was time to hire a full time person to clean the big house and cook. He called Judy and put an ad in the paper.

Two days later he hired an older Mexican woman for the job. She turned out to be a good cook and house cleaner. It was just in time for the upcoming party.

The tables were made, benches made, and a large barbeque pit. They had plenty of wood to cook with. They were ready for the party. All they needed was the meat and other sides. Gary called all his neighbors and several town people he knew and invited them to the party. It was set for the coming Saturday and would be an all-day affair. He decided he would have a dance that night in the house. The dining room was large. He hired a country western band to play.

Friday, Gary went into town and bought all the food needed for the party, which turned out to be a truck load. He was getting to be well known around town and stopped to talk to several people while he was in town. He invited them to the party.

The number coming to the party got larger and larger. Gary wandered if he had bought enough food for the party. He called Judy to make sure she would be at the party. If nothing came up for the paper, she would be there.

When Gary got back to the ranch, all hands met him to unload the truck. They stored his purchases and then went to supper. Maria the cook checked over everything to be sure she had everything she needed for the party. Gary let all hands eat in the house. They discussed the work load for the day and Joe assigned each man his job. Saturday was usually the day off for most of the men. Joe rotated the week-end off for the hands.

Saturday morning was fast and furious. Maria started cooking baked beans, corn-on-the-cob and cornbread. She peeled potatoes to make potato salad. When she had the potatoes cooking, she made a large green salad.

Joe and Ben started the fire in the pit. When they had the fire just right they put on chicken, pork ribs, beef ribs and slabs of beef. Part of the meat they barbequed and the rest they cooked with just the wood smell and flavor. Last they put on hotdogs for the kids.

By ten o'clock people started to arrive. Gary had iced down the beer. There was tea and water for ones that didn't like beer. The young ones had iced down can drinks.

As the crowd arrived the men milled around and talked mostly about ranching. The women went to the house and carried the hot food to the tables. They stacked the paper plates and foam cups with the plastic knives, forks and spoons. Gary set out some paper towels to clean up with.

Twelve o'clock the preacher blessed the food and everybody lined up to fill their plates. For the next hour everyone ate their fill. Gary scanned the crowd for Judy, but she wasn't there yet. He hoped she wasn't called out on a news story. Gary mingled with the crowd with Wolf at his side, letting everybody get used to seeing him. Wolf let little kids pet him, but he wished they would call him Wolf and not dog. Gary smiled every time a little kid petted Wolf and called him dog. He looked at Wolf, "Grin and bear it."

Judy finally showed up and came straight over to Gary. "Sorry I'm late. I had to cover a news story about a robbery." She hugged Gary and kneeled down to hug Wolf. She loved both of them since they were a matched pair. Now that's more like it, thought Wolf. He liked Judy very much.

"Let's get a plate of food and sit down." Gary let Judy go ahead of him in line. Wolf followed close behind. They got their food and sat down at a table. Wolf sat on a bench beside Judy. She cut up his meat in bite size portions. Little kids pointed at them and adults stared. They didn't believe what they were seeing. A huge wolf was sitting at the table eating like a person.

Maria came by the table and put her hand on Wolf's head. She had begun to like the wolf and gave him treats all the time. "Can I get you anything?" she wanted to know. "Thanks but we have everything we need," replied Gary.

Wolf got down from the table and followed Maria to the house to give Gary some time with Judy. "Can you believe that? Wolf left so we could be alone. He is one smart wolf."

"Yes, he is very smart. He can read my mind and I can read his," laughed Gary. Judy smiled at Gary, "Yeah right. If I believe that one, you will tell me another one." She wasn't so sure that maybe he was telling the truth. They always seemed connected to one another.

"I want to know more about you and Wolf. Something is strange about you two." She stared at Gary and he turned his head. "If I told you I would have to kill you," he laughed. "You wouldn't believe me if I told you." He didn't know if he wanted to tell her or not about their connection.

"Try me." Judy stared at Gary. She didn't have a clue what Gary was going to say, but she was very curious. Her heart rate went up and she had goose bumps on her arms. It always happen when she got a great story for the paper.

"What I'm going to tell you can't go any further. You can't use it for a story or I won't tell you." She stared at him. "Ok I won't say a word or print it." She was really curious now. She watched Gary relax and close his eyes.

"Wolf is sitting at the front door watching Maria wash dishes. I see through his eyes and he can see through my eyes." He kept his eyes closed.

"You got to be kidding me."

"Ok, you want more proof, here goes, Wolf will now come out here to us and put his paw on your leg." Judy stared at Gary as Wolf came out of the house coming toward them. She held her breath as he walked in front of her. Wolf put his paw on her leg and stared at her. She thought he was grinning. This couldn't be real, but it was. "Wolf will now run around the area and I will tell you what he is seeing with my eyes closed. You can tell me if I'm right." Gary closed his eyes and described everything Wolf was seeing. Wolf came back and sat in front of Judy grinning.

Judy was dumbfounded and didn't know what to say. This had to be impossible, but she saw it with her own eyes and couldn't put it in the paper, the biggest story of her life. She knew why Gary didn't want people to know. People would think he was a freak and doctors would want to run tests. Well such is life. She wouldn't tell anybody about Wolf and Gary. Wolf went back into the house to give them time alone.

"Does Wolf know what we are talking about?" asked Judy.

"Only if I close my eyes and connect with him."

"What about when we are making love?"

"Only if I close my eyes and connect with him. I don't dare do that," laughed Gary.

They could hear the band tuning up inside the house and knew the dance would start shortly. Gary reached for Judy's hand and pulled her to her feet. It was time to kick up their heels. She was wearing something that smelled good. He wanted to nibble on her body and more. He wanted to be inside her hot body making love to her. Judy smiled at Gary. "I know what you thinking and I would like to very much. Maybe we could sneak away later and check out your big bed."

Her nipples became hard, her heart rate climbed and she knew there was moisture down below. She looked at Gary's fly and knew he had a hard on. "You better get rid of that before we go in the house," she giggled.

The dance was just starting when they entered the dining room. The first rattle out of the box was a fast two-step and everyone was going in a tight circle. Gary and Judy watched and decided to wait for a slower song. After the first song the band played it down a bit.

"Are you ready to dance?" asked Gary.

"Let's do it."

Judy walked into Gary's arms and he guided her around the dance floor. He nibbled on her ear and whispered what he was going to do to her body when they made it in a bed. She blushed red and became hot. "You're driving me crazy, will you just dance?"

"That's the whole idea for you to be hot when we go upstairs to bed." Gary liked to tease Judy and watch her get aroused. They moved around the room making friends and talked about ranching ideas. Gary listened for anything he might use to make the ranch more up to date. When the dance was over and everyone left, they ran upstairs to Gary's bedroom.

Gary opened his arms and Judy went into them for a mind blowing kiss. They undressed each other until they were both naked and were skin to skin. He crushed her breasts against his chest and the sparks started to fly. Gary picked her up and carried her to the bed. He grabbed a condom from the bedside table and started to put it on. Judy reached and took it away from him.

"I want to do that." She sat on the side of the bed staring at his large shaft. Judy didn't put the rubber on, but she wanted to give him a thrill before she slipped it on. She lowered her head until her lips touched the head of his penis. She took as much as she could in her mouth and sucked on it while running her tongue around his shaft. She glanced up at Gary and he looked like he was in pain. He put his hands in her hair while she went up and down on his shaft.

Gary pulled her off before he came in her mouth. She slipped the rubber on his shaft as he lowered himself between her legs. He slammed into her hot folds while she locked her legs around his thighs. She met him thrust for thrust until they both climaxed together. They lay side by side until their breathing returned to normal.

Judy reached over and stroked his dead penis, since she wanted another round of love making before they went to sleep. It didn't take long until Gary had a large erection again.

"Give it to me hard and fast again, cowboy."

"I'll give you all I have left."

They were exhausted after the second time making love. They made a trip to the bathroom to clean up, then lay spoon fashion and went to sleep. They didn't have to work Sunday and could sleep in late. The next day they didn't wake up until almost noon. Judy opened her eyes and the sun was shining brightly through the bedroom window. Gary was still out cold. She lay there watching him sleep, enjoying her fill of him. He was a good looking cowboy and she could never get her fill no matter how long she watched him. She loved him and hoped he loved her as much as she did him.

Judy eased out of bed and went to the bathroom. When she came out Gary was still sleeping and she didn't want to wake him. It was her fault that he was exhausted, she couldn't get enough loving, but Gary wouldn't give up until she had enough sex. She picked up her scattered clothes and went into the hall to dress, before going downstairs to fix breakfast.

Checking the refrigerator for something to cook, she pulled out eggs, hash browns and bacon. She put grounds and water in the coffeepot. She punched the button on the coffeepot and went back to the stove to cook.

The smell of coffee brewing woke Gary. He got out of bed and hunted his scattered clothes He made a trip to the bathroom, relieved himself, brushed his teeth and splashed cold water on his face. After drying off, he went downstairs and found Judy putting the food on the table. Gary got down a couple of cups and filled them with coffee. He stared at the table and food.

"I could get used to this every morning." Everything looked so good.

"Sat down and eat before it gets cold." She hoped he knew what he had said. She put a large plate of food on the floor for Wolf.

They had a late breakfast and stared at each other without talking, each one remembering how good their love making had been last night. Judy blushed at her thoughts. It had been wonderful making love to Gary. He smiled at her and knew what she was thinking, because he was thinking the same thoughts. He had a hard on, but Judy couldn't see it under the table. Gary could see her nipples trying to push a hole in her clothes, bra or no bra, they were hard.

"What would you like to do before you have to go home?"

"I would like to saddle the horses and take a ride. You know how much I like to ride."

"I'll clean up the kitchen while you saddle the horses."

"You got it. I'll meet you at the back door when you finish."

Gary grabbed his hat and went out the back door. He went to the barn, picked two of the fastest horses out of the coral, saddled them and rode back to the house leading her horse. Judy stepped out the back door just as Gary rode up.

Judy sung into the saddle and rode off at a fast pace toward the open pasture with Gary hot on her heels. She loved to ride fast like some people loved to drive fast. Both horses liked to run and they gave them their head's. When they reached the creek they stopped. The horses waded into the water for a drink while Gary and Judy talked.

"You love this ranch, don't you?" Gary asked. He was curious to know her reaction, wandering if someday she would like to live on the ranch. He wandered if she would get tired of being a housewife and mother. Now where did that come from?

"Yes I do, very much." She wanted Gary to ask her to live on the ranch forever. She wouldn't push the point. She wanted him to make up his mind and ask her. She was disappointed when he backed his horse out of the water.

"I'll race you back to the ranch." He waited until she rode up beside him before he took off toward the barn. Judy took off after him. She had the fastest horse and beat him.

"I beat you," Judy laughed as she dismounted from her horse.

"Beginners luck and I gave you the fastest horse." They led the horses into the barn and gave them a good rubdown. They went to the house for something to drink. The phone was ringing when they walked into the house. The call was for Judy. The paper wanted her to go to Houston to cover a story about a robbery.

"I shouldn't have given the paper your number. I have to leave with-in the hour. I guess we don't get to make love again for a while."

Gary walked her to her car. He opened his arms for a kiss and she walked into them. As soon as she drove off, she felt like a part of her was missing. She would quit her job in a New York minute if Gary asked her to marry him, but until he did, she would do her job. She liked her job, but she liked Gary a whole lot more.

Breakfast the next day Joe passed out assignments to the men what each one had to do that day. First thing they had to do was clean up after the party and store everything in the barn for the next time. Gary decided since the party went over so well, they would have one next year. After everything was back to normal the men started their jobs for the day. Gary told Joe he was going to town to make a deposit. He didn't like to keep a lot of cash at the ranch.

Pulling into a parking space in front of the bank, Gary and Wolf got out and went into the bank. Some people stared at them, but a lot of people knew Gary didn't go hardly anywhere without the wolf by his side. Lord, help anyone who tried to harm Gary with Wolf by his side. Several people spoke to Gary while he was in the bank. A young woman that was at the party stopped to talk to Gary. Her little girl hugged Wolf and people stared at them.

Wolf liked the attention. The young woman reached down and hugged Wolf as she was leaving. "Well Wolf, you got two hugs and I didn't get any." Wolf looked up at him and Gary thought he was smiling.

The bank manager came over to Gary and told him if he ever needed anything, just ask. Gary was getting to know most of the employees in the bank. He liked to do business where he was known. All the businesses he used were used to seeing Gary and Wolf together, so Wolf never stayed in the car.

"I guess it's time to get back to the ranch and go to work." They loaded up and headed back to the ranch. When they got back to the ranch Gary saddled a horse and headed out to check fence and livestock. Wolf trotted along beside him.

Chapter Five

Gary and wolf had a busy week finding livestock. They had made good money and Gary decided on Friday to make a trip to the bank and make a deposit. They took the old truck. He pulled into a parking space in front of the bank. A van was parked next to the door with the motor running. Gary noticed the driver was chain smoking and was very nervous. He didn't like the looks of things. He eased up to the driver window and saw the man was holding a gun. The driver looked up as Gary slammed a fist into his face. Gary jerked the door open and grabbed the man pulling him out of the van. He slammed a fist into his gut and then a haymaker to the head. The man went down and didn't get up. Gary took the van keys and the man's gun. He went back to his truck, got his deposit bag and a light jacket. He draped it over his arm to hide the gun.

"Come on Wolf let's see what is happening in the bank."

They walked into the bank. "Come right in and move over with the rest of the crowd," said a man with a gun trained on him. Judy was arguing with another man with a gun. He slapped her sending her to the floor. "Shut up bitch or I'll shoot you."

Judy sat up and stared at the robber as Wolf walked in front of her. She glanced over at Gary and he smiled at her. How could he be so calm with two men holding guns on them? Blood ran down her chin from a busted lip. She wasn't scared anymore with Wolf in front of her.

"Where did this stupid dog come from?" asked the robber.

"He is not a dog, he is a wolf and you had better be very scared. He will eat you for lunch," said Judy. She glared at the robber.

"Yeah right," said the robber as he started to aim his pistol at Wolf. That was a big mistake. Wolf sprang at the robber taking him down as he tore out his throat. He dropped his pistol and lay on the floor bleeding out.

The other robber turned toward Wolf as Gary fired his gun at the robber hitting him in the head. He was dead before he hit the floor. He didn't see the last robber that was coming from the back with the money.

Judy picked up the robber's gun on the floor and aimed it at the last robber. She fired one shot hitting him in the shoulder and he dropped his gun and money. It was over.

Gary went over and picked up the robber's gun and went back to pick up the other robber's gun he had shot. The cashier had pushed the silent alarm button when the shooting started. They heard the cop cars pulling up out front.

Cops charged in the bank and stopped. Gary walked over to the lead cop. He handed the three pistols to the cop. "What's been going on Gary? It looks like a war zone." Gary started to tell him about the attempted robbery as Judy walked over and put an arm around Gary's waist. Wolf was standing guard over the wounded robber.

Judy knew the cop also. "Tom I'll give my statement, but I got to call the newspaper first and give them the scoop." She hurried to find a phone.

"Not much for us to do, but clean up the mess," said Tom. "I can't believe Judy shot one of the robbers. Women are usually scared."

"One of the robbers slapped her and busted her lip. She was pissed." Gary was proud of Judy and he would tell her. He knew she would make a perfect wife on a ranch. She would have his back.

The cops took the two robbers to the hospital while the meat wagon took the two dead robbers. The bank was cleaning up and getting ready to operate again. The bank manager came over to Gary and thanked him. He was glad Gary banked with them. Tom and Gary finished their report as Judy came back.

"I'm ready to give my statement." Tom took her statement.

Gary waited until she was finished. "Do you have time to get a cup of coffee before going back to work?"

"I'll take time, my nerves are still shot. I know why you stood there waiting, you were waiting on Wolf to make the first move so you could take the second robber down."

"Yes, Wolf does make a good distraction."

"You told him to take that robber out."

"Yes, I wanted to be sure he couldn't use his pistol."

"That robber thought he was just a dumb mutt."

"That was his big mistake. Wolf is fast and deadly." Wolf came over to stand beside Gary.

Judy reached down and gave him a big hug. "Thank you for saving my life."

"What's with you always getting the hugs?" Wolf smiled up at him.

Judy threw her arms around Gary and gave him a big kiss. "Now that's more like it," said Gary.

"Are you off Saturday?" Gary asked.

"I am unless something comes up. You know how it is. What did you have in mind?"

"How would you like to camp out at the ranch and we can take my small tent and rough it? Don't you think that would be fun?"

"What time do you want me there?"

"Noon would be fine. It will give me time to take care of anything I need to do before you arrive. Then we can saddle up and head out. Wolf will stay home and guard the house."

"I'll see you at noon tomorrow unless something comes up."

Saturday noon, Judy pulled into the driveway in front of the house. Gary had two horses saddled and was loading their supplies on a pack horse. Judy got out and finished helping him load the packhorse.

"I have coffee on, would you like a cup before we go?"

"It sounds good to me."

They went inside and had a cup of coffee. They went outside and mounted up. Gary took the lead rope for the packhorse. They rode by the barn and told Joe he would be back tomorrow.

"Have fun you two and don't do anything I wouldn't do."

"We won't and if we do we'll name it after you."

Judy blushed and reached over to slug Gary. He touched his heels to his horse and the horse took off at a fast clip with Judy right behind him. As they neared the creek they slowed down to a walk. It was a beautiful day with the sun shining. Gary stopped under an oak tree and dismounted.

"We can camp here by the creek."

Judy loved the spot. She dismounted and came over to help unloading the packhorse. They set up the small tent together. Gary found some rocks to go around the fire while Judy looked for firewood. She brought enough for the night. He built a pile of wood in the circle, but didn't light it. They would wait until supper time. They ate a cold lunch of sandwiches, chips and cokes. Judy went down to the creek and pulled off her shoes and stuck her feet in the water.

"Better watch out, you might catch a fish. Your toes might make a fish hungry."

"Then we can have fish for supper," giggled Judy.

Gary broke out some fishing line, hook and cork. He had brought some blood bait and put some on the hook. He tossed the hook in the water and sat down to wait.

A few minutes later, he got a bite. He played the fish for a while before he sunk the hook. He pulled out about a five pound catfish. He baited the hook and tossed it back in the water. It didn't take long until he caught a three pound catfish.

"We got supper, now all you have to do is skin them and cook them," teased Gary.

"Oh no buster, you skin them and I'll cook them." He took them down by the creek, skinned and gutted them. They decided to eat an early supper.

Judy put the fish on to cook with hush puppies on the side. She had brought bake beans and potato salad for sides. Gary laid out paper plates and plastic silverware. He had tea that they had brought and poured two glasses. He looked at all the food and was ready to eat. Judy filled two plates with food and sat down on the ground on a blanket. They dug in and eat like pigs. Judy was not shy when it came to eating. Gary wandered how she stayed so slim after eating so much.

After they ate, they washed up and put the leftovers away. Judy wanted to take a ride before nightfall. They rode fence lines and checked on the cattle. She loved the ranch life and Gary could tell by watching her. She would make a great ranch wife. More and more Gary decided to ask her to marry him. They had so much in common. He would wait for the perfect time to ask her to marry him.

They watched the sun set from the backs of their horses. "Oh

Gary, isn't it beautiful?"

"Yes it is," but he was looking at her with passion in his eyes. He couldn't get enough of her. She would be his soon.

"Race you back to camp." She dug her heels in her horse and he took off leaving Gary staring at her. That girl sure likes to race. She beat him back to camp and was standing on the ground watching as he rode up. "You sure are a slow poke," she giggled. Gary hobbled the horses for the night.

They sat around the campfire and drank coffee until after dark. Gary teased her about what he was going to do to her tonight.

"Promises, promises is that all I get?" She ran into the tent.

Gary banked the fire and followed her into the tent. Judy was already naked and was on her back with her legs spread wide. "Are you going to join me or do I start alone." She touched her folds and Gary almost lost it. She knew how to make him lose control.

Taking his clothes and boots off as quick as possible he slipped between her legs driving his erection home. Judy arched her back to take all of him. They took it slow and enjoyed every minute of making love until they went over the edge together. It was nice to have all night to make love as much as they wanted to. After the second time Gary pulled a blanket over them and they went to sleep. It was so good sleeping out in the open with nothing to bother them.

Gary woke up first. He eased out of tent putting on his clothes and started a fire for breakfast. He made coffee and started breakfast. He fixed eggs, bacon and warmed some biscuits he had packed. Judy stuck her head out of the tent and stared at Gary. She was still naked.

"Is that coffee ready? I would kill for a cup."

Gary filled a cup and handed it to her. "Hurry up sleepyhead breakfast is ready."

By the time Judy dressed, he had her plate filled with food. She was starved after so much lovemaking last night. "You are going to make some woman a good housewife," she giggled.

"If you keep telling me that I'm going to put an ad in the paper for a job."

They ate breakfast and went back to bed. They slept till noon and made love one more time before packing up and going back to the house. They took care of the horses before going into the house. Wolf was happy to see them. He looked at Gary and knew he had mated last night. He had that silly grin on his face.

Judy had to leave and go home to get ready for Monday. Both of them had jobs and things they had to do. Gary walked her to her car and kissed here before she drove off. He missed her already. It was like a part of him was missing. He went back into the house to check his phone calls and do his books. Joe did a good job keeping up, so all he had to do was answer phone calls. He had a call from his mother wanting to know when he was coming home. He called her first and talked for an hour. He had two calls from ranchers with missing livestock. That would take two days of the week to find them, but the money was good. He never wanted to turn down a job no matter how large or how small.

Judy was walking on air when she went home. All she could think about was what a wonderful Saturday they had. She liked to ride horses, camp out and the good loving they shared. She was in love and hoped Gary loved her as much as she loved him. He didn't ask her to marry him, but she believed he was gun shy from his last girlfriend. She didn't know exactly what happen with her, but it must have been real bad. She could tell he didn't trust women. She hoped to change that. When she got home she checked her phone messages and decided to let them ride until Monday. She had a lite snack, took a shower and worked on her tangled hair. Gary liked to put his hands in her hair and it was a mess.

Monday started like a mad house at the paper and she had a bad day. By the time she got off work she was ready to scream. She fixed a salad for supper and had a beer to drink. After she had a second beer her nerves calmed down. She didn't need any more days like Monday.

Gary and Wolf went looking for a bull that had torn down a fence and took off. He hooked up his trailer to his old pickup and loaded a, quarter horse to ride. He wanted a big horse when he went after a bull. They searched most of the day before they found him. He was mean and didn't want to go home so they had a time with him. Gary threw a rope over his head and Wolf nipped at his heels. That got him moving until they got to the trailer. Gary took the rope and ran it inside the trailer and out the front.

Gary pulled on the rope and Wolf nipped his heels. The old bull finally went into the trailer. When they got him home they had a time getting him out of the trailer. The rancher paid Gary and they headed home.

"Wolf we sure earned the money with that bull. He is one mean S.O.B. and I hope we don't get any more like him."

After they got back to the ranch, Gary and Wolf got cleaned up and were hungry enough to eat the bull they had worked with all day. Gary pulled out steaks and put them on the grill. He fixed a salad and a bake potato for himself. Wolf had two steaks and milk to drink. Gary had a steak, baked potato, salad and beer to drink. After they finished their meal Gary went to the office and Wolf curled up at the door. He checked the books and phone calls.

Tuesday was the same thing except the bull they found was like a kitten compared to the day before. They loaded the bull on the trailer and took him home. After they unloaded the bull and the rancher paid Gary, they headed back to the ranch.

"Well another day another dollar and that was an easy one." Wolf looked at Gary and was glad they were done for the day. Now they would get cleaned up and enjoy the steaks. They both went to bed early and slept in. While they were having a late breakfast the phone rang.

Gary picked up on the second ring. "Hello."

"This is Leroy. They got my girlfriend here at the Renaissance, but I can't find her. I got a gut feeling, I know she is here. Gary I need your help."

"I'll be there in two hours if you will pay my speeding tickets."

"I got you covered, please hurry. I don't know how much time we have before she will be dead."

The renaissance:

Bikers streamed into the parking lot. Leroy never knew there were that many bikers in Dallas. He told Ann's boyfriend to stay with him and Ashley.

Leroy explained, "I want twenty guys inside looking for her. The rest of you surround this place. I don't want anything going out until I give the word."

He gave pictures of Katherine to all the bikers. Leroy left a biker with the car and everybody started to search for Katherine. They searched each booth, storeroom, stage, dressing rooms, closets, bars and barns where the animals were kept. Anything that was locked they cut the lock off. After two hours Leroy went back to the parking lot. A short time later Gary Mitchel drove into the parking lot. He opened his door and got out followed by a huge wolf as he walked over to Leroy. Leroy stared at the wolf. He couldn't believe his eyes.

"Is this your partner you talked about?"

"Yes he is. He is the best and I never go anywhere without him."

Leroy stared at the wolf and he stared back. Gary asked, "Have you found her yet?"

"No, I don't know what to do, I'm lost. I know she is here. She has to be."

Gary said, "I'll take over and you follow me. Do you have some clothes she has worn?"

"No, I would have to go to Dallas to get some."

"Is her car here?"

"Yes, it's over there."

They walked over to the car. It was locked. "Open the car."

Leroy took a bolt cutter and smashed in the driver window. "She's going to kill me for this. What am I saying?"

Leroy opened the door. Gary said, "Wolf" and pointed to the seat.

Wolf smelled the seat and turned to Gary. "Wolf, go and find the girl." Wolf ran inside the Renaissance as Ashley and the biker came out to the parking lot.

"Did you see that big wolf?"

Leroy asked, "Aren't you going to follow him?"

"No I don't have to." He closed his eyes and leaned back against the car. "I see what he sees, I don't understand, but I can, I see what Wolf sees."

Leroy asked, "Where is he now?"

"He is on the back side working his way around that side. He is hot on her trail."

They watched Gary finding it hard to believe what was going on. "When I open my eyes and look at you, Wolf can close his eyes and see you through my eyes."

They thought Gary was crazy. Gary closed his eyes again. Wolf was on the south side working his way toward the front. When he came to the castle he stopped and put his nose to the ground. He went inside the castle. He went down the steps to the dungeon, going to the back wall, he stood up on his hind legs on the wall and scratched.

Gary said, "Wolf has found her, follow me." They hurried to the castle and went inside.

Ashley asked, "Where is Wolf?" Gary ran down the steps with the rest of them on his tail. Wolf was standing at the back wall.

Gary said, "She is behind this wall. I see a fine crack here." They searched for a way to open the wall, but couldn't find a way and the wall was several feet thick.

Leroy said, "We need some C-4 to get in there."

Gary said, "Well I just happen to have some in my backpack."

"You are crazy I can't believe you carry C-4 in your backpack."

"Always, I never leave home without it."

Now where had Leroy heard that expression? Katherine always carried her camera with her. Gary took his backpack off and reached in a pocket. He came out with a block of C-4. He placed the C-4 so it would blow outward. He reached in and got a fuse. Gary stuck the fuse in the C-4.

"Everybody get to the side out of harm's way." He lit the fuse, "Fire in the hole."

Meanwhile in the dungeon on the other side of the wall, Jason said, "It's time to party." He moved up behind Megan, dropped his pants and shorts then slammed into her soft body.

She cried, "Please don't hurt me."

Mark moved into position in front of Ann, dropped his pants and shorts. He leaned over her, put his arms around her waist and slammed into her body.

"May you die today, Ann said as he slammed deep inside her. Mark and Jason laughed.

Chapter Six

All hell broke loose as the C-4 blew the wall out. Leroy charged through the wall with his Colt 45 in his hand followed by the biker, Ashley, Gary and Wolf. Jason went for his gun on the floor in his pants. Leroy fired and hit Jason in the chest. He was dead before he hit the floor.

The biker charged Mark while he tried to reach his gun on the floor in his pants. The biker snapped Mark's neck like it was a twig and dropped him to the floor.

Allen was at the table. He reached for his gun, but Ashley fired first, on target and Allen dropped to the floor.

Bryan turned and ran down the tunnel. Gary glanced at Wolf. "Wolf you can have him."

Wolf charged down the tunnel after Bryan. A bloodcurdling scream came from the tunnel and Wolf came back to Gary's side. Gary knew Bryan was dead.

Leroy said to Ashley, "Now you know why I didn't want the Police to help. It's all over now except cleaning up the mess."

The biker untied Ann and put his coat around her. She kissed him and hung on for dear life. Gary went over and untied Megan, put his coat around her, hugged her close, "It's all over, you are safe and they can't hurt you anymore."

Megan clung to him crying, "I want to go home."

Leroy fished around in Jason's pants pocket until he found the key to the shackles. He unlocked the shackles from Katherine's hands and legs. She fell into his arms. "Ann said you would find us. What took you so long?"

She kissed him with her naked body flat against him. He put his coat around her body. Katherine looked into his eyes.

"You have killed all the bad guys and kissed the girl. Can we go home now?"

Leroy smiled down at her, "Very soon now."

Ann pointed to the hole, "You'll find all the missing girls, our clothes, ands garbage down in the hole."

Gary went over, pulled the lid off and looked down the hole. "It's too deep, you can't see the bottom."

Leroy said, "Ashley would you go find the girls some clothes? The people working at the Renaissance should have some, while I call Captain Curry. Gary would you stay here while I make the call?"

"I got good news and bad news. The good news is the case is closed on the car theft ring and the missing girls. The bad news is the girls are all dead except two. Megan Moore and Ann Mitchel are alive to tell their horrible story."

"Dam, Dam, I was afraid of that. Do you need an ambulance?"

"No sir, just a meat wagon."

"I take it all the bad guys are dead."

"Yes sir, they are all dead."

"Your crime scene people are going to have a hard time. The girls are down a deep hole in the dungeon. They raped the girls over and over until they were tired of them. Then they dropped them down the hole and got a new girl."

"Oh my God," Captain Curry said.

"I don't know how many girls are down in the hole, but probably one for every car that was stolen."

"Why didn't you call for backup?"

"I had plenty of backup, just not your normal type."

"I'm not sure I should hear this."

"When you saw me burning rubber out of here, I just found out Katherine was missing. She had gone to the Renaissance for a story. When I got there and found her car I called for backup."

"I think all the bikers in Dallas, plus Gary Mitchel known as the Tracker and Wolf."

"You mean Wolf like an animal."

"Yes sir a big wolf. He found the girls and Katherine was with them. It will all be in my report when I get back to the Police station."

"The girls will need a rape test done on them at the hospital."

"I don't think we need to do that and embarrass them anymore. They were raped many times by four different men. The four men are dead. Got to go and I'll see you back at the station."

Leroy called Mr. and Mrs. Moore and told them Megan was found and would be home shortly. He went back to the dungeon where the girls now had clothes on. Katherine was looking around the dungeon.

"Found it." She held up her camera. I want a picture of all of you. After she took pictures Gary said, "I'm taking Megan home."

Ann thanked them and she and her boyfriend left. Katherine started taking more pictures and asked Leroy for his notepad. This story will read like a horror book which it is. It would be a big story and she was in it. She would tell the story the way life was.

The crime scene people arrived and Leroy showed them the

hole. The meat wagon came with bags to pick up all the bodies. Leroy didn't want to be around when they started bringing bodies up out of the hole. He was glad he wasn't the one going in the hole.

Katherine took pictures of the crime team. She had her story and what a story. When they got back to the parking lot she demanded, "Who broke my window?"

Leroy laughed, "Ashley did it."

"I did not."

Leroy told her why he broke the window. "The wolf did what?" Katherine got her spare key from a box under the frame.

"I'll drive my car home. I need to go by the newspaper, drop off my pictures and write my story. I'll see you at home."

Ashley drove her and Leroy to the Police station. Captain Curry was waiting for them in their office. He was reading their notes on the blackboard.

"I see the two of you have been busy. Not the normal way Police work, but you sure do get the job done."

The Captain went into his office and waited for the report. He wanted to read it before he went home. He knew it would be some story. He wanted to know how all the car ring died. He would get a shock when he finds out Leroy only killed one of the bad guys.

Gary stopped on the way back to Dallas. He bought Megan some food because she was starving. When they drove into the driveway at Megan's home, her Mom and Dad were outside waiting on them. Gary had her by his side and Megan had her hand on Wolf as they walked up to her Mom and Dad.

"Mom and dad this is Gary and Wolf." She put her arms around Wolf's neck. "Wolf found me and saved my life."

Mr. and Mrs. Moore stared at Gary and Wolf. They had never seen anything like it. Gary was six feet tall wearing buckskins, boots and an old beat up hat. He wore a ponytail and had a rugged complexion. The wolf was huge. They shook hands and thanked Gary for bringing their daughter home to them. He started to leave. Megan hugged him and Wolf.

When they were back on the road Gary had tears in his eyes for Megan and what they had done to her. He was glad they were all dead. If they had lived they would have had a fancy lawyer and might have figured a way to beat the system.

Gary went to Katherine and Leroy's apartment and waited for them to come home. About thirty minutes later Leroy pulled in. Katherine finally got home from the Newspaper. Her boss couldn't believe what happen to her. He looked at her arms where the shackles had made them raw. She showed him her legs that were raw also.

Katherine wanted a beer. The phone rang and she picked up on the second ring. Ashley wanted them to come over for a party and wanted them to be sure to bring Wolf.

There was more room in Gary's truck so they piled into his truck and drove over to Ashley's house. Gary was looking very sad as he stared out the window.

"What's wrong with you?" asked Katherine.

"I was thinking about Megan. She has to go back to school and you know how mean kids can be. They will call her names and the boys will try to hit on her. When she tells them no, you know how they will be to her. If she can't take it she will try to commit suicide."

Katherine said, "I'll take her under my wing and spend as much time as I can with her. Maybe I can get her on part time at the newspaper. I'll try to get her mind off what happened. What about Ann?"

"Ann is as tough as nails, she will be fine."

Gary pulled in the driveway at Ashley's house. Jim opened the door and told them to come in. Ashley served a ton of finger food and beer. She asked if Wolf could have sweet food.

"He eats anything. When I fix dinner or we eat out we eat the same food."

"Good, I got a treat for him. He saved the day and without him we would never have found the girls."

Ashley went to the refrigerator and pulled out a large cake with Wolf wrote on it. She cut slices for all of them and gave the rest of the cake to Wolf. He looked at her with love in his eyes, his tail wagging he ate all the cake.

Jim came in with cards in his hand, "Time to play cards and drink beer."

They played cards until midnight and then called it a night. Back at Katherine and Leroy's apartment Gary was going to a motel, but they wouldn't let him.

After breakfast Gary and Wolf left for home. Leroy thanked him for all his help and told him if he ever needed him just call.

Chapter Seven

Gary and Wolf arrived back at the ranch at noon. Joe was waiting on Gary to hear about the excitement in Dallas. He gave Joe a rundown on what happened. It was a story that was hard to believe. How could anyone be, so mean. The story was on all the news stations. Gary and Wolf went to the house to get cleaned up and eat. Maria was at the grill fixing lunch. She was fixing steaks and all the trimmings.

"Maria, what are you doing here on your day off?"

"Fixing a good meal for you and Wolf after what you have been through. You get cleaned up while I finish the steaks. It's good to have you home Boss."

They washed up and came back to the kitchen. Maria served them and stood back as they dug in. Gary didn't realize how hungry he was until he sat down to, eat. Maria set a plate at the table for Wolf and cut his steak in bite size pieces like she had seen Gary do. Wolf sat in his chair and ate just like a person.

The next morning it was starting to get cold. It wouldn't be long until Thanksgiving. His Mother would expect him to come home for Thanksgiving. His family always made a big fuss on holidays.

Joe, Ben, Sam and Wayne came in and sat at the table as Maria put coffee and food on the table. Gary started off the morning Jobs. "We are going to have to start getting ready for winter. Joe, make sure we have feed, hay, salt and anything else you think we need."

"Yes sir, I'll take care of it." He then handed out jobs for the day.

As they were leaving, Gary asked Ben to stay, "How is your new assistant working out?"

"He is doing great. I don't have to be with him anymore. He is doing all the training on his own. We are getting so much business we need another hand to help with the feeding and grooming of the horses."

"I'll call the high school and see if they have a couple of D.E. students that want a job working on the ranch. I can pay them cheap wages and they can get two credits for the course. I worked at a theatre when I was in school as a D.E. student."

Ben went to work as Gary saddled a horse to check on fence and livestock. Wolf headed out ahead of him. They checked all the livestock and fence. There was a small section that needed to be repaired. Gary carried tools in his saddlebags for small repairs. He got down off his horse and did the minor repairs. A jackrabbit jumped up, Wolf started to chase him. Gary called him back. "Are you going to eat that poor rabbit when you have a steak waiting at the ranch for supper? Bad wolf shame on you."

Wolf tucked his head and lay down to wait on Gary to finish the fence. He didn't want the darn old rabbit anyway.

After Gary finished the repair they went back to the ranch. Maria had cooked them a good supper before she left for the day. The hands joined Gary and Wolf for supper and talked about the day's work. After supper Gary went to his office to check on phone calls. Judy had called and Mike from home. He called Mike first. He had seen the news on Gary and Wolf in Dallas. He wanted the news straight from the horse's mouth. Gary told him the whole story. Mike couldn't believe the horror with the girls. It was hard to believe anyone could be that evil. They talked for thirty minutes. Last thing Mike wanted to know was if he was coming home for Thanksgiving and come out to the ranch? Yes, he would try to make it.

Next, he called Judy and she picked up on the second ring. "I just got home from work and it was another rough day. How was your day?"

"I had an easy day fixing fence. I was thinking about you all the time."

"I heard the news about Dallas. How could anyone be that bad?"

"There are people in this old world that don't care about anything or anyone except themselves. They would sell their own Mother down the drain for a couple of bucks."

"Crime is on the rise here and I get to cover most of the stories. I sure would have liked to get the Dallas story. That was big news."

"Leroy's girlfriend was being held in the dungeon when we blew the wall down. She is a reporter with the Dallas Newspaper. She is the one that broke the story. It was bad and she left out some of the details."

"My question is when are we going to get together again? I miss being with you so much. I need some good loving to keep me going."

"When can you get away from the paper again? I'm going home Thanksgiving and would like to take you with me. That would be a surprise for Mom and Dad."

"I'll try my best to go with you."

They talked for an hour before they finally hung up. Judy was so happy that Gary wanted to take her home with him. Gary wanted his Mother's approval of the girl he was going to ask to marry him. He knew she would love Judy.

Judy hoped Gary's folks would like her. She was so in love with him. She thought about him taking her with him. Did it mean he wanted his Mom and Dad's approval of her? She wanted to be at her best. All she could think about was living on the ranch with Gary.

The next day Gary called the school and talked with the D.E.

teacher. The teacher asked his students if anyone wanted to work on a ranch. He said he had one boy and a girl that wanted a job. He wanted to know if he would hire a girl. He didn't care if she didn't mind hard work. The teacher said they would be out after school. They were both juniors.

They rode out together that evening. Gary thought they might be boyfriend and girlfriend. They were both eager to get the job. They were city kids and wanted to ride horses. The boy's name was Jerry and the girl's name was Kathy. Gary told them they would work Monday thru Friday in the evening. They could start the next day. They wanted to know about riding the horses. He told them Ben would teach them to ride and they could help in the training of the horses. Joe would tell them each day what they had to do.

Judy had to work right up to the day before Thanksgiving. She told the boss come hell or high water she was going with Gary Thanksgiving day. Gary picked her up when she got off work. She had packed a small suitcase for the trip which Gary carried out to his car. Wolf was in the back seat. She reached back and hugged him. Wolf grinned, he loved the affection. He loved Judy as much as he did Gary.

They got to Booneville about ten o'clock. Gary's Mon and Dad were happy to see them. They had drinks and food. They talked until twelve before they retired. Judy was in the guest bedroom while Gary took his old bedroom. Wolf curled up in the hall between the bedrooms. Gary walked her to her door and kissed her.

"I wish we were sleeping together, but I don't think Mom would approve."

"I do to, but I see her point, goodnight."

Thanksgiving morning, it looked like a bee hive with everyone doing something to get ready for the big meal. "Gary, why don't you go ahead and take Judy out to Mike's ranch and I will finish dinner. I'm sure she would enjoy seeing it."

"Thanks Mom."

They drove out to Mike's ranch and as they crossed the cattle guard Lightning and Thunder were there to escort them to the house. "What beautiful horses," Judy remarked.

"They raised them from colts and they are very smart. Mike trains horses for the movies."

Mike and Linda met them as Gary shut off the engine. Gary made the introductions. He told Wolf to stay in the car. He didn't want to scare the animals. Mike and Linda went over to the car and petted Wolf. They sat down in some chairs while Linda brought out some drinks. They caught up on everything except about Judy. Linda looked them over. Gary, do you want to tell me about Judy? Is it serious between you since you brought her home with you?

"I hope it is."

Judy blushed she didn't know what to say. She hoped it was serious. "I hope it is to."

Gary had his answer to what he had been thinking. Sometime soon he would ask Judy to marry him and be his forever. He had finally found the girl of his dreams. She looked at him and he could see the love in her eyes. He wished they were alone right now and he would show her how much he loved her.

"Well it's time to go back to Mom's. She will have dinner ready and waiting when we get back, but before I go I want to pet the horses." He walked over and put his arm around Lighting. Judy put her arm around Thunder. "They are so beautiful," said Judy.

"Yes and spoiled like kids," remarked Mike.

Lightning and Thunder escorted them back to the cattle guard. Dinner was ready when they got back to Gary's house. They had turkey and ham and all the trimmings. Judy had enjoyed the trip very much. She was on cloud nine after Gary's remark. All the way back to Sugarland she dreamed of what their future would be like. Gary glanced at her from time to time and knew what she was thinking. Yes they would have a life together.

When they got to the ranch and went inside the phone was ringing off the hook. It was from the paper. It was for Judy. She took the call and frowned. "I got to go and cover a hot story." There would be no making love this weekend. Gary wanted to ask her to marry him, but he would wait for the perfect time.

Judy hurried to her car and drove off to cover the story. She hated to leave Gary, but she had a job to do and she did it well. It was a robbery at a food store and the cops had the robber cornered. It was a standoff for four hours before he finally came out and gave up. Judy got her story and was exhausted from waiting to see what would happen. She turned in her story at the paper and went home.

Gary called her at home and she told him about her job. Then they talked about what they would do the next time they had time together. "I want to make slow love to you all night. I want to taste you and drive you crazy."

Judy told him what she would do to him next time they were together. She would ride him until he was broken. "I guess we are having phone sex," she giggled.

"At least we will have something to dream about tonight," said Gary.

The next few weeks before Christmas were fast and furious and it got colder each day. All hands worked hard including Gary. Joe brought in a large cedar Christmas tree. Gary wanted to give a Christmas Eve party for his crew. It was only three days before Christmas so it would be a rush to get everything done.

"It's as cold as a well digger's ass in Utah out there," said Joe.

"I second that," said Jerry and Kathy as they entered the front door.

They walked over to Gary. He asked them to decorate the tree and put up decorations in the house while he went to the store for all the food they would need. Maria had made a list for him. It was a big list and would take a while.

"Wolf you can stay out of the cold while I make the trip." No problem, he went and curled up by the stove to wait until Maria started cooking. He knew she would let him sample everything as she cooked.

Gary stopped at a Zale's jewelry store and took the plunge. He wanted the perfect ring for Judy. A young woman helped him make up his mind. He got one that was beautiful, but small enough she could wear it while she worked. Next stop was the grocery store where he thought he would buy them out.

When Gary got back to the ranch, Ben, Sam and Wayne came out to help him unload the food and drink. Jerry and Kathy were just finishing up with the tree and it was beautiful. Maria was just finishing up supper.

"Dinner is ready, come and get it."

All hands sat down and had a good meal before leaving. After everyone left, Gary went to his office to check on phone calls and check his books. He sat the little box with the ring in front of him and opened it. He stared at it, daydreaming about days to come and how lucky he was to find a girl like Judy. He knew she would make a wonderful rancher's wife.

Gary checked his bank account and was happy with the balance. The ranch was way in the black. He decided to give all his employees a good Christmas bonus. He didn't worry about being rich. He just wanted the ranch to stay in the black. He took out his checkbook and wrote a full month's bonus check to each employee. They had earned it.

As he was making out checks, Judy called. Gary answered on the second ring. "What's up, did you have a good day?"

"It wasn't too bad today for a change. I was out of the office most of the day on boring news that has to be covered, but it's my job. How was your day?"

"I'm making out bonus checks for my employees. It has been a very good year and I'm giving them a good bonus. I hope next year will be just as good."

"Don't forget to make me out a check also, I have been a good girl," Judy giggled.

"Yes my love, you sure have been a good girl." Gary thought of the many times they had made love through the year. He became hard just thinking about it.

"I know what you are thinking bad boy. Santa won't bring you anything for Christmas."

"Are we talking phone sex again," Judy giggled.

"Yes we are. Are you hot yet?"

"Yes, I'm burning up."

"All jokes aside, I'm having a Christmas Eve party and you have to be there." He was going to ask her to marry him at the party in front of everybody.

"I'll be there with bells on so you can hear me coming."

After they hung up Judy ran to her closet and thumbed through her wardrobe. She didn't see anything that jumped out at her. She had to have a new dress for the party. She wanted Gary to only have eyes for her. She wanted him to make love to her after the party. Her nipples became hard and her body became hot just thinking about Gary. Tomorrow she would go shopping.

Christmas Eve rolled around and everyone was at the party except Judy. She couldn't believe she had a dead battery on her car. AAA came out and replaced her battery and she finally made it to the party. When Judy walked in and smiled at Gary, all was right with the world. His jaw dropped as he stared at her. She had on a short skimpy black evening dress which showed off her slim figure and curves. Gary just stood and stared at her.

"Aren't you going to say anything?" asked Judy.

"Wow."

Gary came over and kissed her right in front of everyone. Judy blushed, but she loved it. "I missed you."

"I missed you more," said Gary as he led her over to a chair.

The table on the side of the room was loaded with food and drinks. Gary filled a plate for him and Judy. They ate their fill and then everyone talked for a long time.

"Did you notice something different about our party," asked Judy.

"Yes, it's a Christmas party without any little kids."

"Maybe somebody needs to fix that. It's not Christmas without kids."

Gary thought about that and decided his ranch needed kids. He smiled at Judy and she knew what he was thinking. He wanted kids. She hoped he wanted them with her. As the party slowed down, Gary stood up and addressed the crowd.

"Folks I got a couple of things I want to say. I want to thank my crew for all their hard work this year and here is a little something for you." He handed out envelopes with their bonus in them. He walked around in front of Judy and went down on one knee. "I want everyone to witness me as I ask her to marry me. Judy, would you make me the most, happy man on earth and marry me?"

"Judy stared at him with tears in her eyes, yes, yes, yes."

Gary stood up and pulled her into his arms. He kissed her as everyone cheered. This had been the most, happy day of his life. He couldn't wait for everyone to leave. He wanted to make love to Judy right now.

Gary and Judy stood side by side at the door as everyone left, just like an old married couple. As soon as Gary closed the door he led Judy to his bedroom. Wolf curled up at the front door on guard duty.

"Finally we are alone," giggled Judy, as she reached for the buttons on Gary's shirt.

They undressed each other slowly and stood body to body. Gary loved the feel of her body against him with her nipples hard and digging into his chest. His erection dug into her belly. He kissed her and ran his tongue around her lips as she opened to him. He slid his tongue deep into her mouth until she moaned. The sound fired Gary into action. He picked her up and carried her to the bed. Judy lay on the bed and opened her legs for him. He slid between her legs and slowly joined their bodies together. He took it slow trying to make it last all night, but as she squeezed his shaft he couldn't go, slow anymore. He slammed into her as she arched her back with each stroke. They reached the edge at the same time. Judy cried out his name as she climaxed. It went on and on until Gary fell over on her chest exhausted. He turned over with her on top and they drifted off to sleep.

Later on that night Judy woke up as she felt his shaft hard inside her. Gary was still asleep, but he had a smile on his face. She slowly moved up and down trying not to wake him. She was going, slow and it felt so good she wanted to scream. Gary was still asleep until Judy started to squeeze his erection as she came. That got his attention.

"Why did you start without me?"

"You were sleeping and dreaming and I didn't want to mess up your dream. I hope it was me you were dreaming about."

"Yes it was. I was reliving our first time tonight."

"Then I'm glad I didn't wake you."

Christmas morning Judy and Gary slept in until noon. They finally got up and took a shower and put on clean clothes. Judy fixed lunch and they sat and stared at each other while they ate. "Any regrets about last night? You are quite today."

"No regrets ever, I was thinking when we should get married."

"I would like to get married March tenth. That was when my mother got married."

"Then March the tenth it will be. That gives you three months to get ready or back out," Gary teased.

Judy reached over and socked him on his arm. "I want to make love. I got to leave soon to get ready for work tomorrow."

"Race you to the bedroom," teased Gary.

By the time Judy went home she was exhausted from making love, but she smiled all the way home. In less than three months she would be married and the ranch would be her new home. She would start her new life and she wanted to have a baby with Gary. She wanted several children to fill that big ranch house.

New Years, Judy had to work with several breaking news from car wrecks, robbery, and several small stories. She couldn't wait to quit the paper or maybe work part time. She was going to spend her time on the ranch which she loved.

Gary stayed home since Judy had to work. It was cold outside and he only went outside to check livestock and feed them. Things were slow so he told his crew to stay in out of the cold unless something had to be done.

In the month of January they had three colts and five calves born. That gave them something to do, taking care of the young ones. Ben and Wayne worked on their training equipment to have it ready when it got warmer. They were getting behind on their training, but it was too cold to work outside.

Gary got a phone call from Leroy. Katherine and Leroy were getting married on Valentine Day and they wanted him and Wolf to be there. Gary and Wolf would be grooms. Leroy told him to come as he normally dressed. He told Leroy that they would be there.

After he hung up, he pictured the wedding. It would be fun with all his crazy friends attending the wedding. He didn't think Leroy realized what he was doing. They would embarrass the heck out of Katherine. Wolf was curled up by the door when Gary told him that they were going to Dallas to be in a wedding.

Wolf looked up at Gary and grinned. He was ready to go since there would be a lot of good food to eat. He was going for the food.

Gary thought about what Leroy had said about coming as you normally dressed. He laughed, that was what the man said. He had a new set of buckskins in the closet. That was what he would wear. He liked wearing then, when he dressed in buckskins they were soft and felt good on the body.

January went by fast and it was time for Gary to get things caught up before he went to Dallas. He wanted to stop on his way to visit his folks. He had talked to Mike and he would see him and his family at the wedding. He wanted to see their little girl Cindy or should he say big girl. He knew she would be beautiful like her Mother.

February 13, Wolf and Gary left the ranch and headed toward

Dallas. They stopped that night at his folks. His Mom had a feast ready for them when they arrived. Wolf was in hog heaven with all the food he received. They left the next day for Dallas.

They arrived an hour before the wedding and visited all his friends. Punky told stories about the Navy, Mike filled them in on how his ranch was doing. He was still training horses for the movies. Rex was still working at Texas Instruments, Leroy told about life in the Police force and finally everyone wanted to know all about what Wolf and Gary were doing. Rex told Gary about the bachelor party at Hooters and the strip joint they went to after they left Hooters.

Leroy was as nervous as a cat on a hot tin roof. Katherine laughed at him and told him to cool it, but it didn't help.

The wedding march turned out to be a sight to see. Jim Lewis was best man in a suit. The grooms were Rex Johnson in a suit, Punky Wilson in his Navy dress uniform, Mike love in a country western suit, Gary Mitchel in buckskins and Wolf as himself.

Ashley Lewis was maid of honor in a beautiful long red dress. The bridesmaids were dressed in short red dresses. Her bridesmaids were Ann Mitchel, Megan Moore, Linda Love and Cindy Love.

The church was decorated in red for Valentine Day. Red flowers were everywhere. Leroy took his place dressed in a suit. The bridesmaids and grooms took their place. Ashley whispered to the bridesmaids, "Now all we need is a bride. I hope we don't have a run-a-way like in the movies." The girls giggled.

The wedding march sounded and all heads turned to the back of the church. Leroy couldn't believe what he saw. The church was full. Police, Newspaper people and family filled the church. What happen to the small wedding?

Katherine's Father escorted her down the church isle and gave

Leroy her hand. After the wedding vows, the exchanging of rings and kissing the bride it was time now for food and drinks. They went in a back room for that. A newspaper reporter took pictures of the whole wedding.

Leroy and Katherine wanted to get out of the reception as soon as they could. They ran for the front door of the church. As they came out the door the walk was lined with Police in dress uniform, "Present sabers." Leroy and Katherine walked under the sabers.

Mike pulled up in a good-time van as they reached the end of the sabers. People stormed them throwing rice on them. Mike tossed Leroy the keys to the van.

"I thought you would have more fun on your honeymoon with a ride like this."

Leroy handed his car keys to Mike, "Take care of my old Thunderbird."

"I will and you two have a fun honeymoon."

Katherine kissed Mike on the cheek, "Thank you."

She turned and tossed her bouquet over her shoulder and Ann caught it. She stared at her biker.

"We'll see what we can do about it." She opened her arms and he went into them.

Leroy pulled out into traffic and headed south. They were on their way to San Antonio.

Gary said good-by to his friends. Gary and Wolf headed back to the ranch. It had been a different type of wedding, but it was fun. He had got to see his classmates and friends.

They arrived back about midnight tired and hungry. Gary broke out some leftovers, beer and milk to drink. After they finished eating they went straight to bed. It had been a long day.

The next day, Gary opened one eye as sun streamed in through the bedroom window. He finally got up and made it to the bathroom. He heard pots and pans banging downstairs and knew Maria was making breakfast for the crew. Wolf had already left the bedroom looking for food. Gary took a quick shower and put on clean clothes. He walked into the kitchen straight to the coffee pot.

"Good morning Maria."

"Good morning Boss."

The crew came in one by one until they were all there. They wanted to know about the wedding and his friends. Gary gave them a run down about everything. Then it dawned on him. "Judy and I set the date for our wedding. It will be March tenth the same day as her Mother's wedding day. We got a lot of planning before then. We haven't picked a place for the wedding yet. I guess I better buy a new suit to wear."

Maria said, "I'll make up a menu for the reception if you want me to and cook the food. I need to know how many people will be there."

"I have no idea. We haven't sent out invitations yet. We got a short time to get everything ready."

Judy's folks, Mr. and Mrs. Adams moved from Houston to Sugarland. They were tired of the big city and since they retired it was time to move. They bought a modest home in town. Judy could see them anytime now. She didn't see them much when they lived in Houston. Mrs. Adams was happy for Judy and Gary. She started to help Judy plan her wedding. They went shopping for a dress, shoes, flowers and a church. She didn't want a big wedding she just wanted to be Gary's wife.

March 9th, everything was ready. Judy found a small Baptist church in town, all the flowers were delivered and put in place, invitations sent out and Maria was getting all the food ready for the reception at the ranch following the wedding. Judy was walking on cloud nine, one more day and she would be Mrs. Gary Mitchel.

March tenth, wedding day and everything was ready. Mike, Linda and Cindy Love were there along with Mr. and Mrs. Mitchel from Gary's hometown. All the hands and Wolf were there. Mr. Adams would give the bride away. Mike Love was best man and Linda Love was Maid of honor. Cindy was the flower girl and Wolf was the ring, barer. The rings were attached to a small pillow on his back.

The church was filled with friends and coworkers. The Newspaper covered the wedding of one of their own. All was ready.

The wedding march began and Cindy led off with flowers. Judy and her Father followed her to the front of the church. Mr. Adams put Judy's hand in Gary's hand and stepped back. Mike stood beside Gary and Wolf beside him. Linda stood beside Judy. After the preacher preformed the wedding and rings had been exchanged.

"You may now kiss the bride," said the preacher.

Gary took his time and gave her a very long kiss. Judy thought her knees would give way. She would never forget that kiss. Gary was staking his claim. "I love you Judy."

"I love you more."

When they came up for air the preacher said, "I now give you Mr. and Mrs. Mitchel"

Everyone left the church and went to the ranch for the reception. Maria had everything ready when the crowd got there. There was enough food to feed an army. Maria had Wolf a big bowl in one corner of the kitchen. He grinned, that's what he lived for.

After everyone ate, there was dancing for anyone wanting to shake a leg. Gary and Judy started it off with the first dance which was a slow one for lovers. They couldn't wait until everyone left and they were alone. They were going to spend their wedding night at the ranch and go on a honeymoon the next day. They still hadn't decided where they wanted to go.

The party broke up at midnight and they were finally alone. Wolf curled up at the front door and they went to their bedroom.

They slowly undressed one another then stood staring at each other. Gary opened his arms and she went into them. They stood skin to skin her nipples digging into his chest while his shaft dug into her belly. Gary walked her back until her legs touched the bed and she fell back on her back. He dropped down on his knees and lowered his head to touch her folds with his tongue. Judy arched her back and moaned as Gary did a number on her. When he felt her muscles tighten on his tongue, he pulled out before she climaxed. He slid up between her legs and with a fast thrust he was home. She bucked as he rode her hard.

"I'm coming, I'm coming," arching her back with Gary's hands on her butt she came.

Gary thrust one more time and moaned as he came deep in her body. He fell forward on her chest with her nipples digging into his chest. "Oh baby, that was fantastic. I don't want to pull out."

"Then don't."

Gary turned over with her still hanging onto him. She was now on top with Gary's shaft still deep in her folds. It felt so good she didn't want it to ever end. They lay like that until Judy felt his shaft becoming hard again. "Oh Gary," she moaned as she rode him hard. She twisted and turned as she bounced up and down on his shaft.

"Oh Gary, I'm coming again," and she did.

Exhausted they curled up spoon fashion and went to sleep. They woke up as the sun shined through the bedroom window. Judy pushed her butt back against Gary's erection. "I would like you to do me dog fashion before we get up." She raised her rear end in the air for him.

"Your wish is my command."

Later they finally got out of bed and showered together. They dressed in jeans and shirts and went down to fix some breakfast. "I'm so hungry I could eat a horse," said Gary.

"You and Wolf are always hungry."

"I got to keep my strength up since I'm married to a wife that can't get enough sex." Gary grinned at her and she hit him with a kitchen towel.

"I should cut you off, but I would cut myself off to and that won't do. Yes, I love having sex with you as much as you want."

"Then we better eat and keep up our strength."

"What would you like for breakfast besides pussy," giggled Judy.

"I would like the works, two eggs over medium, bacon, toast and coffee."

Judy started cooking breakfast while Gary made coffee. She made eggs, ham, grits and toast for breakfast. She set two plates of food on the table while he poured the coffee. They were tired from making love most of the night. "Where would you like to go on a honeymoon?" asked Gary.

"I don't really know."

"Ok, I'll name a few and you pick one. We could go on a cruise, Hawaii, Mexico, Europe, Galveston, San Antonio or San Diego."

"Let's go to San Diego. It has a lot to do there. It has the world's largest Zoo, Disney World, Sea World, Camping in the mountains and lots of clubs."

"Sounds like a plan to me, let's do it. You want to drive out or fly?"

"Let's take out time and drive. We can sight see on the way. I took two weeks off from work and I want to enjoy every minute of it."

"Then drive we will. "I'll gas up the car and you start packing."

They were on the road by ten o'clock. They stopped in San Antonio to eat and got back on the road. They turned off interstate 10 and picked up highway 285 to Carlsbad. They would spend the night there and go to Carlsbad Caverns in the morning. The motel wasn't the best. Gary pulled back the curtain to the shower and there was a big scorpion in the shower. "Judy we have a pet in the shower."

She looked in the shower and screamed, "Kill it before it gets away."

"I guess you don't like our pet." Gary killed it and put it in the trash.

They didn't sleep well that night. The next day they went down in the big hole. The Caverns were huge. One cave looked big enough to put an aircraft carrier in it. While in the big Cavern the guide turned out the lights for a few minutes. It was the darkest dark they had ever seen. When they reached the bottom they ate lunch. When they finished the guide told them they could walk out or ride the elevator. They were tired and rode the elevator. If you stayed until dark you could watch the bats fly out of the cave. They decided to get back on the road.

They drove to Yuma Arizona and stopped for the night. The next day they drove over the mountains to San Diego. They found a hotel downtown and checked in. After they were unpacked, Gary asked, "What do you want to do for the rest of the day?"

"Why don't we find a nice place to eat and go night clubbing." Judy looked a cub up in the phone book. "They have a big country western club here in town. Not too far from it on the water is a nice restaurant"

They put on country western clothes, boots and all. They found the restaurant close to the water. The waitress showed them a table overlooking the bay. "Oh, I love the view," said Judy.

They both had a large seafood platter. By the time they finished their meal it was close to time to go to the club. Judy said, "Let's go early to get a seat close to the dance floor. I feel like kicking up my heels. When was the last time we danced together?"

"To tell the truth I don't remember, but I'm ready to go now."

Gary parked the car close to the club and they made their way to the front door. After paying a cover charge the waitress showed them a table next to the dance floor and took their order. Gary had beer and Judy had a cocktail. "Let's sit and watch the couples dance for a while. I want to see how good they are. I don't want to make a fool out of myself."

They watched until a medium two-step started. "They are playing our song," said Gary.

He led Judy to the dance floor and they danced in a circle around the floor with the other couples. They danced well together. They danced the night away. Midnight, they went back to their hotel and made love.

The next day they went to Disney Land and spent the day. They rode ride after ride. They even rode the elephant ride with the kids. The best thing they enjoyed was the jungle ride. The animals were so good they looked real. Late that day they ate at a fast food restaurant and went back to their hotel and made love.

They slept late the next day. They were lazy and stayed in their room until noon. After lunch they went to the zoo and spent the afternoon walking. They saw every kind of animal you could think of. Then they saw something different. "Judy do you see that woman over there in the bushes with her ass pointed our way. She has her panties down and is taking a leak."

"When you got to go, you got to go," giggled Judy.

"Would you do something like that?"

"Yes, if I had to go bad enough."

They laughed and went on sightseeing. The zoo was huge and they didn't see all of it that day. They ate a late supper in their room and went to bed. They went straight to sleep and didn't make love because they were too exhausted.

The next day they went to Sea World. It was a lot of fun to see. They watched all the shows and went back to San Diego. They went to a steak house for supper and both had a steak, baked potato, salad and beer to drink. They went back to the hotel and made slow love. "Oh Gary, will we ever get enough of each other?"

"Only when, we get too old to make love anymore."

"You think."

The next day they packed up and went to the mountains. It was still a little cool, but they had a tent and a blow-up bed. They liked to hike and did a lot of it while they were there. They cooked over a camp fire and enjoyed every minute. They stayed two days and nights in the mountains before returning to San Diego.

The next day they packed up and started back home. They had done a lot on their honeymoon and enjoyed every minute. They had made a lot of memories. They spent the night on the road and drove the rest of the way home the next day. All hands were glad to see them back. Wolf was the first to greet them as they got out of the car. They both hugged him. They went into the house to see the crew.

"It's good to be home," said Gary.

"Yes it is," replied Judy.

"Joe, how is everything running?"

"Fine Boss, we got some new colts and cafes. We sold two more quarter horses and Ben is finishing their training. The ranch is growing in leaps and bounds. If we keep on we will need more land and employees."

"Good job Joe."

"Thank you, sir."

"Is there any land joining our ranch that the owner might want to sell?"

"I don't know, but I will check it out. We could grow our own feed if we had more land. That would save us a lot of money in the long run."

"God, how I love this job and ranch," remarked Gary.

Judy had a short time before she had to go back to work, but now she would come home to the ranch. She loved the ranch and everything about it. How had she been so lucky to meet Gary and fall in love with him? Next, she wanted kids to fill this big house.

The honeymoon was over and time to get back to work. Judy went back to the Newspaper and told her boss, in a few months she wanted to go on part time. He didn't like it, but he was happy for Judy. She had been a great reporter.

Gary went back to working on the ranch except for jobs him and Wolf did finding cattle and horses. He still couldn't believe how many ranchers lost livestock, but it was good money for him and Wolf. They had usually at least two jobs of lost cattle every week.

Joe came in the office, "Boss, we can buy a couple hundred acres on the south side of our land."

"Is it good enough to grow hay or corn?"

"Yes, and I think you can get it cheap. The owner died and the kids want to get rid of the land. They want the money."

"I'll go talk to them." By the end of the week Gary had added another two hundred acres to his ranch.

The next month Judy and Gary had fallen into a routine of work and play. During the week they both worked hard, but Saturday and Sunday was their time together. They liked to ride on Saturday to their favorite tree by the creek. They would bring food and drink and sometimes fish. If they caught fish they cooked them there over a campfire. They loved each other so much they were like two joined at the hip. Wolf was always with them like their kid.

"Gary, I would like to have a baby. Are you ready to become a Dad?"

"Yes, I'm ready. We better start now if we want to fill that big old house with kids."

"Judy turned over on their blanket and looked at Gary. Are you ready to start now?" she giggled.

They slowly undressed each other and made slow love. That was the only way to make love. They made love a second time before they returned to the ranch. It was almost dark when they returned to the ranch. They took care of their horses and went into the house.

The phone was ringing off the hook when they came in the door. Judy answered and it was the Newspaper wanting her to cover a late night story. She didn't want to, but she told her boss she would be on her way in a few minutes.

"Gary, I'm going into town to cover a story. Don't wait up because I may be late coming home. I don't know what it is until I get to the paper. I love you."

He pulled her into his arms and kissed her hard, "I love you more." He walked her to her car and opened the door for her. She waved as she drove down the driveway.

He went to his office to check phone calls and check his books. He had just finished checking his books when the phone rang. He picked it up on the second ring.

"Gary, how may I help you?"

"This is the Police your wife was in an accident at the first red light coming into town. You need to get here quick."

"How bad is it? Is she alright?"

"She is still penned in the car and the Fire department is trying to get her out."

Gary and Wolf ran for his car. He drove like a crazy person trying to get to the accident. Half of the intersection was blocked off by the two cars involved in the wreck. Gary and Wolf jumped out of his car and ran to Judy's car or what was left of it. The other car had hit her broadside. She was still pinned in the car. Gary ran up to the car, "Judy I'm here, it's going to be alright." Wolf put his head up at the window.

Judy put her hand on Wolf's head. "No, it's not going to be alright. I love -----and she was gone. Blood ran down from her mouth. "Get her out of the car," screamed Gary.

It took another thirty minutes to get her out of the car. Gary was in shock. He couldn't believe life could be so cruel. He wanted to kill the driver of the other car, but they had already put him in a body bag. He had gone through the windshield on impact. He was drunk as a skunk and ran the light at a high speed. Judy was pronounced dead at the scene and taken to a funeral home. Gary followed the ambulance to the funeral home. He made arrangements for her services at the little church they were married in and she would be brought back to the ranch. He would put her to rest under the tree by the creek where she loved so much. Gary had Joe and Sam build an iron fence around the tree.

Two days later Judy was put to rest under the tree. After everyone left, Gary and Wolf stayed by the grave for a long time. They both loved her very much. They went back to the house. The crew was there and Maria had made food for everyone. Judy's Mom and Dad left early and went home. After everyone left Gary went into his office with a bottle and started drinking. By the time he finished the bottle he was falling down drunk. He cried himself to sleep. Wolf stayed by his side the whole time.

Gary woke up the next morning with a big hangover. The crew had come and gone by the time he came into the kitchen for breakfast. Maria was very, quite as she fixed Gary breakfast. She knew he was hurting, but she didn't know what to say or do. "Boss you have to move on. Judy would want it that way."

"I know that, but I can't seem to get it together. I wish it had been me instead of her. I feel like a part of me is dead."

"Don't say that, God has his reasons for what happen. He has something he wants you to do. I don't know what, but you will know when the time comes."

"I just don't understand why the good die young and the evil live forever."

"Mark my words you will know when the time comes."

"I wish I had your faith. Right now I am totally lost on what to do."

"I have decided to go out in the wild again like I did last time when I was hurting. I will take Wolf with me and he can visit his pack. I know he misses them, but he stays by my side. We are an odd team, but we are good together."

Gary loaded his old truck with enough supplies to feed an army, but it was a pack of wolves he was going to feed. He was going back where he healed the last time when Wolf saved his life. He had to leave the ranch for a while. He went to the barn and told Joe to take care of the ranch until he got back. He didn't know how long that would be. Gary and Wolf loaded in the pickup and hit the road. They didn't stop until they arrived at the same place he spent so much time healing last time. Gary opened the pickup door, "Ok Wolf, go find your friends."

Gary set up his tent, made a place for a fire and unloaded his supplies into the tent. He laid his sleeping bag in one corner. Wolf finally came back with the whole pack of wolves with him. They knew Gary and curled up around the tent. He noticed Wolf had a young she wolf with him.

"You didn't waste any time, did you?"

"Wolf grinned up at him."

"Well, all your friends can stay for supper." Gary put steaks on for him and Wolf. He cut up chunks of steak for the other wolves. Each wolf came up and took a chunk of meat out of Gary's hand. Wolf wanted his cooked. He was spoiled from living on the ranch. After supper all the wolves left, but the she wolf. She curled up beside Wolf.

"Love at first sight," Gary laughed.

Gary banked the fire and went in the tent to get ready for bed. Wolf came in and curled up by the door. Gary motioned for the she wolf to come on in the tent. She finally eased into the tent and curled up beside Wolf. He closed the flap and went to bed. He couldn't sleep at first, but finally dozed off. He was still trying to come to grips with Judy's death. He thought about what Maria said about life. Maybe she was right.

After a good breakfast, Gary took his rifle and went hunting. As he walked, Wolf and the she wolf followed close behind him. After about an hour Gary spotted a bunch of wild hogs. He brought one down on his first shot. He set about butchering the hog. "Wolf, go get your pack and they can finish off the hog."

Wolf took off with the she wolf on his tail. She didn't understand what was going on with Wolf and Gary. She watched as Wolf did everything he was told, but how did he know to do it. She didn't understand a thing Gary said.

He had packed up the meat he was keeping when Wolf returned with the pack. Gary, Wolf and the she wolf left and went back to camp while the pack finished off the hog. Gary made coffee and put some pig meat on for dinner. When it was ready he gave Wolf a large piece. He gave the she wolf a cooked piece and a raw piece. He wanted to see if she would like cooked meat like Wolf. She watched Wolf eat and she ate the cooked piece first, but then she ate the raw piece. She was a little thin, probably from like of food during the winter.

The next day Gary went fishing and caught a mess of trout and catfish. Fishing was good probably because they were so far off the road nobody knew about the place. Gary loved the wild. He liked watching Wolf and the she wolf play. He liked to sit by the fire at night and look at the stars. He could remember Judy now and not go crazy. He liked not having to make any decisions and just relax. He was healing slowly, but he was getting there. He stayed three more weeks. The last night there he had the pack of wolves for supper. He gave them the rest of the meat and anything else they would eat. They were like a bunch of dogs to him. They liked being around him. He had stayed so much time with them they were like family to him. He hated to leave, but it was time to go on with the living. "Wolf, we leave tomorrow."

The next morning, Gary fixed breakfast and packed up their gear. He took one last look around. It was time to leave. He opened the truck door, "Wolf time to go."

Wolf jumped into the truck and turned around. The she wolf came to the door and looked up at him as she whined. Wolf whined and stared at Gary. "I guess you don't want to leave her. What's another wolf in the house?" He motioned for the she wolf to get in the truck. She was trembling and scared, but she finally jumped in the door beside Wolf. They left the wild and headed home. Gary stopped for gas and food. The two wolves stayed in the truck.

They arrived back at the ranch that evening. Gary didn't even know what day of the week it was. He pulled up in front and parked. They got out and went into the house. Maria was in the kitchen cooking supper for the crew. She turned around and faced Gary, Wolf and the she wolf. "Look what the cat's drug in. It's about time you came home and got on with your life. What is this with you?" Maria said, as she starred at the she wolf.

"That is Wolf's girlfriend."

"Well what's her name?"

"She doesn't have one."

"We can't call both of them Wolf. She needs a name. I know what we can name her. We'll call her Sunshine. She brings a new light into this home."

"It sounds good to me. What do you think Wolf?" Wolf barked his approval.

Maria put a dish of food on the floor and Wolf went to eat with Sunshine right behind him. Maria reached down and hugged Wolf. "I missed you around the kitchen." Sunshine watched and didn't know what to think. Wolf was part of this human family. Maria reached down to Sunshine with the back of her hand to let her smell her. "You will get to know me little one. You are now part of a big family around here."

Supper time all hands were at the kitchen table and hungry. They wanted to know about Gary's trip and where he got another wolf. He told them about his trip. Joe looked at Gary, "Are you alright now."

"I think I'm on the mend. I still hurt, but I'm handling it now."

"Good, now you are Boss again. We got lots of work to do."

After supper Gary checked his phone calls and the books. The books were good as usual. The bills were paid and deposits made. He called his Mom and talked about an hour. After he hung up he decided to go to Judy's grave. He went to the barn with Wolf and Sunshine on his heels. He saddled a horse and headed out to the open pasture. He arrived at the fenced in area and walked in the gate. Gary and Wolf stared at the grave. Gary pulled off his wedding band and buried it next to her tome stone. He finally felt he could deal with her death. He would always love her, but she was dead and he was still living. He finally closed the gate and went back home.

Chapter Eight

The next morning before breakfast, Gary went outside just in time to see Ben bite the dust as he was thrown from a big black stallion. He ran over to the fence, "Are you alright, are you hurt?"

"Only my butt and my pride were hurt. I thought I was a good rider until I got on this wild horse. He is one mean bastard. Pardon my French."

"Where did you get him?"

"I bought him while you were gone. I wanted to surprise you with him for your own horse, but the surprise is on me. I can't get to first base with him."

"He is beautiful and since he will be my horse I'll take it from here. Thank you for buying him for me. He will come around very soon I promise you. Come on in the house, it is breakfast time."

Gary had finally got a good night's sleep and was feeling great. As it turned out the whole crew was in on getting Joe to buy the horse. It made Gary feel so humble that they were trying to help him heal. They were trying to get his mind off of Judy. It was nice to have so many friends.

"Thank all of you for getting the horse. He is beautiful. I'll ride him everywhere I go on the ranch and when Wolf and I work to find livestock. There won't be anything than can outrun him."

After breakfast Gary went to the corral to train the stallion. Wolf and Sunshine went with him. Everyone watched from the house thinking he was crazy letting the wolves go with him. They would scare the horse. Little did they know what Gary, was up to. Gary slowly stepped inside of the corral. "Wolf I want you to tell this horse if he doesn't do everything I want him to do that I will let you and sunshine in here and have lunch."

Wolf stared at the horse and he stared back. Gary slowly walked over and put his arm around the horse's neck and petted him. He talked low to him as he slid into the saddle and touched his flanks. The horse started to walk slowly around the corral. He closed his eyes and told Wolf to open the gate. Wolf slid the latch back and opened the gate. "Let's see what you got." He touched him harder in the flanks and the horse shot out of the corral. He went across the pasture like the wind. Gary couldn't believe the horse could be so fast. "You fly like the wind so I'll call you Wind."

Everyone watched as Gary rode back into the corral. "How did you do that," asked Ben.

"I just told him I was the Boss and he had better be good or I would let Wolf and Sunshine, eat him for lunch."

"Yeah right," but he wasn't sure that was what, happen.

When Gary went anywhere on and sometimes off the ranch Wolf, Sunshine and Wind were with him. It didn't take long to train Wind he was a very smart horse. Gary loved running him across the pasture with the wind in his face with Wolf and Sunshine on his heels.

Jerry and Kathy asked Gary if they could bring some friends to the ranch and take them riding. "No problem and you can use the pit to cook steaks. The pit and a table are in the barn. Tell Joe what you need and he will help you get set up."

"Far out," said Kathy. They were two happy kids.

Saturday they brought two boys and two girls to the ranch with them. Jerry and Kathy saddled horses for the ride. The boys and girls couldn't believe they were on a real ranch riding horses. They rode for a couple of hours and returned to the barn. Joe already had the pit fired up and the steaks on. Jerry watched the steaks until they were cooked. Maria brought them a salad, French fries and cokes from the house. They were having a great time when

Gary rode up on Wind.

"Hi kids, are you having a good time?"

They stared at Wolf and Sunshine. "They are wolves," one of the kids said.

Gary laughed, "Yes they are and they go with me everywhere. You can pet them if you want to. They won't hurt you."

Kathy went over and hugged Wolf and Sunshine came to her side for a hug. The kids couldn't believe what they were seeing. After a while the kids hugged and petted the wolves.

One of the girls said, "If only our classmates could see us now."

The other girl said, "Now they will have to believe us," she started taking pictures.

The group finally left and things went back to normal. The only person left on duty was Joe. Maria had cooked some supper before she left. Joe was checking on all the horses before he came in to eat. Gary put supper on the table for him and Joe. He filled a bowl each for Wolf and Sunshine. They chowed down and went over in a corner and curled up to sleep.

Joe came in and went straight to the coffee pot. He filled his cup and came over to the table to eat. Gary and Joe talked ranch problems and new ideas to make the place more efficient. Gary had a few ideas, but nothing jumped out at him.

"Joe do you have anything that feels good?"

"Not at this time, but we can always dream and maybe something will show up."

The next morning Gary was in the kitchen having coffee when he heard a car out front. Joe came in and told him he had a visitor. Gary went outside as a man got out of a Lincoln. "How may I help you sir?"

"Are you Gary Mitchel, called the Tracker?"

"Yes I am."

"Then I have a job for you. It may be dangerous. I want you to find my daughter and bring her home. I think she is being held against her will."

"Why do you think she is being held against, her will."

"She is a little wild, but she always calls us and lets us know where she is. We may not like where she goes, but she never fails to call us."

"Where did she go?"

"She left Dallas with a man called James Lopez. Kristine said they were going Cartagena Columbia on a business trip. I don't know much about the man except he is very rich. He owns an estate in west Dallas. He owns a lot of property around Dallas. I can't find out what he does for a living."

"It sounds like you may have a problem. He may be a drug lord using Dallas as a front to run drugs. I hope I'm wrong for your sake. Your daughter may have seen his operation and he can't let her contact you."

"I just want my daughter back. I don't care what he does. Will you help me?"

"Have you tried to get help from the government?"

"Yes and nobody will do anything to help me. You say you can find anything. Will you help me?" I am rich and will pay anything to get her back."

"I have never done anything like what you want done, but if you want my services I will do it for you. What did you say your name was?"

"My name is Wilson."

"I will need supplies for the trip."

"My company jet will take you to Columbia. Give me a list of what you want and I will have it on the plane when you are ready to go. Anything you need I can get."

"Leave me your phone number and I will call the list to you when I decide what I will need."

"When will you leave for Columbia?"

"I'll be ready in a couple of days. Have the jet pick me up at our airport, unless it is too large to land on a small runway."

"It's not that big, it should be able to land here. I will ride down with you and come back and wait for your call when you have my daughter."

They shook hands and Mr. Wilson left. Gary came into the house. "Wolf we got a big job. I hope I don't get us killed."

The next day Gary built a target range. He bought a bow and some arrows. He didn't want to make any noise when he went to get the girl. He didn't know how hard it would be to find her. He was counting on Wolf to lead him to her. He had shot a bow and arrow before, but it had been a long time. He practiced all day with the bow and arrows plus his 45 automatic. He wanted to be ready for anything.

The second day he made bombs from C-4 with different length fuses. Never leave home without it. He may have to fight a war to get her out. He hoped it was a trip for nothing, that Kristine just got busy and didn't contact her folks. He filled his backpack with food, water, and a first aid kit. He hoped he wouldn't need that. He got his hunting knife and pocket knife and put them with his backpack. He wouldn't need much from Mr. Wilson.

The next morning Gary told Joe to take care of the ranch while he was gone. Gary and Wolf left for the airport. The jet arrived about thirty minutes after Gary got there. Mr. Wilson stepped down out of the Jet. "Are you ready to leave? I have a lot of supplies since I didn't know what you would need."

They boarded the plane and Gary looked the supplies over. He picked out a sniper rifle with a night vision scope with a silencer, a small tent, and a small rubber raft with a tiny troll motor. He wanted the boat in case he went by water.

Mr. Wilson handed him maps and area pictures leading out of the city. He would have to ask around and try to locate Mr. Lopez. If he was as rich as they say he was it shouldn't be too hard. Mr. Wilson handed Gary a set of keys. "These are to a company van with our name on it. That should make you blend in."

"Yes, I want to keep a low profile. Wolf will stay out of sight in the van."

"Then I guess we are ready to take off." He went forward to tell the pilot to take off. Gary strapped Wolf in a seat and strapped in himself. Mr. Wilson strapped in just as they took off.

"I'm going with you to Columbia and return with the plane. When you find Kristine and make it back to the airport give me a call and we will pick you up." They landed in Columbia. "This is a private side, of the airport only for company planes."

"Good, Wolf and I will load into the van and be gone quickly before we draw attention."

They loaded their supplies in the van and Wolf stayed in the van while Gary got last minute instructions. Once the plane was gone they were on their own. Mr. Wilson gave Gary a key to a company house in the edge of town. They would stay there until Gary could find the location of James Lopez. They found the small house. It was off the road and private. That was good as they wanted to keep a low profile. Gary parked the van in the carport and unlocked the side door to the house. They left their supplies in the van. They hoped to be on the road the next day. Tonight Gary would check bars and places he thought he might get information.

Three days passed and Gary still didn't know where to find Lopez. He got the idea people were afraid to give out information. They looked scared every time he mentioned the name Lopez. This was turning out to be harder than he thought. That night as they were cruising around town, they saw a girl being molested by four thugs. Two was holding her down while one man cut her clothes off her body. He was between her legs. He unzipped his pants, pulled out his big erection and tried to enter her as she fought for dear life.

Gary pulled the van up beside them and stepped out of the van. "Let the girl go."

"Buzz off man this is none of your business. Go find your own piece of ass."

"I'm making it my business. Leave now and you won't get hurt." Wolf stepped out of the van and stood beside Gary.

All four men pulled out, knifes. "Ok you asked for it."

Gary pulled out his 45 automatic, "Last chance to live or die."

They stared at the 45 automatic and Wolf. They turned and ran for their life. Gary was so mad he would have killed the men. They were animals.

Gary went over and helped the girl up. She tried to cover herself, but her clothes were torn too bad. He led her over to the van and gave her a blanket to cover herself. "Get in the van and I will take you home."

She only lived a short distance from where she was attacked. Gary pulled up in front of a shack to let her out. "You are looking for this man Lopez?"

"You know him?"

"Everybody knows him. They are afraid of him. He is a big drug lord and will kill anyone who gives out any information about him, but I will tell you where to find him. Do you have a map?"

"Yes, I have a map." Gary spread the map out and she studied it. He handed her a pen. She drew a line along the road and marked the spot where he lived. It was way out in the country.

"He has many men and will kill anyone he catches near his property. I know some of the poor people who work there. He doesn't pay them much, but it will buy food when your family is starving."

"Are they making drugs?"

"Yes they are, but they are hungry and if they don't do it someone else will."

"Is there anything else you can tell me about the place?"

"He lives in the big house with his wife and kids. He keeps a young woman locked up in a cottage behind the big house for his pleasure. He has covered sheds and buildings where they make drugs."

"Are you sure about the woman in the cottage? Is she a young white woman?"

"Yes, I'm sure."

"Bingo," he had all he needed for a go.

Gary pulled out a wad of money and pressed it in her hand. "Spend it very slowly and you won't attract any attention." He didn't give her his name or he didn't ask her for her name. It was better that way. He let her out of the van and waited until she was in the shack.

"Well Wolf, we can finally go to work. We will get a good night's sleep and leave in the morning."

When they got back to the house Gary studied the map and plotted the way he would go. He would follow the main road out of town until he was almost to the turn off to the valley where Lopez lived. He would turn off and hide his van and take the small boat down a small river to the side of the property. They would walk the rest of the way through the jungle on that side of the property.

The next morning, they ate a good breakfast and hit the road. It was slow going even on the so called highway. They weren't too far from the turnoff when Gary spotted a good place to leave the road. He made a left turn into the bushes and drove in a few yards. He got out and erased his tracks where he left the road. He got back in the van and drove slowly toward the river. When he saw the river from a distance of about fifty yards he pulled the van into some thick bushes. He got their supplies out of the van. Wolf stood guard as Gary cut bushes and covered the van.

Gary glanced at Wolf, "Hope we can find the van on our way back. It may be night when we come back." He knew it wouldn't be a problem with Wolf finding the van.

Gary had a harness for Wolf to carry part of their supplies. He had the light raft, motor and tent on his back. Gary was loaded down with his rifle, backpack, bow and arrows. When they got to the river, Gary launched the raft and put the motor on it. They loaded their equipment in the boat and eased in the small boat. They had to be very careful or they would turn the small rubber raft over. Gary eased the boat out into the river. They were on their way.

They traveled downstream at a slow pace as Gary watched his compass. He wanted a straight shot to James Lopez's home. There was very little current so they let the boat drift along. About an hour down the river, Gary checked his compass. It was time to find a place to beach the boat. Gary made an abrupt turn to the right and beached the boat. Wolf jumped out of the boat with a rope in his mouth and wrapped it around a tree. Gary got out of the boat and pulled the boat higher on the bank. He unloaded the boat and pulled it further into the trees. He hid the boat in some bushes and came back for the supplies.

"Well Wolf, let's pack up and go."

Gary loaded Wolf with the tent, bow and arrows. He took his backpack and rifle. He strapped his knife and 45 Automatic on his hip. "Ok, let's head out." He checked the compass one more time.

It was slow going through the woods and bushes. He didn't want to cut anything to leave a trail. "Wolf, you keep track of where we are because we may be coming back at night."

It was starting to get dark and they had a long way to go. "Wolf, we will camp here and go on in the morning."

Gary put up the small tent and put their supplies inside. He checked his bombs one last time. He hoped he didn't have to use them, but you never knew. He broke out some spam and crackers for supper. They flushed it down with bottle water. "That wasn't much of a supper, but it will have to do. We need to ration our food because I don't know how long we will be here."

Wolf curled up at the door of the tent when Gary went inside. He pulled off his boots and lay down to sleep. It was so small Wolf decided to stay outside. Gary didn't close the flap. The night sounds kept him awake a long time before he dozed off.

Chapter Nine

The next morning they ate beef jerky for breakfast and washed it down with water. Gary decided to leave the tent set up and covered it with bushes. He loaded his bow and arrows on Wolf. He strapped on his 45 automatic and knife. He grabbed his backpack and rifle. They headed out.

About two o'clock they reached the rim of the valley. They were high enough they could see the layout of the home and out building. You had to cross a bridge over a moat to get to the house. Gary didn't like the one way in and one way out. The back side was solid woods unless there was a moat which he couldn't tell from the angle. He didn't want to go in that way. It would take too much time to get in and out. He would plan to go in the front.

"Well Wolf, I guess we wait until tonight before we make our move."

He couldn't see the cottage out back behind the big house. He hoped the girl told him the truth. He aimed his rifle with the scope on the area out back. He could see people at work and knew they were processing drugs. They wore masks.

Suddenly, Gary saw a man jerked up in front of a man dressed in nice clothes. The man was held by two other men. He saw the man in charge pull something out of the man's pockets that was being held. They were so loud Gary could catch a few words. "Turn him loose and step back."

The two men turned the man loose and stepped back. The man in charge pulled out a pistol and pointed it at the man. "Nobody steals from me."

The man got down on his knees and begged for his life, but it didn't do any good. He shot the man three times before he hit the ground. He turned to the rest of the workers. "I'll kill anyone who tries to steal from me. Clean this mess up." He turned and headed toward the house where a woman and kids watched.

Gary couldn't believe he had killed the man in front of the woman and kids, but I guess it was a lesson for them to learn. He put his arm around the woman and went into the house.

Wolf and Gary settled down to wait until night fall. He wanted to watch and see how many guards were posted and where. He watched as they changed shifts every four hours. There was one at the bridge, one at the front of the house and two at the work sheds. They were heavily armed.

Gary wandered if there would be more at night or less. He hoped it wouldn't be as many. He planned to take as many out as possible with his bow and arrows. He didn't want them to sound the alarm. He decided to set bombs off all over the place including the bridge. He wanted to put the drug lord out of business at least for a while and give him time to make their escape. It would be slower with the girl alone. She was a city girl and it would be rough on her. He thought about Judy and knew she could keep up with him and Wolf. He missed her.

"Wolf, we might as well take a nap. It is a long time until dark."

They took a long nap until a truck came and woke them up. He stopped at the bridge and the guard flagged him on through. The truck drove around to the back and stopped under one of the sheds. Gary watched as they unloaded the truck. They opened one crate and pulled out automatic rifles with long clips on them probably AK-47's. After they unloaded the crates, they loaded boxes of something back on the truck probably drugs. Nice little business James Lopez had. After it was loaded the truck left and headed back toward the city.

"Wolf, I bet if we check up on Lopez in Dallas he will have an import/export business."

Gary went back to watching the going on at the sheds. The workers were hard at it. A foreman gave orders and the workers carried them out. They had to be making more drugs. It was getting dark and Gary was in a hurry to get going, but he finally decided to wait until after midnight. He was hoping not to have to kill too many men to get the girl. He didn't like killing even if they were the bad guys.

At midnight the guards changed shifts. Two stayed in the back of the house and one at the bridge, but the one in front of the house was gone. He was glad he waited, now he had one less to worry about. He took his rifle and used the night scope to check on the guards one more time.

"It's time to earn, our paycheck." Gary put the rifle down and picked up his bow and arrows. He eased down low and headed for the bridge with Wolf right behind him. He got within about fifteen yards of the guard at the bridge. He would have to take him out with the bow. The man was smoking a pipe and Gary wandered if it had grass in it. He raised the bow and aimed his arrow at the man's chest. He hit him dead on and the man grunted and fell to the ground. He rushed over and dragged him off the road and into the bushes. Gary crossed the bridge with Wolf on his heels. He headed for the house. He eased around the side and peaked around the corner into the back yard. The second guard sat in a chair facing the sheds. He looked half asleep. Gary eased up behind him and clubbed him with his 45 automatic. Two bad guys down and one to go, the third one was in the shed looking things over. Gary closed his eyes and whispered for Wolf to distract the third man. Wolf eased over in front of the man as Gary eased up behind him. The man saw Wolf and swung his rifle up, but Gary clubbed him with his 45 automatic. It was time to find the girl and get out of Dodge. They saw the cottage off to their right and headed for the front door. Gary tried the door and it was locked. He had been told they locked her up all the time and didn't let her go anywhere.

Kristine sat on her bed crying. How could she have been such a fool? James Lopez had been good looking and the perfect gentleman when she met him in Dallas. He had wined and dined her sweeping her off her feet. James was rich and had the best of everything. Kristine thought he lived in Dallas. He had a large estate on the west side of Dallas. The house had twenty rooms and a garage filled with ten expensive cars. Kristine couldn't believe he wanted her. He could have had his pick of any woman he wanted, but he picked her. They had made love many times in the huge bed in the master bedroom. James was a good lover.

James wanted Kristine to take a trip with him on business. He told her it would only be for a week. They took a flight from Dallas to Cartagena Columbia. The city was called the city of romance. Kristine loved the city, but the next day they left by car into the outback. After several hours of driving they came to a large valley. The house looked like something a king would live in. There were many buildings and barns around the back of the house.

Kristine expected to be taken to the big house, but the car pulled around back to a small cottage. She soon found out she would live in the cottage. James lived in the big house with his wife and several children. She would be his mistress.

It was dark and Kristine sat on the bed crying when a man dressed in black busted in her locked door. It scared her. A large wolf stood in the doorway as lookout. "I'm here to take you home."

Gary reached for her hand, "We need to get out of here now. Leave everything except what you are wearing. Do you have boots?"

She had on jeans and a blouse. She reached under the bed and pulled out a pair of boots. She slipped them on and stood up ready to go. She didn't care where she was going as long as it was away from here. "I'm ready, let's go."

Wolf turned and they followed him out the door. "You follow

Wolf to the bridge and wait for me there. I have something I have to do. Wolf led the way and Kristine followed him. She thought how strange it was to see a large wolf with a man, but if he helped them get away then she was all for it. She had been locked up a long time and hated it. She felt dirty like a whore and couldn't wait to try and wash it away.

Gary went about setting C-4 bombs beside the barns, sheds, cars and trucks. He planned to blow the place to kingdom come. All bombs in place he went back and lit the longest fuse on down to the shortest. He ran like hell for the bridge. He set a bomb under the bridge and lit the short fuse. Christine and Wolf were in the bushes waiting for him.

"Let's get the hell out of here."

They headed up the hill just as the first bomb beside a barn went off. After that each bomb went off in order as men poured out of a bunkhouse. They were all guards and mad as a nest of wasps.

They were half way up the hill to the rim of the valley when a truck loaded with armed men were coming to the bridge as it blew up. Too bad they weren't on the bridge. They spotted Gary, Christine and Wolf making their getaway up the hill. They unloaded and started firing at them. Bullets were getting real close. They were still in range. Gary pulled a C-4 bomb out of his backpack and attached it to an arrow. He lit the fuse and raised the bow. He let the arrow fly right into the middle of the men. The C-4 took out six of the men, but the others started up the hill. "It's time to go."

They made it to the rim and over the top. Gary grabbed his rifle with night vision and scope. He carefully took out the closet man to them each time he fired. The last two men turned and ran back down the hill. They decided they didn't want to die tonight.

"Wolf, lead the way out of here." Wolf took point with Christine right behind him. Gary covered their rear. They headed deep into the woods toward their first campsite. It was dark and the going was rough, but they wanted to be as far away as they could by daylight.

They were almost to the campsite when Gary stepped in a hole and hit the dirt. He pulled his foot out of the hole and it hurt like hell. Christine turned around and came back. "What happen to, you."

"I stepped in a hole and broke an ankle or sprained it. It hurts so bad I can't tell. Help me walk it's not too far to our campsite."

Gary leaned on Christine and they started out. This couldn't be happening again. He remembered when Wolf saved him and nursed him back to health out in west Texas. He didn't want to be laid up for six weeks in the middle of nowhere. It was very slow going. Christine was stronger than she looked taking a lot of his weight as he hobbled along.

It was daylight before they finally made it to the campsite. Gary was exhausted as was Christine. Gary eased inside the small tent and Christine went about the job of getting his boot off. He thought she was going to have to cut the boot off, but she finally got it off. The foot and ankle were badly swollen.

"Gary what are we going to do?"

"I got good news and bad news. The good news is we got away and we have supplies to last us awhile. The bad news is we will be here until I can walk again. If they catch us like this we are dead meat. So sit down and take a load off and sleep if you want to."

Christine crawled in the tent beside Gary and curled up for a nap. She was exhausted. Wolf curled up in front of the tent on guard duty. They kept the tent covered so if anyone came hunting them they would walk right by and not see them. Gary handed her his 45 automatic and showed her how to take the safety off to fire the weapon.

"I never shot a gun before, but I'll try if I have to."

Gary liked her spunk. She wasn't as helpless as he thought she would be. He lay on his back and stretched out with his foot on a rolled up blanket with his rifle beside him. It was dark when he finally woke up. Christine was still asleep. He touched her on her arm and she jumped. "I thought I was still being held prisoner, sorry."

"Let's get up and eat something. Are you hungry?"

"Yes, I could eat a horse."

They crawled out of the tent and sat down. "We don't have much to eat, but we will be ok."

Gary gave Wolf a can of spam. He split a can of beans and peaches with Christine. They washed it down with water. They only drank enough to get their food down. They sat around and talked while Christine put a splint on his leg and foot. The swelling had gone down some. They sat for a while and talked before they crawled back into the tent. They slept with their clothes on. Wolf curled up in front of the tent on guard duty. Gary knew if anything came near Wolf would wake him.

Three days went by and Gary was improving, but he still couldn't walk on the foot. They had enough supplies for four more days and then they were in trouble. They hadn't had a bath and they were starting to smell. Gary gave Wolf his canteen and told him to get some water. He raced off to the river and came back with a full canteen. "How did you teach Wolf to do that?"

"He can do a lot to help us stay alive."

Gary pulled a washcloth out of his backpack and handed it to Christine. "What all do you have in that backpack?" He handed her a small bar of soap.

"Would you believe everything, but a kitchen sink." He wet the rag for her. "Let me see what kind of clothes I have in the backpack." He gave her a t-shirt and a pair of shorts.

"You can sleep in them and put your clothes outside to dry. It looks like rain so maybe we will get our clothes washed."

Gary crawled outside to wait while Christine washed up. She handed her clothes out to him. He could smell her female scent on her panties and bra. He had an instant hard on. He could picture her naked in the tent washing with the rag. This was the first time he had thought about a woman since Judy was killed. He felt guilty for doing it, but he was human and there was a beautiful woman in his tent. He had his back to the door when she crawled out. "It's your turn to get cleaned up."

She sure looked good in his shorts and t-shirt. Her breasts were firm and pointed straight at Gary. She crossed her arms over her breasts trying to cover them. She felt like Gary could see right through the t-shirt. Gary smiled, "They look better on you than they do on me."

Christine blushed and turned her back on him. "You look just as good from the back."

Christine knew he was teasing her and enjoying doing it. Well she would get her turn. She felt naked, but the clean clothes felt wonderful. They heard a loud noise and looked up into the trees. There were several small monkeys playing above them. "Meat on the table," said Gary.

"You wouldn't dare kill one of those cute little monkeys, would you?"

"If we get hungry enough, yes I would."

Gary crawled in the tent to wash up and shave. He tossed his clothes out to her. She hung their clothes on low branches around the tent. When he was cleaned up he crawled back outside. He looked up at the sky, "We're going to get a good rain and storm."

As dark rolled in so did the storm. Gary, Christine, and Wolf crawled in the door and closed the flap. Rain pelted the tent for an hour before it finally quit. Everything smelled so clean after the rain. After the rain stopped, Christine crawled out of the tent and squeezed the water out of their clothes so they would dry fast the next day. She crawled back inside and Wolf left the tent. It was cool so she closed the flap. Wolf curled up on watch duty in front of the door.

When they slept with their clothes on the tent seemed fine, but with only t-shirts and shorts on it seemed very small. Christine turned her back to him. He was facing her back. She could feel the heat from his body and it made her body tingle. How was she going to make it through the night with a good looking man in the closed space with her, he looked too good to be true after he shaved and cleaned up. It was so close they touched from time to time if they even moved a little. She trembled each time they touched. Gary turned over on his back and dozed off to sleep.

Sometime during the night Christine turned over facing Gary and threw a leg over him and an arm around his neck. Her face rested on his chest. He woke up with a hard on and knew why with a half- naked, woman on top of him. She lowered her arm from around his neck only to drape at across his stomach close to his erection. He moved just a little and she slid her hand on down his body until she touched his shaft. Gary was about to have a melt-down. She was still asleep and had a smile on her face. She must be dreaming. He moved a little more and she slid her hand down into his shorts. She slowly wrapped her fingers around his shaft and after another few minutes started to stroke his shaft. She was still asleep and smiling. Gary was going crazy and pushed into her hand. She stroked him faster until suddenly she woke up. She was having this wonderful dream of making love to Gary. She jerked her hand back and sat up. She was so embarrassed. "Don't stop now or I'll die," said Gary.

"I was asleep and having a dream. I'm so sorry."

"I'm not," He reached for her and pulled her down on top of him. Her nipples were pebbled and dug into his chest.

His erection was hard against her belly. "Do you feel what you are doing to me?"

"Yes I do," she giggled.

"What are you going to do about it?"

Christine stuttered, "Make love to you."

She pulled her t-shirt off over her head. Gary stared at the two perfect breasts. He reached up and touched one. She pulled back, slid off to his side to pull her shorts off. Gary sat up and pulled off his t-shirt along with his shorts. They sat staring at each other. Finally Gary lay back down. Christine straddled him and sat up. "Be gentle with me I'm a hurt man."

"Yeah right," Christine giggled.

She lowered her body on him until he filled her body with his erection. She didn't move at first letting her body adjust to his shaft. He was large and hard as a rock. She leaned over and covered his mouth with her own. Gary opened his mouth and she plunged her tongue deep as their tongues mated. She started to move up and down at a fast pace. She had never felt so good making love. Why was she so attracted to Gary, since she barely knew him, but she wanted to know all about him and why he was traveling with a wolf? He didn't seem to trust women. Had he been, burned bad by some woman? She was going to find out. Right now she was having the time of her life. "Oh, I'm coming, I'm coming."

Gary thrust up hard and they went over the edge together. Christine was as contented as a cat. She slid off and lay on her back spreading her legs in invitation. "Give me a minute to catch my breath, you wore me out."

"What's the matter? You getting old and can't cut the mustard anymore," she giggled. After that he was wandering if he was getting old. Christine had him totally exhausted, but he would be ready soon. She reached over and took his shaft in her hand. She stroked it until it was hard again. Gary eased in between her legs and thrust into her folds. She moaned as he picked up the pace. Gary didn't want it to end, but all good things come to an end. She wrapped her legs around his body and cried out as she came again. It was wonderful making love with Gary. They lay spoon fashion and went to sleep.

They stayed in bed the next day until their clothes dried. It was almost noon when they dressed and ate beef jerky with water to wash it down. They had caught some rain water last night, but they were getting low on food. Gary still didn't think he was well enough to travel. He was walking around with a home-made crutch. He decided they had to hunt to get some meat.

"Christine, I need you to learn how to shoot a bow and arrow. We need some meat. You can go hunting with Wolf. I don't want to use the rifle because it might bring the bad guys."

"I'm game if you will teach me." She picked up the bow and an arrow. Gary stood behind her and gave her instructions. She was a quick learner. About an hour later Christine and Wolf went hunting. She didn't know he could see through Wolf's eyes as they went hunting.

About an hour later they spotted a young deer. Christine didn't want to kill the deer, but her stomach growled. She took aim like Gary taught her and let an arrow fly. She brought down the deer. Wolf and Christine dragged the deer back to camp. "I got a deer she screamed," as they entered camp. Gary acted like he was surprised, but he had watched her bring down the deer through Wolf's eyes. "Now all you have to do is dress out the deer." He thought she would flip.

"Ok, if you will show me how." She was enjoying herself. Gary was liking, this beautiful young woman more and more as the days went by. He thought about last night and got a hard on. Not now, they had work to do.

They hung the deer up on a tree limb and Gary started skinning the deer. He cut the deer to bleed out. Then he handed his knife to Christine and showed her how to cut up the deer. It was a small buck without any horns yet. He would make tender meat. They would eat well tonight.

"Wolf, go find some dry wood for a fire. I don't think the bad guys are still looking for us." Gary made a fire pit while Christine finished cutting up the deer. Wolf came back with a large limb to cut up. Gary found some leaves and small twigs to make the fire burn. He built a fire and put two cups of water on. He had instant coffee, but they hadn't been able to make a fire.

Christine smelled the coffee, "I would kill for a cup of coffee." Gary handed her a cup.

Gary made sharp sticks with his knife and put chunks of meat on the sticks to cook. He kept the fire small and it gave off very little smoke. When it was done he passed it around to Wolf and Christine. He took a large chunk and enjoyed it.

"Doesn't Wolf eat his meat raw?"

"No, I spoiled him since he came to the ranch."

This was the first time Gary had talked about himself. Christine wanted to know all about him. Do you live and work on a ranch. He didn't like talking about himself, but for some reason he didn't mind talking to Christine. He didn't talk for some time and she thought he had shut her off. Finally, "I own a ranch at Sugarland Texas. We raise cattle and horses. We train and sell the horses from birth to old enough to ride. I started small, but the ranch is getting larger all the time. I have a good crew working for me."

She was as curious as a cat about everything. "Then why are you on a mission to save me with a big ranch to run?"

"It is a second job Wolf and I do. It's called you lose it and we find it. People lose cattle, horses and sometimes we find people when nobody else can. The pay is very good. It helps to keep the ranch in the black."

"So I'm just a paycheck to you," Christine looked very sad. She was hoping he liked her because she was falling in love with him.

Gary saw how he broke her heart and felt like a louse. "It was at first, but to be frank I don't know now. I guess I'm still in love with my wife."

"Are you married?"

"No, my wife was killed by a drunk driver. I guess I haven't fully got over her, but I can at least talk about her now. I'm trying to move on, but it's hard."

"Oh Gary, I'm so sorry." Now she could understand him a lot better with his mood swings. She could see the love in his eyes when he talked about his wife. Christine wished she had someone who loved her as much.

"That's enough about me, now it's your turn."

She hadn't expected that. Christine started with her story. "I was a little rich kid raised by a nanny. My folks didn't have the time or didn't want to take time with me. I was always trying to get their attention by doing things to piss them off. That only got me sent to a boarding school when I was old enough. This was the last straw. I guess they are really pissed off now. When I get home I'm going to start over. I'm going to get a job and live off what I make. Then nobody can tell me what to do."

Gary liked her spunk. "It's hard to make it on your own, but you will feel great when you do. I left home and made it on my own. It feels so good when I ride over my land and know it's mine."

"But how did you get started?"

"I worked for a large real estate firm in Houston and was lucky. I bought some prime land and sold it to a big company. I bought the ranch and end of story."

"I have one more question since you are in a talking mood. Why do you travel with a wolf?"

"To make a long story short, he saved my life and now we are a team."

"I want to hear the long version sometime. Something is very strange about you two. He always knows what you want and does it. I have never seen anything like it."

Three days later Gary was walking pretty well on his foot. It looked normal now. It was getting time to go back to the living. They stayed another day and Gary made the decision.

"Christine, it's time to walk out of here. I think I can make it now. Tomorrow we head out to the river where I hid a small rubber boat."

"Are you sure you are alright? We can stay longer if you need to heal more."

Chapter Ten

The next morning they packed up and headed out with Wolf taking point. Gary took his time, but they made it to the river by noon. "I think we will make camp here and go on in the morning. It will be harder going up stream than it was coming down." They set up the tent and made a small fire pit. They were a short distance from the river, but they were in some bushes and would be hard to see from the river. Gary pulled some hooks from his backpack and attached the line and hooks to a pole he cut.

"Wolf, find us some wood while I go fishing. If I'm lucky we will have fish for supper." He had a small amount of blood bait in plastic bag in his backpack. He baited the hooks and went to the river.

Christine couldn't believe everything he pulled out of the backpack. He must have been a Boy Scout when he was young. She made a fire pit and got the wood ready that Wolf dragged up. Two hours later Gary came back with a mess of fish. They weren't too big, but they would taste wonderful.

"Have you ever scaled a fish?" he asked.

"No, but I will if you teach me." He thought where was that little rich girl? The more they were together the more he liked her. She was game for anything including making fantastic love with him. What more could a man want?

Gary showed her how to scale a fish and gut it. He handed her the knife and went to get the fire started. By the time he had the fire going she had the fish ready to cook. He put the fish on sticks and put them over the fire. It didn't take long and they were eating fish. The fish were small and they had to pick the meat off the bones, but it was delicious. They were hungry and ate their fill. After the meal Christine made coffee. They sat around the fire and talked. This would probably be their last night together alone. Christine wanted Gary to make love to her, to make some memories in case she never saw him again.

She decided to be bold tonight. She went in the tent early and got ready for bed. She closed the flap and stripped off all her clothes. She lay on her back naked and waited until Gary came to bed. Gary wandered why she turned in so early. Her opened the flap and crawled into the tent.

"I wandered why you went to bed so early. Does this mean what I think?"

"Yes, I want you to make love to me. We may never see one another again. I love the way you make me feel when we are making love." She wanted him to tell her he loved her, but she would take what she could get.

Gary pulled off his clothes and joined her. She spread her legs wide inviting him to take her. He eased up between her legs and joined them with a deep thrust. Christine moaned and locked her legs around him. He took it slow and easy trying to make it last as long as possible. Christine bucked as he slammed into her hot body, but they both lost control and too soon they both came. He flipped over with her on top and waited until their breathing returned to normal. She lay on his chest with her nipples digging into his chest. He loved that part of making love. Soon, she could feel him filling her again with his big shaft. She sat up and slammed down on him taking all of him. She rode him hard until he felt her clinch his shaft and come around it. Gary kept slamming into her body until he came. Christine finally rolled off him and curled up beside him. She was always like a contented cat after they make love.

The next morning they ate the last of the fish and finished the rest of their coffee. It was time to tackle the river. Gary loaded the boat while Christine put out the fire. The boat was only designed for two people so they had to be careful not to turn the boat over. Gary used the tiny motor and rowed to keep them moving. It took them until about four in the evening before they reached the point where he had hid the van. Gary beached the boat and they unloaded it. They loaded all their things in the van and were ready for their last leg back to town.

Gary slowly eased up close to the road and let Christine out. She checked the road and it was clear of traffic. He pulled onto the road and she got in.

"We are finally on our way home," said Gary.

They made it to the airport without any trouble. Christine called her Father and told him to come get them. "I'm on my way." He sounded liked he really cared. She needed to patch things up with her folks, but she had made up her mind she was going out on her own. The bird was leaving the nest.

The plane arrived that night and they loaded everything on the jet. They refueled the jet and took off for home. Gary was thinking how much he was going to miss, Christine. The jet landed at his airport and Gary unloaded his gear.

"Mr. Wilson I would like to keep the rifle, I'll pay you for it."

"Keep it, you have earned it." He handed Gary a check and shook his hand. "Thank you for bringing my daughter home."

Christine stood in the jet hatch and watched as the love of her life was gone. She had tears in her eyes as her father boarded the plane.

"Christine, are you alright?"

"Yes, I'm just happy to be going home," she lied.

It was still dark when Gary and Wolf reached the ranch. As he came in the kitchen Maria was fixing breakfast for the crew. Joe sat at the table drinking coffee. Wolf went to see Sunshine. Gary poured himself a cup of coffee and sat down across from Joe. Sunshine nudged his leg for attention. He reached down and petted her. It was good to be home at last.

"I wandered when you were coming home," said Joe.

"We had a little trouble along the way. The place Christine was being held was a drug lord's home and business. I had to take out a few bad guys before we made it to the woods beside the house. I also destroyed his business for now. This guy has a big estate in Dallas and a lot of property. To them in Dallas he is a rich businessman. His name is James Lopez. Be on a sharp lookout in case he decides to get even with me. I hope it is over, but I have a bad feeling in my gut."

The crew came in for breakfast. After breakfast Gary said, "I have a drug dealer mad at me and I don't know if he might try to find me and get even. If anyone wants to quit I won't hold it against you. I think I messed up on this job. The good news I brought Christine home. He had a big smile on his face.

"So it's Christine, is it?" Ben smiled at Gary.

Gary realized too late what he had done. He missed her already. "Ok, we had to spend a lot of time together."

"Yeah right," Maria smiled at him. She had seen that look before when Judy was alive. She hoped Gary was heeled and ready to move on.

"Joe, how is everything going on the ranch?"

"Everything is going great, but we have a big workload every day." He handed out assignments to each crew member.

Gary stood up, "I have one more thing to say, I want everyone to have a weapon on them at all times. Joe, I want you to teach Jerry and Kathy how to shoot and handle a weapon. I don't want anyone working by himself. I want two people together at all times until I say different."

He thought some of the crew would quit, but they all stayed. Most times when trouble, happened the ones that were scared would quit. He was so proud of his crew for staying with him. "Ok, everyone do your job."

The crew filed out to do their assignment for the day. Joe stayed until last and talked with Gary. It had been a long time since they had time to talk.

After their talk Joe went to the barn and Gary went to ride fence and check on cattle. Wolf went with Gary, but Sunshine stayed in the kitchen with Maria. She had adopted Maria as the one she liked to stay with. She let Sunshine taste all her cooking and she loved it.

Gary took his sniper rifle with him and put it in his saddle scabbard. He would carry it with him from now on while riding on the ranch. He had some lost cattle to find and planned to start on that tomorrow. Several ranchers had called while he was gone. Gary and Wolf checked cattle and fence all day. There were new calves to be branded and checked over. There was some fence that needed mending. Joe would assign the work tomorrow. Jerry and Kathy met Gary on his way back to the house. Ben had them riding two new horses he had trained. The new owner would pick them up in a couple of days.

Gary and Wolf washed up and went to the kitchen where they smelled food. "What's for supper?" Gary asked.

"We are having chicken, mashed potatoes, gravy, corn-on-the-cob, green beans and biscuits. There's tea and coffee to drink." Maria started putting it on the table. Gary and Wolf were starved since they didn't break for lunch. The rest of the crew came in and sat down for supper.

After Gary finished supper he went to his office and checked his books. He couldn't believe the profit the ranch was making while other ranches were going broke. He hadn't put his check from Mr. Wilson in the bank yet. He sat and stared at the check and knew he didn't need it. He thought about his time with Kristine and how they had made love. For a little rich girl she had spunk. He liked everything about her. She would make a rancher a good wife. Now where did that come from? He relived every minute he spent with her and now he missed her. He decided one thing that he would send the check back to Mr. Wilson.

Chapter Eleven

Mrs. Wilson was waiting at the Airport when the jet landed. She hugged her daughter and told her how happy she was that she was home safe. They went home to their estate on the west side of Dallas. When they drove into the driveway Kristine should have been very happy, but all she could think about was Gary. She realized that she was head over heels in love with him. She wandered if he missed her as much as she missed him. When they made love his eyes said he cared for her or was it just lust? She wanted him, but did he want her? What was she going to do?

Kristine went to her room as soon as they got in the house. She threw herself on her bed and cried herself to sleep. She opened her eyes at about two. She had missed breakfast and lunch. She took a shower and put on clean clothes. She put on shorts and a blouse since she didn't plan on leaving the house today. She went to the kitchen and fixed her a sandwich and had a diet coke to drink. Her Mother and Father were gone as usual. He would be at work and she would be at a charity.

After she ate, she decided to go to the Public Library. She wanted to look up news articles about Gary. Her Father had told her very little about him except he was the best and only man who would come after her. When she got to the Library she asked the librarian if she knew Gary Mitchell. She said she did. She pulled out newspapers from Sugarland and Dallas. She read the Dallas story first about Wolf finding the girls in the dungeon. She read about him helping catch a prisoner in Houston, about them finding a lost little kid and stopping a bank robbery. The stories went on and on. She couldn't believe everything that happened to Gary and Wolf. Finally she read about a drunk driver killing his wife. It was so sad. They had only been married a short time. His wife had worked for the Newspaper in Sugarland and that was how they met. She was laid to rest on the ranch. Kristine had tears in her eyes for Gary.

She left the Library and headed home. She didn't know what she would do, but she had to do something. She loved Gary and hoped someday he would love her. "I would make him a good rancher's wife," she said to herself.

That night after supper, Kristine had a talk with her father. "Dad I want to work at the company for now until I find what I want to do."

"What do you want to do?"

"I thought about doing public relations for the company if you have an opening."

"I'll make one for you."

"Thank you Dad, I'll do a good job and make you proud."

Mr. Wilson wandered what had come over his daughter since she had come home. She wanted to work like everyone else. She didn't want to play the little rich girl anymore. He owned an oil company and always had room for another employee.

The next morning Kristine was up early and drinking coffee when her Father came into the kitchen. He was surprised again. She was ready to go to work. After breakfast they drove separate cars to work. When they got to work Mr. Wilson showed Kristine to her office and gave her a secretary. Before lunch her name was on her door. By closing time she had already contacted people to start her public relations with the company. Two weeks later she was in big demand at the company. Mr. Wilson couldn't believe what was going on. He was proud of his daughter.

That evening Mr. Wilson was going through his mail when he noticed a letter from Sugarland. He opened it and found his check marked void across it. Kristine looked over his shoulder at the name. Kristine's heard beat faster, it was from Gary. The note simply said I can't accept this check for damaged goods.

Mr. Wilson stared at the check and at Kristine, "I don't understand."

"I do," screamed Kristine, "It means he loves me and won't take payment for my return. I'm sorry Daddy, but I quit. I'm going to Sugarland and find a job. I'll give you a two week notice to find someone else to take my place."

"Have you lost your mind?"

"Maybe I have, but I love the man and I'm going to try and win his heart. Wish me luck Daddy."

The next day she was on the phone looking for a job in Sugarland. The Newspaper had a job opening for a reporter. She thought she could handle it since she was in public relations.

The Editor said, "The job you will be taking was Judy Mitchell's before she was killed by a drunk driver. She will be a hard act to follow. She was Gary Mitchell's wife. Do you know him?"

"Yes, I know him very well since he came to Columbia and rescued me."

That got his attention, "I didn't know he went to Columbia. He was gone for a while, but I thought he was on vacation. Will you write the story?"

"I will if Gary says it's ok. It was a secret mission and I don't want him to get into any more trouble over me. It was like a war to get me out of there."

"You have the job, when can you start?"

"I can start in three weeks. I'll give the company I work for a two week notice and I need a week to find a place to live in Sugarland."

"I'll see you in three weeks ready to go to work."

"Thank you sir, I'll be there."

Kristine looked up Gary's phone number and called him right away. What if he didn't want her to take Judy's old job? What if he didn't want her to write the story? What if he didn't want her in Sugarland?

Gary answered on the third ring, "Gary Mitchell here."

Kristine was nervous just hearing his voice, "Gary this is Kristine, I need your advice on something. More, like I need your, ok."

"Do you care if I live in Sugarland?"

"Come on down I would love to see you again."

"Here comes the hard part. Would it hurt you if I take Judy's old job?"

Gary thought about it for a second, "No, someone has to fill the position so it might as well be you."

"One last question, may I do the story on my rescue?"

"I don't see how it will matter. James Lopez will find me anyway."

Kristine was like a kid that had just got some candy. "I love you. I'll see you in about three weeks." What did she just say?

Gary caught the three little words and smiled. She hadn't meant to say them, but in her excitement she had. He was looking forward to seeing her again. Call it love or lust, but he wanted Kristine in his bed. He had a hard on thinking about the last time they made love.

James Lopez would find him anyway. Gary thought about that a long time. He had made a big mistake tangling with a drug lord. They tended to kill whoever got in their way or their business. He had taken a woman from the drug lord and ruined his business for a while. He wouldn't rest until he found Gary and made him pay.

Gary decided that from now on he would wear a gun belt with a pistol on his hip like in the old west. He would get a gun permit to carry a concealed weapon when he was out in the public. The town didn't know what he had done yet, but when Kristine wrote the story in the Newspaper they would know. The next day Gary went and got a gun permit. That was all he could do for now. He made sure guns were handy in the house. He didn't lock the gun cabinet anymore.

Monday, Kristine started to train her replacement. She had the Public relations office running like a, new oiled engine. Betty, her new replacement was a fast learner. She gave the lectures for the next two weeks. Kristine spent as much time as possible with her folks, but that wasn't much. They were too busy to spend time with her. They didn't want her to leave Dallas, but her love was in Sugarland and she would do anything to get him in her bed. Maybe he didn't want her, but she had to try. What could she do to make him love her? She knew he was still in love with his wife, but she was dead. How could she compete with a dead woman? She thought about James Lopez and wandered how she could have been so stupid. If it's too good to be true, then it usually isn't. She wandered if he would come back to Dallas. Maybe her leaving Dallas was a good idea. Maybe he wouldn't come after her. She had the feeling she was stupid again. He would come after her.

At the end of her second week she traded her sports car for a plain compact car that got good gas millage. She bought clothes and shoes that were a working girl style. She put her hair in a simple ponytail. She bought jeans, shirts and a pair cowboy boots. She didn't want to look rich to Gary, but she did have a large trust fund. She didn't want to use it unless of an emergency.

Monday, Kristine packed her car and left for Sugarland. She couldn't wait to see Gary. Her nipples pebbled just thinking about him. She was in love with the man. She wandered what the ranch looked like. She was a greenhorn about ranching but she had read as much as she could find on the subject. She didn't want to look totally stupid about ranching. She wanted to learn to ride most of all. She just hoped she wouldn't break her neck. She didn't want to be a rich little city girl anymore. She wanted to lead a common life like most people.

She arrived in Sugarland in the evening and started to look for a place to live. After looking around she found a small furnished cottage in the edge of town and rented it. The utilities were on, but she had to call to get them changed into her name. She unloaded her car and carried her things inside. Kristine unpacked and was ready to call the place home. It wasn't much, but it was hers. She didn't have any food in the house so she went to a fast food place for supper. She ordered a hamburger, fries and a coke. After she was full she went grocery shopping. She didn't want to eat out unless she had to. This was all new to her. She would have to set up a budget to live on. She had never done that before. I guess being a little rich girl had its benefits, but she was going to make it on her own.

Her Mother and Father gave her a few weeks before she called for money or wanted to come home. That pissed her off to no end. She would starve before she would ask for help. She wanted to call Gary, but she didn't want to be a pushy woman. She knew men didn't like that. They liked it to be their idea to do things and they wanted to be in charge. She was going to take her time and win him over. She wanted him to want her as much as she wanted him.

Kristine put her groceries away and had some tea. She was tired and it had been a long day. She showered and put on her pajamas. She would sleep naked when she ever got Gary in her bed again. She lay on her back and dreamed about making love to Gary.

Since talking to Kristine, Gary decided to call the sheriff and give him a head ups on what he had done. The Sheriff answered on the second ring. "How may I help you?"

"Sheriff this is Gary Mitchell, I need to tell you a story about my trip to Colombia."

"I heard you were on vacation."

"No, I was on a mission to bring a young woman back to her parents. I didn't know until I got to Colombia that she was being held by a drug lord. He has a large estate in Dallas and is a respected business man, but I know he deals in drugs and weapons. His name is James Lopez. Do you know him?"

"No, but I have heard of him. He is rich and respected in Dallas. Do you know for sure what you are saying?"

"I rescued a woman and destroyed his business while I was rescuing her in Colombia. He lives in a house big enough for a king and makes drugs to trade for guns which he sells for a huge profit. His business was behind his house in a valley in the middle of nowhere. I'm sure his business in Dallas is a front, but you would probably never get the law to believe it and issue a warrant. A young woman by the name of Kristine Wilson is the one I rescued and her Father is in the oil business. "Do you know the name?"

"Yes I do. He is a rich oil man."

"Kristine is starting to work at the Newspaper next Monday and will be writing the story of her rescue. She won't use Lopez's name in case of a lawsuit. It will give the details of my mission to rescue her."

"Why would a rich woman like her come to Sugarland for a job? What is she thinking?"

"She wants to make it, own her own. She wants to make her own money and have pride in her job to do her best." Gary didn't tell the Sheriff why he thought she was coming to Sugarland. He didn't know for sure, but he suspected it was to see him. They had unfinished business. Was she in love with him? Was he in love with her? He didn't know for sure, but he sure missed the spunky little woman. He wanted to explore the fact if he was in love with her.

"If you have any trouble at the ranch, call me and I will come running. You are respected in our town."

"Thank you Sheriff. I wanted to let you know that they may come after me at the ranch. My crew is armed and we will defend ourselves. I'm sure he won't do the dirty work himself, but if he does come to the ranch I will not be responsible at what I will do in Dallas."

"You can't take the law into your own hands."

"If he harms anyone on my ranch I will go after him myself because you know the law won't do anything to a respected citizen. He has his own army of thugs. I killed several of them in Colombia, but I'm sure he has replaced them by now. I watched him kill a man at his home for stealing from him. He will kill anyone who gets in his way. He is a mad dog."

"Gary, you take care."

"Thank you, Sheriff for your time."

Gary hung up the phone and stared at the wall. What else could he do to protect his crew? He would discuss it with the crew the next day. The next morning at breakfast, he told the crew, don't try to be a hero, when trouble comes try to hide. The men who come will be trained killers and won't care who they kill. If anyone wants out now is the time. When it's over you still have a job. You aren't paid to take on a bunch of killers. Nobody left. Joe handed out the assignments for the day. Everyone left with a weapon on them. It was like living in an armed camp waiting for an attack.

Monday, Kristine was at the Newspaper ready for work. She was nervous, but she was ready to do her job. Her boss told her to write the story of her rescue. She had a desk and typewriter so she sat down and started on the story. When she finished about noon, she called Gary at the ranch. He answered on the third ring. "Gary Mitchell."

"Gary this is Kristine at the Newspaper. I finished the story about my rescue. I would like to come out to the ranch and let you read it before I submit it to be published."

"When did you want to come?"

"I would like to come out as soon as possible."

"How about six o'clock? You can eat with the crew and get an idea about what ranch life is about. Another day you can come out to the ranch and I'll give you a tour of the ranch."

"I would like that very much."

"Good I'll see you at six o'clock." He gave her directions to the ranch.

After Kristine hung up, she sat and thought about Gary. She couldn't wait to see him again. She went in and told her boss he would have the story tomorrow. "I'm going to the ranch tonight and make sure Gary approves of the story."

"Gary is it?" Her boss smiled at her.

Too late she realized her mistake. She blushed, "We spent a lot of time together while he was rescuing me."

"He's a fine man. He was in love with his wife and I hope he's over it by now. He needs to move on."

Gary told Maria they were having one more for supper. When he told her who was coming she smiled at him. "It's about time you had a woman in your life."

"Her name is Kristine and she is coming out on business. She is writing about her rescue at the Newspaper."

Maria smiled, "History repeating itself. Judy did the same thing. Is she gorgeous like Judy?"

Gary hesitated, "Yes she is, but she is a rich kid."

"Then why is she here and not back in Dallas?"

"I don't know," he lied. He hoped she was here because of him.

"Gary you are a fool if you don't know why she is here. She is here because of you."

Maria could read him like a book. "Maybe, he admitted."

Kristine pulled her car up in front of the ranch house. As she got out of the car Gary came out the front door with Wolf on his heels. She hugged Wolf and stared at Gary. She wasn't sure what to do next but she went to Gary and hugged him to. He hugged her back. "I'm glad you came," said Gary.

"I'm glad you would see me."

"Come on in the house, supper is ready." He reached and took her small hand in his and led her into the kitchen. He sat her down beside him and the crew sat down. He introduced the crew, "This is Joe my foreman at the end of the table is Ben, my horse trainer and Wayne his assistant. Sam, Jerry and Kathy are the hands that do most of the work around the ranch. Crew, this young lady is the one I went to Colombia to rescue." Maria walked in the kitchen, "This is the cook, cleaner and anything else I need her to do. Maria meet Kristine, She is from Dallas."

"I'm very glad to meet you since I've heard so much about you." Gary squirmed in his chair. Maria didn't waste any time playing cupid.

"I'm sure everyone is starved," said Gary, "Dig in."

Kristine liked everyone and enjoyed her meal. She praised Maria, for her cooking and made a friend for life. After the meal was over and everyone left Gary showed Kristine to his office. She sat in the chair in front of the desk and handed him her story. He read it slowly and handed it back to her.

"Well what do you think? Did I get it right?"

"Yes, except for one thing."

"What did I leave out?"

"You didn't have any sex in the story. Every action story should have a good love scene in it," teased Gary.

Kristine blushed, "I thought you had, forgot about it."

"How could I forget about the most wonderful sex we had. I still think about it all the time."

"You do? I do to. It was fantastic."

"We need to explore it some more," teased Gary.

Kristine surprised him, "Yes we should."

"Why don't you come out to the ranch Saturday for a cookout? We can go riding and I can show you the ranch. Would you like that?"

"Yes, but I don't know how to ride. I have never been on a horse. I'm a city girl, remember."

"No problem, I will teach you to ride."

"Ok, I'll be here Saturday. What time do you want me here?"

"Make it about noon. We can go riding and have a cookout when we get back. After everybody leaves I'll show you my etchings."

"I had rather you show me something else," Kristine giggled.

"I can do that."

They talked awhile before she left to turn in her story. Kristine was on cloud nine. She had her first date with Gary. She hoped he took her to his bed Saturday night. She was on fire just thinking about it. Her nipples were hard and her folds were moist. It had been wonderful the first time they made love. It couldn't get any better, could it? She went to the paper and turned in her story. Her boss was still at work and looked it over.

"It will be on the front page tomorrow. You did a great job and I don't have to edit it. Keep up the good work and you will be our number one reporter in a short time. Go home and get some rest and I'll see you Monday."

Kristine went home, fixed her a salad and a glass of tea. She didn't want to get fat. Most men didn't like fat girls. She didn't know much about Gary's likes and dislikes, but she would find out. After a shower she went to bed and dreamed about Saturday night. Gary would make love to her. She would dress sexy and hope it worked. Then she remembered that they were going riding. She would dress in jeans and a blouse. What the heck, she would be like a ranch girl and even put her hair in a ponytail. If he wanted her he could make the first move.

Chapter Twelve

Saturday noon, Kristine drove up in front of the ranch house. Gary, Wolf and Sunshine came out to meet her. What a reception, she had never been to a place like the ranch. She hugged Wolf and Sunshine then turned to Gary. He opened his arms for her. She went into them and he brushed a light kiss on her lips. Gary could see the love in her eyes and hugged her tighter. They stood like that for a while, both of them not wanting to let go.

"I'm glad you could make it, come on in the house." Wolf and Sunshine ran ahead of them for the door. Gary put his arm around her shoulders and guided her into the house. They went into the kitchen where Maria was cooking. "Maria we will have a light lunch and head out. Sandwiches and tea will be fine. I'm taking Kristine riding."

After lunch they headed for the barn. Wolf went with them, but Sunshine stayed behind with Maria. She got to taste all the food being cooked and she loved Maria. Joe had saddled Gary's horse and a gentle mare for Kristine to ride. Gary secured his rifle to the saddle and turned to help Kristine mount her horse. He showed her how to make the horse go, stop and turn. Gary swung into the saddle and headed out with Kristine beside him. She was a quick learner and was riding like a pro in no time. They rode for an hour before Gary stopped beside the creek than ran through the property.

"The creek has fish in it and I'll bring you fishing sometime."

"I would like that."

After they rested they rode for another hour. Kristine loved the ranch. She could see the pride Gary had in his ranch as he talked about how he started small and now it was a big operation. There were cattle everywhere. They rode back to the barn and dismounted. Gary led the horses into the barn and showed Kristine how to give them a rub down. Then he gave them a ration of feed. He took her through the barn and showed her the horses in training.

"This is where the big money is made. We raise our own horses. Ranchers buy them when they are young and we train them until they are old enough to ride. Then they come and get their trained horse. Quarter horses are in big demand."

They left the barn and went back inside. Maria had left for the day and Sunshine was happy to see them. Maria had left out two big T-bone steaks and potatoes. She left a note, two salads in frig.

Gary put the steaks on the indoor grill. He wrapped the potatoes in tin foil and put them on with the steaks.

"What can I do to help?" asked Kristine.

"Set the table and pour us some tea."

She set the table and poured them some tea. They sat down to wait on the steaks to cook. They sat and stared at each other. Kristine looked deep into his eyes. Was that love or lust in his eyes? She hoped it was love. She was in love with Gary and couldn't hide it from him. She knew he saw it in her eyes.

When the steaks and potatoes were done they ate in silence. Kristine was nervous as a cat on a hot tin roof. She was thinking about what would happen when they finished eating supper. When they finished eating, Gary stood up and took her hand. He led her to his bedroom and turned to face her. He pulled her tight against his body and kissed her. She melted against him, her nipples digging into his chest. She could feel something hard against her belly and knew Gary wanted her now. He stepped back and reached for the buttons on her shirt.

Kristine moaned, "Let me do it." She started taking off her clothes.

Gary watched her as he started taking off his clothes. In record time they both stood naked before each other. He stared at her, "You are so beautiful."

"You're not so bad yourself." He had a big hard on and it stood at attention.

She went into his arms and they kissed. She clung to him to keep from melting at his feet. He eased her back to the king sized bed and they fell on it. Gary kissed his way down her body to her nipples where he nibbled on each one before going on down her body. He was on his knees and slipped a leg over each shoulder. He touched her folds with his finger and she moaned swinging her head from side to side. He replaced his finger with his tongue and she came unglued. She grabbed his head and pulled it harder to her. She was on fire. Finally she had a climax.

Gary moved up between her thighs and touched her entrance to her hot body. They gazed at each other as he entered her. Never taking his eyes off her he gave her all of his, shaft and started to move. Kristine didn't think it could get any better, but it did. She arched her back meeting him thrust for thrust. Gary finally lost control and slammed into her faster and faster until she cried out. "Oh Gary, I'm coming, give me all you got."

He felt her tighten around his shaft as she had a climax. Gary slammed into her one last time and came with her. They were hot and sweaty, but it had been so good. Kristine curled up next to Gary and was asleep immediately. He lay there thinking, I'm in love with a city girl and a rich one at that. Then he remembered her vow to make it on her own. It was sad that parents didn't have time for their children. He had seen some like that in school. He was grateful he had parents that loved and supported him.

Kristine woke to sun coming in the window. For a minute she didn't remember where she was until she turned over and Gary was watching her. "Good morning sunshine." He pulled her into his arms for a morning kiss. She melted into his body. They were both still naked and she trembled from the heat of his body. She wanted him again. Gary reached down and touched her and set her on fire. She moaned and reached for his shaft. "I want you in me now."

Gary pulled her on top raising her up so she came down on his erection. She took all of him and started to move. She rode him hard and they both came and she fell on his chest with her nipples crushed between them. "I want to stay this way all day," giggled Kristine.

"I'm sorry, but I have run out of gas. I got to have some food."

"You must be getting old," teased Kristine.

"Right now I do feel old. I'm taking a shower do you want to join me?"

"I thought you would never ask."

They showered and got dressed. Gary went down and started breakfast. Kristine joined him shortly and set the table. He cooked eggs, bacon and made toast. She made the coffee and poured them a cup. They sat across from each other and ate their breakfast. Kristine looked like a woman that had been well loved the night before. She had a glow on her face and when she smiled at Gary he knew he was lost. He had lost his heart to this beautiful young woman. He was still afraid of his bad luck with women. Would it be right to love again?

Kristine watched Gary and knew something was wrong. "I'll give you a penny for your thoughts."

"I was just thinking you should run not walk away from me. I have bad luck with women. You know about my wife, but you don't know about the others before her."

"I'll take my chances. I'm stronger than I look."

"I just wanted to warn you. I'm starting to care very much about you. I don't want you hurt because of me."

They spent the day lounging around the house enjoying each other. They watched television, listened to music and took a nap in the afternoon. It had been a relaxed fun weekend, but all good things have got to come to an end.

"I guess I had better go home and get ready for work tomorrow. Did you see the newspaper yet? The story was on the front page."

"The paper came, but I haven't read it yet. I'll read it tonight after supper. I had better things on my mind than a newspaper."

Kristine blushed, "We did have something better to do than read a newspaper."

Gary walked her to her car and kissed her one last time. She waved as she drove off. She was still on cloud nine. She had been in his bed as planned and he cared for her. He would say those three little words yet. She would bide her time and take whatever he gave her. She wanted to prove to him she could make it on her own without her Daddy's money. She had made a fool of herself once over a man and it wouldn't happen again.

That night after supper Gary went to his office and read the newspaper. He hoped Lopez would let what happen go and go on with his import of drugs and export of guns. The law could deal with him if they ever found out what he did for a living, but he was good at using a regular business for a front. Dallas thought he was an upstanding citizen. He gave regular to several charities in Dallas and they thought he was great. If only they knew how he made the money. That was enough thinking about Lopez. He switched his mind over to more important things like Kristine and how he was falling in love with her. He hadn't told her he loved her, but he knew it was coming. He could tell she was in love with him, Wolf and the ranch. She was like a ray of sunshine. She hadn't been gone long and he felt like a part of him was missing. It was the way he had felt about his wife, but she was dead and he was alive. Maria was right, he should move on.

Monday, Kristine was at her new job and loving it. She was sent on two stories to cover. One was a follow up on a robbery and the other one was a child abuse case. She finished her stories by that afternoon for the next day's paper. The Editor loved her work. She made his job easy, all he had to do read the story and turn it in to the printer. He would tell her the next day and in a month he would give her a fat pay raise if she kept up the good work.

Monday was very busy at the ranch. Joe passed out assignments for the day. Gary and Wolf had a job finding the crazy bull they had tangled with before. What was his problem? He had a herd of cows to service and he ran away from home. He also had plenty to eat. If it was his bull Gary would give him an attitude adjustment and if that didn't help he would get rid of him.

They found him in another rancher's field with his cows. Maybe he wanted something different. They rancher didn't care if he serviced his cows. He was a prize bull and would deliver good stock. Gary had to rope him and Wolf nipped at his heels all the way back to the trailer. They delivered him back home to his ranch. After the bull was back in his own field Gary talked to the rancher.

The rancher paid him again for his services. He scratched his head, "I don't know what I'm going to do with that crazy bull. I guess he thinks the grass is always greener on the other side of the fence."

"May I make a suggestion?" asked Gary.

"I'm open to anything."

"I would build an electric fence around a small area and build a second electric fence around that fence. If he makes it through the first fence I think after he gets his dick knocked stiff a couple of times he will stay in that fence. When you want him to service a cow just put her in with him. That should take care of your problems.

"By golly I think you are right, I'll start on it tomorrow. Thanks again for your help."

The next day they were back on another job. Cows had torn down a section of fence and made their escape. It took Gary and Wolf all day to round them up and bring them home. Wolf made a real good cow dog or should he say cow wolf. That did sound funny, but Wolf didn't like to be called a dog.

The next two days Gary worked on the ranch. He checked fence and livestock. Jerry and Kathy were riding two new horses Ben Had finished training. The owner would pick them up tomorrow. They would ride them like you would test drive a car. Ben didn't want anything to go wrong with the sale. You were talking big bucks for the pair.

Friday night after work, Gary called Kristine at home. She had just got home from work. She had a rough week, but she loved her job. She answered on the third ring. "Hello, Kristine speaking."

"What do you have planned for this weekend?" asked Gary.

"Nothing, what do you have in mind?"

"We could go out of town somewhere or we could eat out and take in a drive-in movie. I haven't been to a drive-in since I left home. I worked at a drive-in when I was in High School."

"The drive-in sounds like fun. I have never been to one."

"If we don't like the movie we can always neck."

"Now I know for sure I want to go to the drive-in," giggled Kristine. She got hot just thinking about what they could do in the car.

"Then I'll pick you up at five. We can go out to eat and then go to a movie."

"Gary, have you ever made out in a drive-in in your car?"

He started to lie, but changed his mind. "Yes I have a few times."

"I was told by some of my friends that they had done it in a drive-in and lost their cherry. Did the girls you made out with lose their cherry?"

"Most of them, but some had already lost it."

"Getting a girl for the first time isn't what it's cracked up to be. It is very messy when you pop her cherry."

"Well I lost mine a long time ago."

They talked awhile longer before they hung up. Gary sat and thought about tomorrow night. It would be fun going to a drive-in movie. It would bring back old memories when he worked at the movies. He had made out a lot at the drive-in movie except when the parents insisted their little girl double date. That caused a big problem. You could neck or play stink finger, but that was as far as you dared to go. The girl had to be home at a certain time. He laughed out loud as he thought about the times he missed out. All a young guy had on his mind was getting a piece. The girls were curious and if you could get them hot enough you scored. He remembered the first time he bought condoms. He was nervous and the cashier was a woman. She, ask him how she could help him? He stuttered as he finally got out he wanted some rubbers. They were kept behind the counter.

"What size can I get you?"

"Medium, I guess."

She handed him a box of medium rubber bands. "Is that all you want?"

Gary stuttered, "I mean the other kind. The kind used for sex."

She put a box in a sack and handed it to him. "That will be one fifty."

He paid her and left the store. The cashier glared at him the whole time. You would think she thought he would be having sex with her daughter if she had one. After that he went in and asked for condoms. He didn't want to get a girl in trouble. If he was lucky enough to score he wanted to protect the girl. He noticed as he got older most guys didn't care. It was up to the girl to protect herself and they liked to brag when they scored. That pissed Gary off. He didn't believe in show and tell.

Gary checked the icebox for food. Maria had made supper for him. He ate and went to his office to check his phone calls and books. He had two more lost cattle jobs for next week. They had been gone some time already so what was a couple more days. He showered and went to bed. He dreamed about Kristine and woke up in the middle of the night with a big hard on. He went to the bathroom and relieved himself. He slept like a log the rest of the night.

The next day he worked around the ranch until time to get ready for his date. He shaved, took a shower and dressed in jeans and a country western shirt. He put on his good boots and hat. He left in time to pick Kristine up and go out to eat before the theatre opened. They decided to go to a Dairy Queen for supper. Gary pulled into the parking lot. He had elected to use his pickup for the big bench seat. It was higher off the ground and they could make out if they decided to. Gary helped her out of the pickup. She was wearing a skirt and blouse and her hair in a ponytail. He liked the way the skirt hung to her curves. The blouse showed off her nice set of boobs. His mouth watered and it wasn't for food. They went in and got a booth.

"What would you like to eat?" asked Gary.

"I'll take a chicken sandwich, fries and a diet coke."

Gary elected for a hamburger, fries and a coke. He went up to the counter and ordered for them. It didn't take long and he was back in the both with their food. They wolfed down their food and left for the drive-in theatre. At the entrance he bought their tickets and drove half way down to the screen. He reached out and got the speaker and put it on the door inside. It was playing country music while waiting to get dark enough to start the movie. "Gone with the Wind" was playing for the second time around. Gary had worked it when he was in High School. Kristine had missed it the first time and was delighted to get to see it. Gary knew it was a fantastic movie, so there wouldn't be any necking at the movie.

"I caught tickets sometimes at the drive-in in High School. Kids used to try and sneak in, in the trunk of the car. You could always tell when someone was in the trunk. The driver would look guilty and be nervous."

"What would you do?"

"I would drop back and pound on the trunk and they would scream. Then I would make the driver open the trunk. After they paid I would close the trunk and tell them to drive on."

"Do you want a coke and popcorn?" asked Gary.

"Sure, let's go all the way."

Gary got out of the car and went to the con-session stand. He ordered a large coke and large popcorn. A coke and popcorn was seventy five cents. Prices just kept going up. He got back to the truck just as the movie started.

"I got a large coke and popcorn. I thought we could share."

"The popcorn smells delicious."

They watched the movie and enjoyed their coke and popcorn. "Gone with the Wind" was a long movie with a break in the middle. "I love Clark Gable swooned Kristine. He was a real man."

"Well my favorite hero is John Wayne. Anything he does on screen is possible. I love all his movies and can watch them over and over." The first half ended and they had a fifteen minute intermission.

"Do you want anything else to eat?" asked Gary.

"I'm full and I don't want to gain any weight. Most guys don't like fat girls."

The second half started and they cuddled up and watched the movie. Gary slipped his hand under her skirt close to her panties. He left it there. He wanted her hot when they got back to her apartment. He wanted some loving tonight. It had been too long since they had made love.

The movie finally let out and it was past midnight before they got back to her apartment. Gary got out and came around to help her out of the truck. They went up the sidewalk hand in hand. They were both thinking about what was about to happen. Kristine's nipples strained at her blouse and she was moist down below. She was ready to make love. She didn't need any foreplay. Gary's pants were standing out because of a big hard on. She opened the door and turned on the lights. As soon as they were inside Kristine went into Gary's arms. He reached for the snap on her skirt letting it drop to the floor. Next he unbuttoned her blouse and slid it off letting it drop to the floor. She kicked off her shoes and stood in her panties and lacy bra.

"You have on too many clothes."

She unbuttoned his shirt and slid it off dropping it to the floor. He kicked off his boots and waited as she unbuckled his belt and dropped his pants. He stepped out of them and stood before her in his shorts. The crotch was standing out showing a big hard on. He had left his hat in the truck. Kristine dropped his shorts and stared at his big erection. She dropped to her knees and put her fingers around his shaft. She wanted to show Gary how much she loved him. She slowly stoked him and took as much as she could in her mouth. She wrapped her tongue around the head as she sucked on his erection. He put his fingers in her hair and pulled her to him. It felt so good he thought he would faint. He didn't want to come yet so he pulled her back to her feet. He unsnapped her bra and pulled down her panties. The bra hit the floor and she stepped out of her panties.

They stared at each other. He opened his arms and she went into them. She jumped up and locked her legs around his waist. "Gary I want you in me now."

Gary backed up to the wall and lowered her until she took all of his, shaft. She started to move up and down and cling to him for dear life. They both lost control and acted like dogs in heat. She moaned and screamed as she had her first climax. Gary didn't slow down and kept pumping into her soft body. Kristine felt Gary as he reached his climax and shuddered and strained as he shot his load deep into her hot body. "Oh Gary, I'm coming again." They clung together for a long time before he lowered her to the floor.

"Why didn't we use the bed?" asked Gary.

"I couldn't wait. I wanted you now."

"I'm hot and thirsty, let's take a break and then take it slow and easy. We got all night to make love and get it right."

"Are you worn out already?" Kristine teased.

"Woman you may make me have a heart attack before the night is over."

They padded into the kitchen naked. Gary had a beer and Kristine had a glass of wine. They sat at the table naked staring at each other. They had cooled off and got their strength back. "Is the old man ready to make love again?" she giggled.

Gary got up and grabbed her hand. "Yes, it's time to do some serious love making."

"Can I be on top this time?" Kristine asked.

"Go for it if you think you are good enough."

In bed and Kristine on top she was riding this old cowboy to death. She didn't stop the ride at eight seconds. Was she trying to set a record at how long she could ride him? She would bring them close to coming and then slow down or stop. She was going to give him a heart attack if she didn't finish it.

"Kristine finish making us come or you're going to kill me."

"Ok, hang on cowboy." She bounced up and down sliding around on her way down. Gary gritted his teeth as he had a powerful climax. Kristine came a couple seconds behind him. She laid on his chest trying to get her breathing back to normal. She didn't want it to end so she stayed coupled to him. They were so tired they drifted off to sleep still coupled.

Kristine woke first and was still coupled to Gary. She moved just a little and felt his erection grow hard inside her. She slowly sat up and started to move. It didn't take long for Gary to wake up. "What a way to wake up in the morning. I could get used to making love in the morning."

Gary arched his back going deeper into her soft body. They didn't do slow and soon they both climaxed. Kristine squeezed his shaft until she had every drop from him. They finally got out of bed and headed for the shower. Gary washed Kristine all over from head to foot and she did the same to him.

"That was a fantastic night. Did we sleep at all last night?"

"Not very much, we spent most of what was left of the night making love."

They had to go to the living room to retrieve their clothes. After they were dressed Kristine made breakfast while Gary made coffee and set the table. They had slept almost until noon. After they ate she walked him out to the pickup and kissed him long and hard. Without thinking she said, "I love you."

He had his back to her when she said it. She didn't know if he heard her or he just didn't want to reply. He was her cowboy and one day he would say those three little words. He waved as he drove off toward the ranch. She missed him already.

Gary had heard her and played like he didn't. He was falling in love with her so why didn't he tell her he loved her. It was quiet at the ranch when he arrived home. Wolf and Sunshine met him at the door to be petted. "It's good to be home," said Gary.

Chapter Thirteen

James Lopez stormed into his estate home. The staff met him and several thugs at the front door with drinks. "I'm back," he told the staff. "I want to have a party tonight, see to it."

The head of staff said, "I'll take care of the arrangements sir."

"Be sure you have plenty of girls for our pleasure."

"Yes sir."

"Men, come into my office, we have some business to discus." The thugs followed him into the office.

"Willie, I want you to go to Sugarland and scout out the Mitchell Ranch. The owner is also called "The Tracker." He is the one who raided my home in Columbia and took my mistress. Her name is Kristine Wilson. She is working for the newspaper. Find out her routine and when would be the best time to kidnap her. Nobody destroys my property and takes anything that belongs to me. At the same time we take the girl another group will raid the ranch and kill Mitchell and anyone else on the ranch at that time. It will be a lesson that nobody comes up against James Lopez and lives. We will make our plans when Willie gets back from Sugarland. Is everything clear?"

"Yes sir," they said in unison.

"Pedro, you take five men to the warehouse and get things set for a business meeting. The drugs we brought in will buy a lot of guns. We will sell them at a big profit. I may use some of the money to start a cat house in Dallas. I should say an escort service. That sounds better."

"Will we get a discount price on service?" asked Pedro.

"That will be part of your benefits for working for me," laughed

James.

"Snake, you will stay here on guard duty with two men. Ok, time to get to work. Willie, take as long as it takes in Sugarland. I don't want any slipups when we raid the ranch." Lopez went to check on the party and food.

Party time and Lopez took first pick of the girls at the party. She was a good looking redhead and he thought she would make his day, but she didn't.

He banged her only one time and sent her packing. She didn't have the fire. He thought about Kristine and how good she was in bed. He would have her one more time and then let his men have her to play with. That would teach the bitch not to mess with James Lopez. He was tired of the party and got a bottle on his way to his room. He thought about Kristine as he got drunk. His men got a girl each and found an empty bedroom to finish off the night.

Monday, started a new work week. All hands were at the table eating breakfast when Gary joined them. Joe had already, gave out work assignments for the day. Gary poured himself a cup of coffee and Maria set a plate of food in front of him.

"Ladies and gentlemen I have an idea. Why don't we have a cutting horse contest, a chili cook off and a dance that night? We have been working hard and it's time for some fun and relaxation. What do you say?"

"Speaking for the crew I think we would love it," said Joe.

"Good, Joe you get everything set up. Ben, take charge of the chili cook off and Maria will fix the rest of the food. The rest of you will help out as needed. We will have it this coming Saturday. I'll put it in the newspaper and on the radio. I'm sure that will get us a bunch of people. Jerry and Kathy would you like to ride in the cutting horse contest?"

"Yes sir," they said in unison.

"Who makes the best chili?"

"That would be Sam," said Joe.

"Sam would you like to be in the contest?"

"Yes sir, I will try to make you proud."

"It doesn't matter if we win or lose it's the fun of it."

That night Gary called Kristine and told her to place an ad in the paper for him. "Will you be able to come?"

"A team of wild horses couldn't keep me away, I'll be there. I'll tell my boss I need to cover the event and get pictures. Am I sleeping over?" she giggled.

"Yes, I can't wait until the party is over. We may have to sneak off and have a quickie someplace and return to the party."

Kristine's heart rate increased thinking about Saturday. She needed some good loving.

Everyone worked hard getting ready for the party Saturday. Gary answered calls all week about the cutting horse and chili cook off contest. He wandered if they could handle that many people at the ranch. They would soon find out. Friday at breakfast everyone gave Gary a progress report.

"It looks like we are going to have a full house Saturday. People are coming from other states. The cutting horse completion is going to be something else. We have several coming from Oklahoma. I bought a trophy for the winner and cash for first, second, and third places. That should stir up some talk and be good for business."

"I guess we are as ready as can be," said Joe.

"Ok, everyone take the day off and be here early in the morning." said Gary.

"What about our work today?" Joe asked.

"Sam and Jerry feed and water the horses, then go on home."

"Yes sir."

Saturday morning all hands were there bright and early as pickups with trailers came up the driveway. Jerry showed everyone where to park. They took their horses out of the trailers and put their horses in one of the corals until time to ride. The pickups loaded with chili cookers and supplies were lined up with their tailgates down to unload and use the tailgate for cooking supplies. Before long the chili smell was everywhere and made your mouth water. By ten o'clock people started to arrive from everywhere young and old. By eleven Maria and Kathy started bringing food from the house. Before long the tables were loaded with anything your heart could desire. A preacher gave thanks and everyone sat down to enjoy their food. People sampled the chili until they voted on the winner.

Gary announced the winner and gave him his trophy and cash. Second and third place winners received a cash prize. Kristine stepped up and took their picture. That was the first time Gary had seen her. She had on short-shorts and a long white shirt. That made his mouth water and not for food.

Kristine watched Gary as he stared at her, "What's for lunch?" she smiled.

"You if we didn't have all these people around."

"We could scream fire," she teased.

"Are you hungry?"

"Starved, I thought you would never ask. I didn't get up in time to eat breakfast."

They filled their plates and wolfed down their food while they stared at each other. They didn't need to talk to know what the other one was thinking. Kristine blushed at her thoughts. Gary smiled and knew what she was thinking.

After lunch everyone surrounded the coral that the cutting horse contest would take place in. Ben had several, young calf's in the coral. The rider rode the horse, but let him have his head and do the work. The horse would cut out the calf selected and keep him from the herd. The fastest time won the contest. A cowboy from a ranch in Oklahoma won first place. Second place went a Texas cowboy and third place went to Kathy. She was thrilled to death. Gary smiled as he handed her the cash prize, "Nice going Kathy."

"Thank you, boss."

Kristine took pictures of the winners for the paper. She hugged Kathy, "The girl's won something. That is so great. I'll send you a picture."

Everyone snacked on leftovers and got ready for the dance. The floor and tables were set up. A live band tuned up getting ready for the dance.

Gary hunted Kristine, "I claim the first dance before you fill up your dance card."

She hugged Gary and they sat down at a table waiting for the music to start. The first dance was a fast two-step and they hit the floor. That was Gary's favorite dance. Gary and Kristine two-stepped around the dance floor, in a circle. The next dance was a slow belt buckle shining song. Kristine shined Gary's belt buckle, good. After the slow dance they went back to their table and watched the couples dance.

They sat and stared at each other, each one knowing what was on their minds. At nine o'clock Gary asked, "Do you think anyone would miss us if we sneaked out for a while?"

"I'm game if you are."

They got up and eased around to the back door. "Let's use the guest bedroom at the far end of the hall. Nobody should come there."

Just as Gary was about to open the door he heard voices. "It won't hurt, but just a second and then it will feel good."

"Jerry, are you sure?"

"Trust me, I won't hurt you."

"Have you ever done it with a girl?"

"No, but my friends said it didn't hurt long. Hasn't your Mother told you about the birds and the bees?"

"No, I guess she thinks I'm too young. Has your Father told you about it?"

"No, I guess we will just have to hum it."

Gary pulled Kristine back down the hall and they both laughed. "I guess they are like me. Nobody told me what to do either. I just jumped in with both feet."

"Was it good your first time?" giggled Kristine.

"I don't know, I came so fast I don't remember."

"Well I guess we better go back to the party," complained Kristine.

"We can continue after the party. Let's go back and dance."

The party lasted until midnight. By one everything was put away and everyone was gone. Kristine stared at Gary and ran for his bedroom. "I want to make love in a bed tonight."

He took off after her pulling off clothes as he went. Kristine was in bed naked by the time he got there. "There won't be any foreplay the first time," said Gary.

Kristine spread her legs and arched her back to receive his shaft. Gary thrust deep into her and she groaned his name. She matched him thrust for thrust until she went over the edge with Gary right behind her. "Oh baby, I needed that."

They were tired and curled up together and went to sleep. They didn't get up until noon the next day. Kristine put on Gary's pajama top and Gary wore the bottom to make breakfast. Kristine cooked eggs, bacon and toast while he made coffee and set the table. They sat and stared across the table at each other. "I could get used to this," said Gary.

"Me too," Kristine looked deep into his eyes and thought she saw love in his eyes hoping it wasn't just lust.

"What would you like to do after breakfast or should I say lunch?"

"Sorry, but I got to go home and write my story for the newspaper. Maybe we have time for a quickie," giggled Kristine.

After their quickie, Gary walked her to her car and kissed her as he opened the car door for her. She waved to him as she left the ranch. Kristine smiled as she drove home. She could tell Gary was, liking her more and more. She was still waiting for those three little words.

Gary was missing Kristine and she had only been gone a few hours. He dreamed about how madly they mad love. They couldn't get enough of each other. He went to his office to check phone calls and check the books. He only had one missing bull call which Wolf and Gary would take care of Monday morning.

Chapter Fourteen

Monday, Willie reported back to Lopez. "I got it all worked out and the best time would be to hit the ranch Friday and kidnap Kristine at the same time. She takes a morning coffee break at ten. We can hit both places at ten."

"It sounds like a good plan. Willie, take five men and hit the ranch at ten. Pedro, take three men and pick up my little mistress at ten. Don't hurt her, she is mine until I'm tired of her and then the men can have her."

"Are there any more questions?"

"Where do we bring the girl when we get back to Dallas?" asked Pedro.

"Bring her to the warehouse. Snake leave three men at the house and come with me to the warehouse. We got a business to run. We got to get everything running smooth again. We still have drugs to sell and guns to pack for shipment. We run an import and export business," Lopez laughed.

"Willie, you and Pedro get your weapons and cars ready to leave Thursday. You can look the area over Thursday and hit your targets Friday. I don't want any slipups. I want Mitchell dead and I don't care how many more you kill while you are there. I want the ranch shot up good as a warning to anybody else who messes with me. Take automatic weapons to do the job."

They broke up the meeting and went their separate ways. Lopez and a crew worked at the warehouse while Willie and Pedro got their equipment together for their trip to Sugarland. After they were ready the men were off to party until Thursday.

Thursday, Willie and Pedro took two cars and headed for Sugarland. Thursday they roamed around looking things over. They made their final round checking things out. Willie drove by the ranch several times during the day while Pedro watched Kristine take her break as usual. Everything looked perfect for Friday.

They gassed up their cars and went out for a big supper. After supper they picked up some beer and got rooms at a motel for the night. They gathered in one room, played cards and drank their beer. At midnight, Willie went over their job one more time.

"Ok boys, let's get some sleep. We don't have to get up too early. Nine o'clock we will get into position and ten o'clock we will carry out our mission."

Monday and Tuesday Gary worked on the ranch. Tuesday morning Gary got a call from a hunter who had lost his best bloodhound. He lived close to the Trinity River and wanted Gary to find him. He told the man he was on his way. "Wolf, where are you?"

Wolf came trotting into the kitchen where Maria was fixing breakfast. Gary was drinking coffee and waiting on his eggs and bacon. "Wolf, eat your breakfast, we have a job and it is different from any we have done before. We will be hunting for a bloodhound."

Wolf stared at him and Gary knew what he was thinking. "I know, the bloodhound is usually the one looking for someone, but this one is lost so we will find him, I hope."

After breakfast, they loaded their gear in the pickup, hooked up the trailer and loaded Wind his black stallion in the trailer. They headed for the Trinity River at the place where the hunter lived. The hunter introduced himself as Jake Simmons. He had a nice home out in the country and worked in town as a lawyer. He was still an old country boy who liked to fish and hunt. He loved that old hound and wanted him back. "Where was the last place you seen the hound?"

"We were hunting on my neighbor's ranch down the road. He caught sent of a coon and took off after the coon. I heard him way in the distance and then nothing. I looked and looked, but never could find him. My dogs won't track another dog so that's why I called you. He is the oldest dog I have, but he is still the best, hound."

"We'll find him." They followed Simmons down to his neighbor's ranch. Gary unloaded Wind and swung into the saddle. He strapped on his 45 automatic and fastened his rope to the saddle. Gary pointed which way to go and Wolf took point.

"I wish you luck," said Mr. Simmons.

Gary waved and followed Wolf. They made a sweep back and forth trying to pick up the trail of the bloodhound. After an hour Wolf picked up his trail and took off at a run. Gary closed his eyes and watched Wolf as he ran. He saw Wolf stop, but he didn't see the bloodhound. Gary rode up beside Wolf and watched him. He was looking down in a hole. It appeared to be an old well that had been covered over. He hoped there wasn't any water in the well. Gary got down and pulled the rest of the boards aside. He looked down in the hole and the hound looked up at him and howled. It was a pretty good drop, but his rope should be long enough. Gary hooked his rope to the saddle horn and dropped it down the hole. The hound didn't move, so he must be hurt. "I don't like this, but I'm going to have to go down after him. Wolf if I get in trouble, you go for help."

Gary put his gloves on and slid down the rope. The dog had broken a leg, but seemed alright otherwise. He looped the rope around his waist and pulled the dog into his arms. "Ok, Wind back up slowly."

Wind backed up slowly on command until Gary reached the top. He used a piece of wood and set the dog's leg. He always carried medical supplies in his saddlebags. The dog seemed to know Gary was trying to help him. After Gary covered the hole with boards he loaded the dog across the saddle and swung up behind him. "Ok guys, let's go home."

Mr. Simmons was waiting beside Gary's truck for them to return. He ran out to meet them smiling from ear to ear. "You found him."

Gary carefully handed the hound down to his master. He noticed his leg and looked at Gary. "We found him down in an old well. You need to let the rancher know about it before a cow breaks a leg or something else falls down the well."

"I will do that. How much do I owe you?"

Gary figured how long it took for the job and Mr. Simmons paid him. "Thank you again for finding my dog."

They shook hands and Gary loaded up. "Well Wolf, another satisfied customer, let's go home."

It was late by the time they got back to the ranch. Wolf and Gary chowed down on cold chicken, potato salad and a salad. Gary had a beer and Wolf had a bowl of milk. Wolf had got to where he ate almost anything. He gave Sunshine several pieces of chicken. She still liked her meat raw.

After supper, Gary called Kristine. She had just got home from a hard day and had to go to Houston on Wednesday to cover a convention. She wouldn't be back until late that day. They missed each other and their love making.

"I hope we can get together this weekend, I'm getting to be a horny old man."

"Well I guess that makes me a horny old woman," she giggled.

"You want to go out of town or stay here this weekend?"

"I don't care as long as we have a bed at night."

"Honey I'll make sure we have a bed."

"Let's wait until Friday night to make up our mind where we want to go. I don't care as long as we are together."

"I'll call you Friday night after you get off work. Good night and sweet dreams."

Friday morning, Willie, Pedro and thugs were eating breakfast next door to the motel. After they finished eating they went their separate ways to set up for their strike.

Pedro and his thugs parked across from the newspaper and waited for Kristine to take her morning break. She came out the door at ten o'clock. Pedro made a u turn right in front of her. Two thugs jumped out of the car and grabbed her dragging her to the car. A young man saw what was happening and came to help her. Pedro shot the young man. "Get her in the car now."

The thugs shoved her in the back seat and jumped in the car. Pedro drove off at a high rate of speed. When he turned the corner he slowed down to the speed limit. They passed a cop car and headed out of town. The Police stopped in front of the newspaper office. The young man was dead. Another witness saw what happened and had called the cops. They still didn't know who the woman was that was kidnapped.

When the thugs got out of town, Pedro said, "Tie her up and put a gag in her mouth. I don't want to listen to her screaming all the way to Dallas."

Kristine put up a fight, but they were too strong for her to do any good. She finally gave up and sat staring at them. "The boss wasn't done with you when you took off. Now you are in big trouble."

She now knew who had kidnapped her and why. She was scared to death, but she wouldn't let them know. Her bonds were hurting her, but she couldn't do anything about it. She sat as still as possible so they wouldn't hurt as bad.

"Your boyfriend should be dead by now. Willie was going to hit the ranch the same time we kidnapped you. He won't be coming after you, nobody will."

Tears formed in Kristine's eyes. She hoped Gary was still alive. She just as soon not, live if he was dead already. She knew what Lopez was going to do to her. She knew she would soon be dead. Her only hope was that Gary was still alive.

Gary took part of the crew to fix a section of fence that was falling down. He left Joe and Ben working in the barn feeding horses and cleaning out stalls. Maria was in the house cooking with Sunshine waiting to taste her food.

The fence Gary and crew were working on was just over the hill from the ranch. They started tearing out the old fence to make room for the new. It would take most of the day to put up new fence, but it had to be done. Wolf sat on top of the hill watching them work and keeping an eye on the ranch house. He saw a strange car drive past the ranch and then circle back. He pulled into the road to the ranch. Wolf felt something was wrong. He turned and barked at Gary. While digging a hole for a post he looked up at Wolf. "What's wrong," he yelled. He closed his eyes and looked through Wolf's eyes. Gary pulled his rifle from his saddle and walked up the hill toward Wolf. He got to the top of the hill just as the car stopped in front of the ranch house.

Willie and the thugs got out of the car. "Santana, come with me and the rest of you wait here." They went to the front door and opened the front door. They went in with weapons drawn toward the kitchen. Maria looked up as they entered the kitchen. Sunshine got to her feet and stood beside Maria. "What do you want?" asked Maria.

"Where is Mitchell?"

"I don't know. I just do the cooking and he doesn't tell me anything."

"Wrong answer you bitch." He slapped her across her face almost knocking her down. Sunshine instantly attacked the man. As Willie turned to fight off the attack, Maria ran out the back door. The two men had their hands full fending off Sunshine. Finally they shot Sunshine several times killing her. Willie yelled, "Stupid dog let's get out of here."

Joe and Ben ran out of the barn with rifles in their hands, but as they came out they met a wall of bullets from automatic weapons. Joe was dead before he hit the ground and Ben went down. They sprayed everything with automatic fire, killing two horses.

Gary watched in horror at what was happening. The rest of the crew hurried to the top of the hill as Gary lay down and took aim at the thugs. He hit the first one dead in the chest. The others turned toward the hill and fired their automatic weapons.

Everyone dropped to the ground. "Don't worry we are out of range, but they aren't out of range for this sniper rifle. He squeezed of another shot and thug number two went down. They kept firing up the hill, but hadn't realized their target was out of range. Gary lined up on another target and fired killing the third thug.

"Just like shooting fish in a barrel," said Gary as he picked another target and fired killing the fourth man.

Willie screamed, "Let's get out of here."

As Willie got in the car, Gary shot the fifth man as he opened the car door. Willie started the car and turned around headed out. He thought he was home free when Gary fired at the gas tank. The first one missed, but the second one hit the tank. The car exploration rocked the area killing Willie. It looked like a war zone in front of the ranch house.

Gary and his crew got their horses and charged toward the ranch house. Maria ran from the back of the house screaming.

"Wayne, check on Joe and Ben." Gary went in the house and

saw Sunshine dead on the floor and the place shot up. Wayne came in the house, "Joe is dead and ben is shot up bad. They even killed two of our best horses."

Gary went in his office and called for an ambulance. He then called the Sheriff. "I got a mess out here at the ranch. Joe is dead, Ben is shot up, Sunshine is dead and I killed six thugs. I know who sent them, but I can't prove it."

"I have some more bad news." The Sheriff said.

"What else do you have?"

"I just got a call from the Police that Kristine Wilson at the newspaper has been kidnapped."

"I know who kidnapped her. It's the same thugs that hit the ranch. I guess you know this means war. I'm going to Dallas. I hate to leave you with this mess, but I got to go now. Their boss doesn't know I'm still alive so I have that advantage."

"You need to let the law handle it."

"The law won't do anything because they think he is a good guy and a business man. This is personal now. This is between him and me and one of us has to go down. He sent men to kill me today and now it is my turn."

Gary hung up as the ambulance arrived. They took Ben off to the Hospital and Wayne went with him for support. Jerry, make arrangements for Joe. He doesn't have any family that I know of. We will bury him on the ranch with Judy. Tell Sam to bury Sunshine alone beside Joe. Our little plot is filling up. "I got to leave for Dallas right away. I got a score to settle."

"Kathy, you and Maria hold down the fort until the men get back. Tell Sam, Wayne and Jerry to keep the ranch going until I get back and if I don't come back, call my Dad. I got to load up and head out to Dallas. Always keep some weapons handy in case more thugs come back."

Gary loaded his sniper rifle, 45 automatic, bow and arrows. He carefully packed some blocks of C-4 with fuses. He was going to war. Maria packed him a basket of food and drinks to eat on his way to Dallas. He went to his office to call Leroy in Dallas. He was in his office at the Police station and answered on the third ring. "Detective Cooper, how may I help you?"

"Leroy this is Gary. I got a big problem and I need your help."

"Anything you need you got it."

"I need to know everything you can dig up on a James Lopez. He is a drug and gun dealer from Columbia. Everybody in Dallas thinks he is an honest business man and is very rich. He is the one I rescued the girl from. His thugs raided the ranch and killed Joe, put Ben in the hospital and killed the little wolf Sunshine. His thugs kidnapped Kristine again and I don't know where he took her."

"I'll find out all the property he owns in Dallas. He has several warehouses he calls Import and Export Inc. He has a large estate on the west side of Dallas. I'll have a list by the time you get to Dallas."

Gary and Wolf loaded into the pickup and headed for Dallas. Gary was thinking about Kristine and wandered if she was dead or still alive. He hoped Lopez would keep her around for a while before he did away with her. He gripped the steering wheel so hard his knuckles were white. If anything happened to Kristine he didn't know how he would cope with it. She was his life and he loved her. He admitted he had to have her in his life. He lost his first love to a drunk driver and he wasn't going to lose Kristine to a drug dealer. Wolf sat beside Gary wired just as bad. He wanted blood for the person that had caused him to lose his mate. They would have their revenge. Gary pulled into a roadside park to eat something and rest a moment. It had been a long day so far.

As Gary opened his door to get out a man in a ski mask stuck a gun in his face. "Give me your money or die."

"Mr. I have had a very bad day and I don't have time for this. Why don't you just take off and you won't get killed?"

"And just who is going to kill me?" he laughed.

Gary glanced at the pickup door, "Wolf."

Wolf caught the man by surprise and he screamed as Wolf slammed into him taking him down with a broken arm. He stood on the man's chest waiting for Gary to give thumbs down or up. The man pissed his pants and his gun was on the ground beside him. Gary walked over and picked up his gun. He should let Wolf have him for supper, but the man was scared to death already. He pulled off the guy's ski mask. "If I ever see you again I will let Wolf have you for lunch. He kills on command."

"Ok Wolf, let's get out of here. We got larger fish to fry." They got back in the truck and drove off. The would-be-robber lay there for several minutes. He thought he was going to die. Where did that huge wolf come from? He finally got up and dragged himself over to his hidden car. He had to get to a hospital and get his arm fixed.

Chapter Fifteen

Gary stopped at a service station south of Dallas and called Leroy. He was still at the Police Station searching information for Gary. "What do you have for me?"

"I haven't found much on him. He hides behind other names and business names. It's going to take time to find everything about Lopez."

"I don't have time to wait. He may kill Kristine before we find anything on him. I'm going after him. Do you have his estate address?"

"You can't go barging into his home. He can kill you and call it trespassing and the Police can't do anything about it."

Gary laughed, "Look who is talking about following rules. You never follow rules unless it is to your advantage. Now give me the address."

"Ok, but I am going with you."

"Thanks, but no thanks. I'm not letting you put your job on the line for me."

"You think I'm going to let you go alone after you saved the love of my life. By the way is Wolf with you?"

"Yes, and he is after blood the same as me. They won't know what hit them when Wolf and I attack the place."

"I suppose you brought weapons and C-4 with you."

"Never leave home without it. I might want to blow up something."

"Ok, if you must do this, get a motel room and call me. I'll meet you at the motel as soon as I get off work. I don't want Ashley to know about this. She would want to come along to protect my back. We been watching each other's back for a long time now, but I don't want her to lose her job over this."

"I don't want you to lose your job either."

"No problem, they know I'm a maverick and never follow rules."

"This is not a case of rules, you may get killed. This guy Lopez has a small army and plenty of automatic weapons, enough to start a war."

"Look at it this way, if they have weapons or dope and we bust them I'll get another pay raise or a bonus."

"I guess we are two crazy people."

"Gary, we need to wait until it is dark before we raid his home. He will probably have only a few thugs on guard duty."

"He will be wandering where his crew is that hit the ranch pretty soon. I want to surprise him, before he starts looking for his goons."

"Call me when you find a motel." They hung up.

Gary drove over on the west side of Dallas and found a motel. He called Leroy and told him the location. "I'm going to drive around looking the area over until you get here. I don't know my way around Dallas, but I will learn."

He found the estate of Lopez and looked it over. It had a high metal bar gate in the driveway and a high fence around the estate. It would be hard to penetrate the estate. He heard dogs barking on the grounds. "This place is built like Fort Knox."

Wolf and Gary went back to the motel and waited on Leroy to get off work. "Wolf I hope I don't get us all killed on this job."

Leroy was searching the computer for anything he could find on Lopez when Ashley walked in. He changed screens on the computer. "What are you still doing here?"

"I was just catching up on some reports. I'm leaving shortly," he lied.

They left the parking lot and went in different directions. Ashley had got a look at the computer before Leroy switched screens. She saw the items on James Lopez. Why did Leroy lie to her? Something was fishy and she didn't like it. As soon as she got home she ran to her computer and brought up the page Leroy was on. Why was he checking out James Lopez? She was going to find out. She found Lopez's address and decided to go there.

Leroy met Gary and Wolf at the motel. He had his Colt 45 and a shotgun for close range. Gary filled him in on Lopez's estate. "It's going to be hard to get in that place."

"Where there's a will there's a way. We can use a chain to pull the gate open or you can use some of that C-4 that you always carry with you."

"C-4 would be faster and we could rush them as soon as the gate blows."

"By the way they also have guard dogs. Wolf will take care of them. I bet when they see him they will run the other way."

"If they don't run we will have to blow them away," said Leroy.

"Then let's get the show on the road," said Gary.

They loaded into Gary's truck and headed out. Ashley drove by Lopez's estate and parked a half block away. She didn't know why she was here, but she had a bad feeling something bad was about to happen. What was Leroy up to or getting himself into? He didn't want her with him tonight so it had to be something that was illegal. She watched the gate.

Gary stopped his truck in front of the gate. Leroy and him got out and approached the gate. Gary placed a small package of C-4 on the gate so it would blow the gate forward up the driveway. He lit the fuse and they got back in the truck. "Fire in the hole," yelled Gary.

Ashley watched them as they set the charge. She knew one of them was Leroy because of the fast-draw rig on his hip. She sat and watched as the gate was blown open.

Gary stepped on the gas and they shot up the driveway. They got out and two guard dogs stepped in front of them. Wolf stepped in front of Gary and Leroy. The two dogs stared at Wolf and turned tail and ran. "I thought so," said Gary.

Snake and one other thug charged out the door with automatic weapons. Leroy slapped leather and both men hit the ground dead. "I'm the firepower and you are the tracker," said Leroy.

Ashley heard the gunfire and knew someone was dead when she heard the Colt 45. She was going to call it in to the Police Station, but she was out of her area and would have to call the Dallas Police. She decided to wait.

Gary and Leroy charged in the front door and met one more thug. The thug dropped his weapon on the floor and raised his hands. "Are you the only one left in the house?" asked Gary.

"Yes, I'm the only one left in the house."

"Where is the girl?"

"I don't know anything about a girl."

"Wolf, talk to the man."

The man stared at the huge wolf. "I'll tell you anything you want to know."

"Where is the girl?"

"Lopez has her at one of the warehouses, but I don't know which one."

Wolf moved closer to the man. "Please, I'm telling you the truth."

Gary pulled out a pen and a notebook. Ok give me the address of all his warehouses. Lopez had five warehouses. Leroy pulled the phone cord out of the jack and tied up the thug. "That should hold him for a while."

They walked out the front door and Gary stopped. "I'll be right back."

Gary went around the side of the house to the garage. He stared at all the beautiful new cars. He had to blow something up. He placed a block of C-4 in the garage and lit the fuse. He ran back around to the front of the house. "Let's get out of here."

"What did you do?" asked Leroy.

"Don't ask."

As they got in the truck as the garage was blown away. Gary looked over at Leroy, "The devil made me do it."

Gary pulled out into the street and took off. He handed his notebook to Leroy. "Where is the closest warehouse from here?"

Leroy gave him directions and Gary followed them. It was about ten miles to the first warehouse. He hoped this would be the right one. Time was running out for Kristine.

Ashley watched the truck leave and she followed at a safe distance as she tailed them. Where were they going now? She would be there if she was needed. She knew the fire department and Police would be at the place they left.

Gary pulled in close to the warehouse and saw some goons on guard duty. "What do you think asked Leroy?"

"That's a lot of guards for one warehouse. I would say they have something to hide. I wish we knew which warehouse Kristine was being held in, but since we don't we have to try them all. They got out and walked up to the guards. "We would like to see Mr. Lopez."

"What do you want to see him for?" He stared at Wolf.

"He's not here."

"Do you know where he is?"

"I don't give out information to strangers."

"Do you mind if we come in and look around?"

"Yes I do." He started to raise his automatic weapon, but Wolf nailed him. Gary and Leroy had their weapons drawn on the rest of the goons. They dropped their weapons.

"Wolf and I will take a look inside the warehouse while you watch these thugs." They went inside and found it full of weapons, but nobody else. They came back outside. "Leroy, call the Dallas Police and tell them about this place. It is full of weapons enough to start a war. Tell them you got a tip and wanted to be sure before you called the Police because of who owned the warehouse. We will stay here until they get here and take off as they enter the warehouse area."

"Wolf, go in the warehouse and find some duck-tape." He came back with a roll. Leroy kept an eye, on the hoods while Gary tied them up.

Ashley sat a distance away watching them. The hoods were tied up. Gary and Leroy got back into the truck and waited. As they heard the Cops coming they drove out of the parking lot and headed south. Ashley followed them at a safe distance. By now she guessed they were looking for something, but what?

"Leroy, give me directions to the next warehouse."

"It's about a mile from here. I'll give you directions as we go."

They had four more warehouses to check and it would be daylight soon. They liked working at night better. They didn't think there would be as many guards. Gary pulled into the next parking lot for the next warehouse and saw only two guards. "What do you think?"

"It must not be much in this warehouse since they only have two guards, but let's check it out anyway."

Gary pulled in close to the door and all three got out. The two guards stared at Wolf. He always got the attention. "Is this one of Mr. Lopez's warehouses?" asked Gary.

"Who wants to know?"

"I do, he has something that belongs to me."

"He isn't here and I don't give out information."

"Maybe I can get you to change your mind, Wolf."

Wolf moved in front of the two men. "Have you changed your mind?" Gary asked.

"What do you have in the warehouse?" Leroy asked.

"Nothing, it is empty."

"I don't think so, drop your weapons or Wolf will have you for a night snack."

They stared at Wolf and dropped their weapons. Gary and Wolf went inside the warehouse while Leroy watched the guards. What they found was a big surprise. Locked in several rooms were young girls to be sold into prostitution. They came back outside. "Leroy, call the cops. You won't believe what they have in this warehouse. They have young girls. Isn't there anything this guy isn't into?"

"Just think we have three more warehouses to go that we know of. I'm curious to know what is in the other warehouses."

While Leroy called the Dallas Police again, Gary tied the guards up. They got back in the truck and waited until they heard the Police coming and pulled out into traffic. "Maybe the third time is the charm," said Leroy.

Ashley watched again and waited. As usual Gary took off again. He didn't find what he was looking for. She followed again.

"Leroy, give me directions again."

"This one is only a couple blocks over." Leroy gave him directions. Gary pulled up in front of the warehouse. There weren't any guards or lights on. Gary went around the building and broke a window. He crawled inside and looked around. It had the regular goods that were normally sold at stores. He crawled out the window and came back around to the front. It was starting to get light out. "That one had normal goods for sale in stores. This is probably the warehouse he uses as a cover for his operation."

They got back in the truck and headed out again. Ashley watched them leave and followed. How many places are they going to she wandered. Then it hit her, he must be looking for Kristine. She must have been kidnapped again. She called the Police Station and asked if there had been any kidnapping reported. The dispatcher came back on the line. "There isn't any here in Dallas, but there is one reported in Sugarland."

"What's the name?"

"It is a reporter by the name of Kristine Wilson."

"Thank you very much." Now everything came together. That

was why Leroy was with Gary and they weren't going by the book. Leroy never followed rules. There was no backup, just Gary, Leroy and Wolf. They didn't know it, but she had their backs. She called her husband and told him she was on stakeout. She would be home in the morning.

"Leroy, give me directions to the next warehouse." It was only a few blocks away. Gary pulled into the parking lot and it was the same as the last warehouse. It was a front for the operation. They pulled back out into traffic. Ashley watched them and followed.

"We only got an address for one more warehouse," said Leroy.

"This had better be the one. I'm worried about Kristine and I'm sure Lopez knows or suspects his thugs aren't coming back from Sugarland. It is sure to hit the national news this morning. This had got to be the right warehouse."

"It's the next turnoff to the right. It is way back off the road."

It was light out and there was no hiding in the dark. Gary turned right and eased up the driveway. Automatic fire came from the warehouse. Gary turned the truck sideways and they jumped out using the truck for cover. "Well I guess they were expecting us."

"Yes they were and my Colt-45 isn't much good or my shotgun at this distance."

"I got something that will reach them." Gary reached in the truck and pulled out his sniper rifle. As the automatic fire died down, Gary raised and picked a target. He fired and dropped a man. "One down and who knows how many men they got in the warehouse. They will probably try to flank us. You watch for that and let me work on them." They barley had the doors open to the warehouse. Gary raised, up and picked another target. Another man hit the ground. Lopez sent two men to flank them. They got close, but Leroy was watching for them. He slapped leather and dropped both of them.

Ashley was just around the corner listening to the heavy gunfire. She eased her car around the corner just as she seen Leroy drop the two men. She pulled her car up behind them and got out of the car. "Ashley what are you doing here?"

"I'm here to cover your back." Leroy knew not to argue with her.

"Cover our right flank. This is war. I think you better call for backup. We may have bit off more than we can chew."

Ashley went back to the car and called the Dallas Police. She said, "Officer needs backup now. We are taking heavy automatic fire." She gave the address. She got out of the car and covered their right flank.

"Looks like we have a Mexican standoff," said Leroy.

"Let's see if I can shake them up." Gary got his bow and arrows out of the pickup. He pulled a block of C-4 from his backpack. He wrapped a small block to his arrow and stuck in a short fuse. He raised his bow up and set his arrow. "Light the fuse."

Leroy lit the fuse and Gary let the arrow fly. It hit the double doors of the warehouse and blew them down. Gary picked up his rifle and looked for a target. He dropped another man just inside the doors.

"That should get their attention."

Lopez was getting worried as he watched his men drop like flies. He decided to cut his losses and run.

Chapter Sixteen

"You two men get the woman and meet me out back. The rest of you keep firing and keep them pinned down."

The two men dragged Katrina out the back to the car. Lopez was in the front seat on the driver side. As soon as they were in the car Lopez spun out. He took the back way away from the warehouse. As soon as he left the rest of the thugs called to Gary, "We give up."

They walked out of the warehouse one by one dropping their guns on the ground. Gary walked slowly toward them as Leroy and Ashley covered him. The Police showed up just as Gary reached the men. The police stormed the warehouse, but it was empty of people. Lopez had got away. The warehouse was full of weapons and drugs. The Police put out an ATB on Lopez, but they didn't know what he was driving. Gary was fit to be tied. He knew Lopez had Kristine.

"Well, we lost Lopez for now. I'm going back to my motel and make some phone calls. Leroy, you and Ashley go get some rest and we can brainstorm later."

"Gary, we'll find Kristine some way. At least the public will know Lopez is a bad guy now. He is well known and maybe the public can help. We will put his face on television and in all the newspapers. The airports will be on the lookout for him," Leroy explained.

"Thanks, I'll call you guys later."

Gary went back to his motel. He called Mr. Wilson first and told him his daughter had been kidnaped by Lopez. "Lopez is a very dangerous man now that he has been exposed for what he is. He is on the run now. Did Kristine every mention any place he might have taken her?"

"She said something about him taking her to a lake house. It was right on the lake with a boat dock and large cabin cruiser. She said they stayed a weekend there, fished, water skied and partied. I don't know which lake it was at."

"It's at least a start if he hasn't gone back to Columbia."

"If you need anything, my plane, weapons or money for supplies let me know."

"Thanks, I'll keep it mind." They hung up.

Gary called the ranch to see what was happening. Maria answered on the second ring. He asked how she was holding up. She was doing the housework, cooking and answering the phone. "Let me talk to Wayne." Maria went outside and got Wayne.

"Wayne, how may I help you?"

"This is Gary give me a rundown on what is happening."

"Ben is still in the hospital in I.C.U. He is stable, but will be out of action for a while. Arrangements are being made for Joe to be brought back to the ranch. Sam is running fence and checking on livestock. Jerry and Kathy are taking care of the horse barn and helping me with training. Maria is doing her usual job and anything else to help out. What is going on up there in Dallas? There was a lot of action going on last night. Was that you in the shootouts? Did you find Kristine?"

"Hold on and let me catch you up. Yes I was in some shootouts, but we didn't find Kristine. Lopez still has her or has killed her already." His voice broke and he thought he would cry. "I'll be gone as long as it takes to find her. I want you to take charge and take care of the ranch until I come home. I know it a lot to ask, but I love Kristine and won't give up on her."

"Boss, we will all take care of things until you return."

"Thanks Wayne. I'll talk to you later." They hung up.

Last he called his Mom and Dad. His Mother answered on the second ring. "Mom I'm in Dallas."

"Gary what is going on?"

"Lopez kidnapped Kristine and attacked my ranch killing Joe. Ben is in the hospital. They even killed our little wolf Sunshine when she tried to protect Maria. The shootouts you seen on television today, I was in them, but Lopez got away and took Kristine with him. I'm working with Leroy to try and find Lopez. Don't worry, I'll be alright. Wolf is with me."

Gary went to bed for some needed sleep. He woke up at three in the evening. He called Leroy to see what he was doing. Leroy and Ashley were at the Police Station trying to come up with the location of the house by the lake. "I'll be there shortly as soon as I get something to eat. My stomach thinks my throat is cut."

When Gary got to the Police Station, Leroy was looking over Ashley's shoulder as she hunted for the information on the computer. "Nothing yet," said Leroy.

Captain Curry walked in while they were searching for the house. "Leroy, how do you and Ashley always end up in some kind of trouble? What were you doing on the west side of Dallas or should I ask? I saw it on the news this morning."

"We thought it was too quiet on this side of Dallas so we went in search of some action. Actually I went to help Gary. His ranch was attacked by Lopez's thugs and they kidnapped Kristine. She was the one he brought back from Columbia. While searching for Kristine we happen to fine warehouses full of weapons, drugs and girls being sold for prostitution. This guy is a real upstanding citizen so everybody in Dallas thought. He is on the run and has Kristine with him we hope. He may have killed her already, but we won't give up until we know. I need time off to help Leroy. I owe him my wife's life."

"Ashley what's your story?"

"I followed Leroy when he was in the firefights. I always have his back. I need time off to go with him."

"You two are something else."

"Thank you, sir."

"Permission granted, but I don't want to know what you are doing. I know it wanted be by the book whatever you're doing." He left the room and they went back to work.

They worked the rest of the day and into the night without finding anything. "This is too slow, we need a break from the public," said Gary.

The next day they got a break. Lopez was spotted at Lake Palestine by a neighbor. It was off highway 155 at a boat launch. It was time to hit the road. They piled in Gary's truck and headed for Lake Palestine. It took them about two hours to get there. When they got there they started to drive around the lake looking for Lopez and his hoods.

They finally broke for lunch and ate at a joint close to the boat launch. They spread out and talked to the fishermen. After about an hour they got lucky. The house was about five minutes from where they were at.

"Ok let's pay Mr. Lopez a visit." said Leroy.

They went along beside the lake until they spotted the house. They all got out with Wolf in the lead and eased up to the front door. Gary kicked in the door and Wolf charged in. There were only two guys in the house. "Where is Lopez?" asked Gary.

"We don't know anybody by that name?"

"Then why are you in his house?"

"That's our business."

"Now it's my business, Wolf." Wolf advanced on the men.

"I'll only ask one more time before I feed you to Wolf. Where is Lopez?"

"He left last night for Houston. He has his own private plane there. He is going back to Columbia. That's all I know."

"Where is the plane parked?"

"I don't know and that is the truth."

"Did he have a girl with him?"

He stared at Wolf as he came closer. "Yes and she is a hellcat. She tried to get away the whole time they were here."

"That sounds like Kristine."

"What do we do now?" asked Ashley.

"We head for Houston. Call the Police and have them check every airport around Houston. It will probably be at a small private airstrip. Also call the Palestine Sheriff department and tell them to pick up these two men."

"What do you mean by pick us up? We haven't done anything."

Gary found some cord and tied the two men up while Ashley called the Sheriff's Office to have them picked up.

"Leroy, you and Ashley better call home and check in or you will be in big trouble. As soon as you finish we'll head to Houston. It will probably be midnight before we get there."

Ashley called her husband and he was not a happy camper about her chasing around the State, but he knew she would follow Leroy and have his back. They were a team like no other.

Leroy called his wife and she didn't like it either, but she owed her life to Gary and Wolf. "Please call and let me know what is going down."

"I'll keep you up to date as we hunt down Lopez. I'm worried he will get tired of Kristine and do away with her. Our only hope is he will keep her to piss off Gary. I got to go we are leaving for Houston and hope we catch up with Lopez before he flies back to Colombia."

"Ok, we are good to go."

"Then let's get on the road," said Gary.

They loaded up in Gary's truck and headed for Houston.

Gary tried not to break too many speed limits. If they got stopped it would only slow them down. Half way there they stopped and gassed up and ordered some food at a fast food place. Then they were back on the road again. They arrived in Houston about midnight and decided to find a motel for the night. They got one room with two queen size beds. Ashley didn't mind staying in the same room with Gary and Leroy. Ashley and Wolf took one bed. Gary and Leroy took the other bed. They were tired and fell asleep in just a few minutes.

Gary was up first and went to find them some breakfast. He got breakfast at another fast food place. At least the coffee was good. When he got back everyone was up and dressed. Ashley called the Houston Police Department and asked for their help in finding Lopez. They were on it right away checking air strips for his plane.

Ashley checked for air strips. "You won't believe how many air strips there are around Houston. It is like looking for a needle in a haystack. We will never find them before they take off for Columbia."

"We have got to try," said Gary.

They started checking airstrips for the plane. By noon they still didn't have any luck. They went to a fast food joint for food. After eating they were on the road again. Around four o'clock they got a call from the Houston Police. They were at a small airstrip where they think Lopez had taken off from. They got a call about a woman fighting off men. They got directions and headed for the airstrip. When they got there Gary talked to the witness, Bob Jones.

"Mr. Jones, tell us what you saw."

"There were several men and one woman that got out of a car close to a small jet plane. The woman made a break for it, but two men went after her. Her hands were tied behind her back. They caught up with her. She kicked and screamed, but they were too much for her. One of the men knocked her out and they carried her back to the plane. I called the Police, but they had taken off by the time the Police got here. I wanted to help her, but I could see they both had guns. Was it a kidnapping?"

"Yes and I know where they are going."

"What are you going to do?" asked Leroy.

"The only thing I can do. The Police in Columbia won't lift a finger to help. I will have to go and get her again. When I went last time it was a job. This time it is personal. Lopez has the love of my life. She knows I will come for her. If he has harmed a hair on her head I'll kill him on the spot and he knows it. He will be expecting me this time and it won't be as easy as last time."

"I'll call Mr. Wilson and he will have his plane at an airstrip close to Sugarland. He will send me anything I need. Thank you and Ashley for helping me, but you need to go back to Dallas. If I got you two hurt or killed you wife and her husband would never forgive me."

"I'm not letting you go alone," said Leroy. "I'm with you all the way."

"I'm going to," said Ashley. "We had better make our calls to Dallas."

Gary knew there was no way to talk them out of it. "I'll call Mr. Wilson."

Mr. Wilson answered on the second ring. "This is Gary I'm going back to Columbia to get Kristine. You know by now we love each other."

"I already knew that a long time ago when she told me she was moving to Sugarland to be near you and hoped you loved her as much as she loves you."

"I will give up my life to keep her safe."

"What do you need this time?"

"I'll need some heavy weapons this time because they know I'm coming. I want something that will do some real damage. I need several throwaway rocket launchers and automatic weapons. Can you come up with them?"

"Money will buy anything if you have enough and I have enough. I'll send food, drinks and weapons. Just get my daughter back."

"I'll get her back or die trying. We will be waiting at the airstrip when you get there. I'm going by the ranch to check on things. Give me a call when you are on your way here."

"I'll see you at the airstrip. I better get cracking and get your supplies together. I'll see you soon." They hung up.

"I got it set up. We'll go to my ranch and wait for his call. I need to see what is happening at the ranch before I leave." They loaded up and headed for Sugarland.

When they got to the ranch Gary got a big surprise. There were six men sitting at the kitchen table drinking coffee and eating apple pie. They were dressed in old clothes. He knew a couple of them. One was a Highway Patrol, two Policemen from Houston and one from the Sheriff's Office and two more Policemen from Sugarland. "We heard you were going hunting and could use some manpower."

"I can use the manpower, but I am going to Cambodia and you will lose your jobs if you go with me and I don't want that."

"Dirty Harry is going and I want see him shoot to see if he is as good as they say. We know all the risks we're taking, but we decided to go. Four of us are single and the two married men know if you were needed you would go."

Gary's eyes had tears in them, "Thank you all for caring. It is going to be hell because they know we are coming."

"We are all ex-military and have been under fire. We know what to expect and we'll go with the flow and get the job done."

"Then I'll draw up a map of the place and we can make our plans. We will have a plane coming from Dallas with weapons and supplies. I'll go in the office and make a map. Maria will cook food for a good meal before we leave." Gary went to his office to make a map and check his books.

Chapter Seventeen

Gary went to work on his books. They hadn't been touched after the attack on the ranch. Joe had been laid to rest on the ranch. Ben was still in the hospital, but was improving every day. He should be home soon. He decided he had time to run to the hospital before they left for Cambodia. He came back into the kitchen. "I'm going to the Hospital to visit Ben. I'll be back before the plane leaves."

Gary made a fast trip into town to the Hospital. Ben was sitting up when he went into his room. Ben was glad to see him. "Did you find Kristine?"

"No, but I know where she is. Lopez took her back to Cambodia. I'm leaving shortly to get her back. It will be hell getting her back unless he has killed her already. Then I will level his home and everything he owns. I think he is using her to get to me. He knows I will come after her. What he doesn't know is I am not coming alone and will have enough firepower to level his place. There will nine of us plus Wolf. You get well and come home. I want you to take over as foreman as soon as you get back to the ranch."

"Are you sure about that? I have never been in charge before."

"I'm sure you can handle it since most of the work revolves around the horses. Wayne will move up to trainer and Jerry to his assistant. We will hire another hand later."

"I'll do my best."

"I've got to run. You get well quick and come home."

Gary walked into the kitchen. "Mr. Wilson called about fifteen minutes ago and is on his way to the airstrip," said Maria.

"Then we better get on the road," said Gary." They loaded in their trucks and cars and followed Gary to the airstrip.

The jet landed and came to a stop. Mr. Wilson met Gary at the hatch. They shook hands, Gary and his crew loaded on board. "I got everything you ordered," said Mr. Wilson.

"Good, then we can takeoff." The jet lifted off and they were on their way.

Gary introduced his crew to Mr. Wilson. "I'll have two vans waiting for you when you get off the plane. I'm staying with the plane and as soon as you get back we will takeoff for home."

It was three in the morning when they landed. Two vans pulled up next to the jet and they unloaded their supplies. They loaded up and raced away from the airstrip. Money sure talks, no customs. Gary rode in the lead van and Leroy in the second van. It would be close to daylight when they arrived at their destination. Gary decided since they knew they were coming they would attack in the daylight.

Lopez was in the big house and mad as a caged cat. While he was in Dallas his wife had left and taken the kids with her. She took a large amount of cash with her. She had told the staff she had, enough of his chasing women and wasn't coming back. His cash flow was in trouble and he couldn't deliver all his products. Everything was falling down around him. He still had Kristine and raped her when he wanted sex. He would have killed her already, but she was a hellcat and was fun to rape. He would get rid of her when he found another woman. He knew Mitchel would come for her. He had an army of thugs and wasn't afraid. He had guards stationed everywhere. Nobody would get on the property.

Gary had information that Kristine was locked in the cottage behind the big house and his wife and kids had left him. That gave him a big advantage. He hoped the information was correct. It was close to daybreak as they approached Lopez's estate. Gary pulled off the road followed by Leroy and they hid the vans in some bushes. Everybody got out and huddled around for last minute plans.

Gary told four of the men to go to the top of the hill. "Take four sniper rifles and four rocket launchers with you". They took water and something to nibble on while they waited for their part in the attack.

"You two, cover us from down here. Leroy, Ashley, Wolf and I will charge the place. Make sure all of you wear a vest. It will stop most of the bullets except a high powered weapon. They have better weapons than the Police in the U.S. Maybe the Police should buy from Lopez. Ashley, I wish you would stay behind, but I know you won't. Stay close to Leroy and myself. Is there any questions?"

One of the four on the hill asked, "When do we open fire?"

"As soon as Leroy and I take out the guards at the bridge, pick your targets and fire at will. If Lopez calls for more men use the rocket launchers to take them out as they come down the road."

The four men went upon the ridge and the rest of them sat down to wait for daylight. As the sun slowly started to rise, the rest of the crew eased down toward the bridge. Four men came out to relieve the night guards.

They watched as other guards relived the ones about the area. "They got a small army guarding the place. We are going to have to take out a lot of them before we can make an attempt to get to the cottage," said Gary.

"We could drop a rocket in their drug sheds. That should get their attention," suggested Leroy.

Kristine sat on her bed as Lopez unlocked the door and came in. She hadn't slept good last night and she was starving to death. "If you are good today I might feed you."

"You can go straight to hell. Gary will be coming for me and he will kill you for what you did at his ranch. If you had left us alone none of this would ever have happen. He didn't come to Dallas after you or tell anyone about you. Why couldn't you leave us alone?"

"Nobody takes anything from me unless I am ready to give it up."

"Your wife and children have left you. Don't you care about them?"

"If she wanted me she should have stayed here. She had everything a woman could want."

"Not everything, she would want a husband to love her and the children. You have to have a mistress right here under her nose. How do you think that makes her feel?"

"If she was better in bed I wouldn't need a mistress."

"What makes you think you are so hot?"

"You liked me until you found out I was married."

"I was stupid, but not anymore."

Lopez slapped her and then punched her in the face. She hit the floor hard and curled up as small as she could hoping not to get hit again. She didn't want to anger him anymore.

Chapter Eighteen

"It's time to get the show started," said Gary. He put his rifle to his shoulder and took out one of the guards at the bridge.

The four men on the ridge took out the other three. "Time to make a little noise," said Leroy. He raised his rocket launcher and fired hitting the drug building that was newly built. Guards came out of the house in force.

Gary raised his rocket launcher and fired at the front of the house killing several guards. The rest continued to rush them. The four on the hill using the sniper rifles kept cutting them down to size. Five almost made it to the bridge before Leroy, Ashley and Gary cut them down.

The rest turned and ran back into the house. "Ashley do you know how to use that launcher?"

"No, but tell me what to do, I want to do this." Leroy gave her instructions as she raised the rocket launcher to fire. "Drop it in the front door of the house."

Ashley fired the launcher and put the rocket in the front door. The front of the house went up in fire and smoke. "I did it."

A couple of seconds later a man stepped out the door and dropped his automatic weapon on the ground followed one by one of the men inside. Gary yelled to them, "Put your hands over your head and come toward me."

When they got to the bridge, Leroy searched them for any weapons they might be hiding on their body. Some still had knifes on their body which he tossed into the water. "Ok, they are clean."

Gary looked them over and decided they weren't a threat anymore. They had cuts and bruises from the rocket. "Ok, I'm letting you go. Walk on down the road until you can get a ride into town. Don't come back because we will kill you on sight."

"Thank you," said one of the men.

"Ok, get on down the road."

"Ok, let's go find Kristine. I know where Lopez will be. He will be inside the cottage with Kristine. He will be very dangerous since he doesn't have anything to lose. He has lost everything already."

Gary, Leroy, Ashley and Wolf slowly worked their way toward the cottage. When they reached the cottage Gary reached for the knob on the door. The door was unlocked. He opened the door and stepped inside followed by Leroy, Ashley and Wolf. "Welcome to the party," said Lopez.

Lopez was holding Kristine in front of him with a gun pointed at her throat. "I'm going to kill Mitchell and then her. You can watch and do what you have to do after. I'm not going to be taken alive, but I will kill them first. I hate them that much."

Leroy stepped over to the side away from the others. "Kristine, do you remember the woman I kissed in front of the bank."

"Yes, I remember, it was so sweet."

"What kind of bullshit is that?"

Kristine tilted her head away from the gun just a little. Leroy slapped leather and nailed Lopez right between the eyes. He was dead before he hit the floor. "You did it again," yelled Kristine.

She ran over and kissed Leroy. Gary couldn't believe what had just happen. Everybody stared at them.

"Leroy, we have killed all the bad guys and you have kissed the girl, can we go home now?" said Ashley. Everybody laughed as Kristine ran into Gary's arms.

"You look a mess, I'm not sure you are worth taking home," but he kissed her just the same. She had a black eye and bruises all over her body. She also had a cracked rib which hurt every time she moved.

Gary looked at everybody, "Let's go home."

"Good idea," said Leroy.

When they got outside the cottage the house was totally in flames. By morning there wouldn't be anything left. They looked back as the cottage caught fire. By the time they got to the vans the four men on the ridge was waiting for them.

"I guess we put Lopez out of business. He was horrible man," said Gary.

Kristine looked down at herself. "I need a bath and something to eat. The bastard starved me while he waited for you to come. I don't like to say it, but I'm glad he is dead and can't hurt anyone else."

They loaded up and headed for the airstrip. It was quiet on the way back. Gary was driving and Kristine sat beside him with Wolf curled up behind her seat. She loved Gary and Wolf.

When they reached the airstrip, everyone loaded aboard the jet as quickly as possible. Mr. Wilson welcomed them aboard as the pilot fired up the engines and prepared for the takeoff. They were in the air within minutes. With a sigh of relief Kristine said, "We're on our way home." She hurt all over where Lopez had punched her in the face and her body.

When they were airborne, Kristine moved over into Gary's lap. "Please hold me."

She slept almost the entire flight until they were about to land. Gary helped her back into her seat and buckled her in for the landing. She looked like hell. Her eye was black and swollen shut, face bruised and swollen and her ribs hurt. "I must look terrible to you, but I love you. I don't know if you still love me after I was raped by Lopez."

"Baby, I love you. I don't know how I would have gone on if I had lost you. Let your Dad take you back to Dallas and get you well. I'll be at the ranch when you are well again. We have the rest of our lives to love each other."

When they landed and unloaded the plane Gary tried to kiss her before she left for Dallas. Her face was so swollen he could only peck her on her lips. "Call me as soon as you are ready to come back to the ranch."

Mr. Wilson was so sad for his daughter. "As soon as she is ready I'll bring her to you on the Jet. You get your ranch back in order while you wait."

Gary thanked Leroy and Ashley for their help as they loaded back on the plane. He stood and watched as the jet took off, then he turned to his team. "I don't know how to thank you. You can't even tell anyone what you did."

The Highway Patrol spoke for all of them. "If one of us was there you have come for us. That's the kind of person you are. All we ask is you invite us to your wedding."

"You got it."

They all loaded up in their cars and trucks and headed home. When they went back to work it would be work as usual. It would be a little different with Leroy and Ashley. Their boss would want to know or he may say I don't need to know what you two have been up to. He would know it was something not by the book.

As the plane landed Leroy said, "Time to face the music."

Mr. Wilson said, "I hope you don't mind but your wife and Ashley's husband are waiting at the airstrip for your arrival. I called them when we were on our way home."

Katherine and Jim waited at the airstrip as the plane landed and pulled to a stop. As Leroy came down the steps Katherine ran into his arms followed by Ashley as she ran into Jim's arms.

"I must smell pretty bad we haven't had a bath since we left." She did look pretty bad, but so did Leroy.

Mr. Wilson helped his daughter down the steps and into a car that was waiting for them. "Hi Mom" Kristine said as she got in the car. The car headed for Baylor Hospital. There she was treated for her injuries and put in a room.

Gary arrived at the ranch to find all his crew waiting to see him and Wolf. He was happy to be home. Maria had food waiting for him and Wolf. She set a big steak, baked potato and salad in front of him. She put two steaks in a plate for Wolf. She handed Gary a cold beer and put a bowl of milk on the floor for Wolf. Everybody wanted to know the full story of what happen. Gary told them the story as he ate. "Kristine will be coming home when she is patched up. Her face was so swollen I couldn't even kiss her."

"Will we have any more trouble?" asked Wayne.

"No, Lopez and his operation are wiped out."

"Good, now everything should get back to normal."

Gary went to his office to catch up on his books and phone calls. About an hour later he had his books in order. There hadn't been much going on since the attack on the ranch. He made out checks to pay the bills and balanced his checkbook. Wolf curled up on the floor close to him. Gary watched him and could see he was grieving from the death of Sunshine. He would have to do something about that. After answering his phone calls he took a shower and went to bed. He didn't wake up until noon the next day. Maria made him breakfast. He decided to visit Ben in the Hospital. "I'm going to the Hospital"

"It's no need to go to the Hospital. Ben is coming home this evening. He called and gave me his order for supper. He said the food was terrible and wanted my home cooking."

"Then I'll ride over the ranch and check things out." Wayne was working a horse in the coral when Gary went to the barn. He watched him for a while before he saddled up and rode out with Wolf in the lead. They checked the fence and livestock for any problems. His crew had kept everything in ship shape. He noted they had several new calves that needed branded.

When he walked in the kitchen Ben was at the table drinking coffee. "Hi boss, is everything ok on the ranch?"

"Good to have you back. We have some calves that need to be branded. Other than that everything is fine. You can start tomorrow assigning the jobs and I will start you learning the books. We have accounts at a lot of places where you can buy supplies. I want you to be able to run the ranch while I'm away."

"Are you sure I can handle everything?"

"I'm sure you will as soon as I have time to teach you. I want your input on anything that will make the ranch run better. Joe and I brain stormed from time to time. We will do the same."

"I'll do my best."

"That's all I ask of you."

"As of now you will be receiving foreman salary."

"Thank you, sir."

Gary went to his office and called Kristine at the Hospital. "How are you feeling?"

"I'm bored and want to come home to you. I miss you terribly."

"I miss you to. I can't wait until you come home."

The next morning at breakfast Gary told Ben he was going to west Texas on a trip. He decided to do something about Wolf. "I'll only be gone a few days. Take care of everything."

"Yes sir, I will."

Gary loaded the truck with enough food to feed an army, tent, and fishing gear. He took a rifle and his 45 Automatic. He called Wolf and he came running. "We're going on a little trip."

They hit the highway west. He didn't tell Wolf where they were going. He wanted it to be a surprise. When Gary turned off the highway onto the pig trail Wolf knew where they were going. As soon as the truck stopped under the same tree they used before, Wolf was going nuts. Gary opened the door and he hit the ground running. "You can bring your pack for supper," yelled Gary.

Gary set up camp, set up his tent, unloaded the truck and built a place for a campfire. As the sun sank in the west Wolf returned with his pack of wolves. Most of the wolves had been to the camp before and sat down to wait for supper. Gary cooked steak for him and Wolf and gave the wolf pack chunks of raw meat which they wolfed down. After supper the wolves lay around a long time before they left for their cave. "You can go with them if you want to," said Gary. Wolf trotted off with the pack. Gary banked his campfire and turned in. He slept like a rock. This was his third time he had come here to get his life back in shape.

The next morning Gary was up early. He cooked some breakfast and then went fishing. It was so relaxing. He sat and thought about Kristine and how much he loved her. Maybe this time he could build a life and not have anything bad happen. A jerk on his fishing pole brought him out of his thoughts. He had a big catfish on his line. He brought him in to shore and took him off the hook. He was at least a ten pound catfish. Today was going to be a beautiful day.

"It's about time I had a good day," said Gary.

Gary sat around and killed the day fishing. That evening he came back to camp, skinned and gutted the fish. He built up the fire and started cooking fish. He cooked some and saved some raw for the wolf pack. They showed up at dark. Gary gave Wolf his fish cooked. He gave the wolf pack more chunks of meat and fish raw. After they left for the night Gary noticed a young female wolf stayed with Wolf. He looked over at Wolf. "You like your mate young, don't you?"

Wolf grinned at Gary and they curled up together. Gary was glad Wolf had found a new mate. That was what the trip was all about. Now if she, would leave with them when they left. He decided to stay a couple more days and give her time to adjust to being around people. He hunted and fished to relax. He hated to leave when it was time to go. He loaded the truck and told Wolf it was time to leave. Wolf came to the truck and Gary opened the door. Wolf jumped in and looked back at the female. She hesitated and didn't know what to do. Gary gave Wolf time to get her in the truck. She looked back and looked at Wolf. She finally jumped up in the truck with Wolf. He had him a new mate.

After a while Gary said, "We got to give her a name." Wolf stared at Gary and back at his new mate.

"She is so small I think we will call her Baby. What you think of that name?" Wolf barked his approval of the new name.

Gary looked over at the young wolf. "Your name is now Baby and welcome to our family."

Baby whimpered, Gary laughed and Wolf barked. They would be home soon.

Gary pulled the truck in front of the ranch house and shut off the engine. He loved this ranch and got a lump in his throat every time he came home. He went in the front door, Wolf and Baby right behind him. When they got to the kitchen Maria was cooking. She looked down at Wolf and Baby. "Well what do we have here?"

Wolf barked and Baby whimpered. "Baby is Wolf's new mate. She is small and you will have to fatten her up."

She hugged Wolf, "I can do that." Baby backed away as Maria turned her hand over for her to smell. She loved the little wolf already.

Gary got a cup of coffee and sat down at the table. "Would you like a piece of apple pie to go with your coffee?"

"Yes thank you."

Maria cut him a quarter of a pie and put in front of him. She got some chunks of beef for Wolf and Baby. Wolf made fast work of his food, but Baby had never eaten cooked meat and sniffed it. Wolf took a bite of her food and she decided to eat it before Wolf did. Maria watched her and laughed, "Baby isn't going to let Wolf eat her food."

By the next day Baby had learned to follow Maria around the kitchen and she got to taste all the food Maria was cooking. She was curled up close to Maria when Wolf went with Gary. They started their routine again, finding lost livestock and horses. Bulls were the worst at staying at home. They always thought the grass was greener on the other side of the fence and the cows hotter. That just made more jobs for Wolf and Gary.

The next morning Ben handed out jobs for the day. While they were eating breakfast Gary thanked them for standing by him with all the trouble he had been having. "I would like to let you know I am going to ask Kristine to marry me when she is well enough to come home."

That didn't surprise anyone. The way he looked at Kristine and she looked at him you have to be blind not to know they were in love. After breakfast everyone went to their assigned job for the day. Gary had another cup of coffee.

The phone rang and Maria answered it. "It's for you."

"Hello, what can I do for you?"

"You can meet me at the airstrip. I'm coming home," said Kristine in a very sexy voice, "That is if you still want me. Daddy is bringing me down by Jet."

"I guess I'll take you if nobody else wants you," teased Gary.

"You better want me. I don't know what I would do without you in my life."

"What time are you arriving at the airstrip?"

"We are loading on the plane now. I'll see you shortly."

Chapter Nineteen

"Come on Wolf, we are going to meet Kristine at the airstrip." They loaded into the truck and headed for the airstrip.

As they waited for the plane to arrive, Gary passed back and forth in front of the pickup. He was as nervous as a teenager on his first date. He loved this woman more than life. He remembered how he had almost lost her in Columbia. He remembered the good times and the bad. He watched as the Jet flew into a landing pattern. The jet made a smooth landing and came to a stop close to Gary's pickup.

The outside hatch was lowered and Kristine came running down the steps. She screamed Gary's name as she ran to him. Gary opened his arms and she ran into them. They kissed and clung to each other. "Gary I love you."

"I love you more."

Mr. Wilson came down the steps and smiled at them. "Well all's well that ends well. Gary, take care of my little girl. I have to go straight back to Dallas on business. I didn't tell you where I got the weapons you needed. I got them on black market, but I'll take care of it."

"I hope we never need weapons again," said Gary.

The jet took off and Gary put his arm around Kristine, "Let's go home."

"Good idea, I miss the ranch and everyone there."

When they arrived at the ranch the whole crew was out front to meet them. As they got out everyone rushed around Kristine. She loved every minute of it. Her beautiful home in Dallas never felt the love she felt here.

Maria had made a big feast for Kristine's home coming. She had cooked big juicy steaks, baked potatoes and a big salad. This was a ranch and steak was the number one staple. She had pies for desert, tea, water and beer to drink.

Gary said, "I would like everyone's attention. I want everyone to witness what I have to say." He got down on his knees in front of Kristine.

"Kristine I love you with all my heart. If you will marry me I will love you for the rest of our, lives."

"Yes, yes, yes I will marry you. I love you." She dropped down into his arms for a kiss.

Wolf came over for his hug and Baby stayed behind him. Kristine hugged Wolf and stared at the little wolf behind him. "What have we here?"

"That's Baby, Wolf's new mate. He robbed the cradle."

Kristine laughed, "Some men like their women young."

"Dirty old men," said Gary.

After the party was over, Gary and Kristine sat at the kitchen table staring at each other. "Finally we are alone," said Gary.

"What's on your mind cowboy?"

"When do you want to tie the knot?"

"Just as soon as possible, I want to be in your bed every night," Kristine giggled.

"How about, Sunday after next will that give, you enough time to get ready for the wedding?"

"I'll be ready, but right now let's go to bed and make slow love all night."

"I 'm ready," Gary took her hand and led her to the master bedroom. They made love two times and got up to eat.

Epilogue

Sunday arrived and everyone was getting ready for the wedding. For what was to be a small wedding there were a lot of people arriving by the minute. Jerry was parking cars and wandering where all the people were coming from. Maria and Kathy were in the kitchen cooking and putting icing on the wedding cake. Wolf and Baby were standing by for anything that was dropped on the floor. Ben was outside cooking on the grill. Wayne and Sam were setting up more chairs for the rest of the guests.

Mr. and Mrs. Wilson arrived and separated. She went to help Kristine get ready for the wedding and he went into the master bedroom when he found Gary trying to tie his tie. Gary was so nervous he couldn't tie a knot.

"Here let me do that." Mr. Wilson tied his tie for him.

"Thank you, I can't believe I'm so nervous since this is my second time around. I guess I thought I would never get the chance to love again. I will love and protect your daughter with my life."

"I got something for you and Kristine." He handed him an envelope. It had a hotel key and tickets to all kinds of things. "I own part of a hotel right close to the beach in Hawaii. My Jet will take you there and stay until you come back. Have a nice honeymoon. Kristine doesn't know about it yet."

"This is too much," said Gary.

"If it wasn't for you I wouldn't have a daughter to give it to. Enjoy your honeymoon."

Jerry stuck his head in the door, "Ten minutes till time."

Gary assumed his place in front of the preacher. Leroy was best man and Ashley stood up for Kristine. Mr. Wilson walked her in and placed her hand in Gary's. Kristine was in a trance looking at her husband to be.

After they were declared man and wife, the party started. Mr. Wilson came over to Gary, "We are going back to Dallas and I will send the jet straight back. Take care of my little girl."

Kristine was shocked that her Mother and Dad left so soon. "I'm sorry they left so soon. I guess Dad had some business to take care of."

Gary smiled at her, "They left so we could have the Jet for our honeymoon."

"You got to be kidding," she screamed. "Where are we going?"

"We are going by private jet to Hawaii. Your Dad is giving us the honeymoon."

She flew into his arms, "I love you so much."